ATLAS
IN
CHAINS

AMERICA IN DECLINE

BOOK I

GREGORY C PHILLIPS

Blue M Publishing, LLC - Chicago

Library of Congress Cataloging-in-publication data
Names: Phillips, Gregory C.
Title: *Atlas in Chains*
Description: First edition | Blue M Publishing, LLC, Chicago, IL [2016] | Series: Book one of three of multi-volume series| Contents: *Atlas in Chains – America in Decline* | Summary: A couple fight the government and a big, corporate competitor to keep their doors open. Meanwhile, America sinks into a totalitarian state with the imposition of central planning, replacing capitalism | Audience Note: Recommended for readers fifteen and older | Language Note: Infrequent offensive language.
Identifiers: ISBN 978-1-945385-00-1 (Paperback)
Subjects: LCSH: sh85001072 Adventure stories| BISAC: FIC031060 FICTION / Thriller Political | FIC055000 FICTION / Dystopian | FIC037000 FICTION /Political | GSAFD: 00000cz a2200037n 45 0 680 Dystopias
Classification: LCC PS370-380 | DDC 813/--dc23

Phillips, Gregory C.
Atlas in Chains: America in Decline, Gregory C. Phillips
Contents: Part one – Patent Pending

ISBN 978-1-945385-00-1 (Paperback)

Fabulous Book Cover Design by HIP Distribution
Published by Blue M Publishing, LLC, Hammond, IN

Blue M Publishing
6205 Indianapolis Blvd
Suite 100
Hammond, IN 46320

Printed in the United States of America
www.blueMpublishing.com

CONTENTS

ATLAS IN CHAINS:
AMERICA IN DECLINE

BOOK SUMMARY

Patrick and Shea develop a revolutionary combustion engine that improves operational efficiencies so dramatically that it threatens the government's on-going war against fossil fuels. In this dystopian future, the pair battles an increasingly authoritarian government bent on destroying capitalism and the underlying democratic principles upon which the country was founded. Bullied and tormented by federal authorities who have teamed up with big business, the couple fight back against the great powers in Washington.

However, out-gunned and out-financed, the Disones' world collapses. It is only when they team-up with a feisty senator from Wyoming that they find renewed courage to fight back. This sets the stage for a titanic clash the nation hasn't seen in nearly two hundred years, and one which no one wanted – then or now.

*****

Rating: PG-15* for use of harsh language and graphic images of violence and threats of violence. Some drug and alcohol use is described. There are scenes with sexual references or implied sexual activity.

*Rating is provided by the author as a parental guide and is not based on any established rating systems.

ACKNOWLEDGEMENTS

Growing up, the author read extensively from a variety of nonfiction tomes – from Aleksandr Solzhenitsyn's *The Gulag Archipelago* to the classic WWII narrative by William L. Shirer, *The Rise and Fall of the Third Reich.* Although mainly attracted to history, the author was surprised when his older brother gave him a copy of *Atlas Shrugged* by Ayn Rand and *The Wealth of Nations* by Adam Smith . Although all of these books had an impact, *Atlas Shrugged* has held a special place in the author's heart and helped shape his views about capitalism and its symbiotic, albeit sometimes conflicting, relationship with democracy.

Written in the 1950s but set in the future, *Atlas Shrugged* presents a female protagonist fighting an on-going battle against the forces of socialism and tyranny that wish to destroy her company and the very foundation of capitalism upon which it was built. Rand's philosophy, referred to as Objectivism, continues to be ridiculed and scorned to this day by those on the Left, but considered relevant and prescient by those on the Right. Still, whether right or wrong, such a philosophy warrants a place in our discourse largely because the power of capitalism has proved itself through the years to be the most effective wealth-creating system yet devised by man.

The author of this book series recognizes the contributions made by Rand and in no way suggests that the ideas expressed herein are perfectly true to her philosophy (and he apologizes in advance for any deviations that may cloud this series and its title). However, it is hoped that the series will reignite the discussion about the place capitalism and democracy have in the nation and in the world. For most of recorded history, man has been subjugated by systems of trade and governance that favored authoritarian rule and central planning. Indeed, the world is threatened now by theologies and political philosophies that are antithetical to the ideals of freedom as we know them as originally penned in the *U.S. Constitution*. Only with dogged vigilance can we hold on to these principles; otherwise, they will be taken from us and not returned without great conflict and strife.

*****

PREFACE

The question currently presented to denizens of the United States is whether the country has embarked on a new, more promising experiment than that initiated in 1776 or whether it has completely lost its way.

This three-part story, *Atlas in Chains, Atlas in Revolt* and *Atlas in Ascendance,* is fiction. It presents a narrative when all democratic and other non-violent approaches to change the nation's course have been exhausted, and there are few alternatives other than those more extreme. The author neither endorses nor condones extreme measures and believes there *are* peaceful solutions to the challenges that confront this country.

But a failure of democracy goes hand-in-hand with the repudiation of capitalism, which in concert with democracy has created an engine of wealth the world had never seen before. This is not to say that complete *laissez faire* capitalism is the solution – at least where its definition includes big-company *corporatism.* Where unfettered corporatism permits big companies to crush all competition with impunity, losers always outweigh winners. As a result, there is a role for government to play referee and ensure there is free competition, allowing the rights of consumers to determine the winners and losers in the marketplace.

The author presents a future where the iron fist of the government falls hard on capitalism and the freedoms of its citizenry, especially when it teams up with the special interests and lobby groups of big business. Crony capitalism results. In the not-so-distant future, he presents a nation which is oppressed by an authoritarian administration and the unscrupulous actions of monopolistic companies. Not only do the ideals of socialism and cronyism rise up to crush small business, but they also strip away the last vestiges of freedom and liberty to which the American people cling.

In this fictional account, there is one leader who has the courage to step forward and risk everything to guide his people out of the darkness and into a world of hope. It is not without sacrifice and strife, but it is a path that he and others in his close-knit group believe must be taken.

*****

AMENDED PREFACE

Nothing is constant. The world today is not the world of yesterday, nor is it the world of tomorrow. It is changing faster than ever before, and by the time one blinks, it's changed once again.

This amendment to the original preface was necessary after the events of a recent presidential election. We are always hopeful when there is a new chief executive in the White House. However, vigilance is required. It is still up to the American people to hold their representatives accountable for what they promise during campaigns and not let them suffer amnesia from these pledges as they hide behind their walnut office doors on Capitol Hill.

Too many of our brave men and women have died in the service of this country fighting to ensure the preservation of our rights as free men and women. Freedom and liberty -- and our right to vote for those who pledge to defend them on our behalf -- are virtues that have always been and will always be worth fighting for.

*****

PART I – PATENT PENDING

CH A A BLEAK FUTURE

May 2051

(Flash forward)

"But Madam, the Canadian Prime Minister wants answers!" said her chief of staff. "You can't expect him to sit by idly after you ordered a military offensive at his border!"

"I don't have to answer to him," said the First Citizen, whose position had replaced the president as head of what once was the United States of America. "Our military can and will crush them! They've made their choice as to which side they're on, and since they've chosen the rebels, then they must live and soon die by that decision. The same hammer I'll use to eliminate the rebellion and those who think they can secede will be used to destroy them as well."

"But millions could die?"

The First Citizen only shrugged. "Just as Lincoln faced the possibility of hundreds of thousands dying, so do I."

The chief of staff understood the stark differences in the two situations, but valued his neck enough not to raise them. "But it's Canada, First Citizen! They've been an ally of our country since its founding!"

"That's not true, and you know your history well enough not to say something so stupid. The French Canadiens were *not* with the Americans and the other seven British colonies in Canada were too weak to join the lower thirteen," she snorted back to him. Then, thinking about the French, she added, "What about the Quebecois Prime Minister?"

"What about her?"

"The French are usually more understanding of our socialistic ways. Are they willing to join us?" asked the First Citizen.

"With what is happening with the Republic of Canada, I didn't think it wise to approach their newly separated neighbor, Quebec."

"I want the Quebecois Prime Minister on the phone now!" Standing next to the windows, the First Citizen stopped and looked out from the Oval Office and across the South Lawn to the hole where the Washington Monument once stood. "Also, get me General Crawford out of Malmstrom right away. I want our nuclear bombers airborne at once. If Canada wants to get *pissy* with me over sending a couple armed divisions to the Ontario border , then so be it."

*****

CH 1 AFTER YEARS OF TOIL

October 2047

(Present Time)

The night was foggy and damp. Meteorologists had warned all day that the weather would be changing and that the warm spring air would be replaced, albeit temporarily, by a blast of colder gusts from the northeast. It seemed that each year the weather was getting cooler rather than warmer, but that was for the global climatologists to argue about – something they'd done for over seventy years. Yet, that wasn't a concern of Shea Disone as she drove her six-year-old, white Mercedes toward her company's headquarters. It was a humble building situated along the Charles River just outside of Boston. Built-out from a renovated 1934 brick warehouse constructed just before the war, it had undergone many transformations and near-death experiences during the previous hundred years.

For tonight, Shea just wished to be late, but not too late. Unfortunately, she was on time to be *really* late. The celebratory party that she had arranged for her husband, Patrick, had already started, and she had gotten delayed at their attorney's office going over the ramifications of a letter she had received earlier that day. It was from the government, and it meant a lot to their business. It had taken them over twenty years and their life's savings to build their business – sacrifices they were more than willing to make. It was true that it had almost taken away their marriage, with the endless hours and pressures to make the business work, scrimping on personal luxuries and canceling dinner plans to address company needs. But the possibility of selling their company or part of it would make them more than comfortable in retirement and provide additional funds to expand research and development on the next generation of products.

And it was all about an engine – a simple combustion engine, one that had first been developed back in the nineteenth century by a man named Etienne Lenoir in Belgium in 1858. His design became the prototype for all the others that were to come later – from Mercedes and Benz to Henry Ford and Enzo Ferrari. Patrick had been the brains behind its development – a highly-efficient combustion engine, capable of converting power from gasoline or diesel at an amazing level of efficiency. For automobiles, this meant cars capable of four hundred or more miles to the gallon.

Right out of law school, Shea would not have believed anyone if they had told her that in thirty years she would be married and working with her husband to develop a simple, yet revolutionary engine that could change the world. At Harvard, she had studied constitutional law rather than getting immersed in contracts, torts, patent law or other more lucrative legal endeavors. Shea had pursued her dream of serving in Congress, being elected twice to the House of Representatives while in her twenties. However, her dream quickly turned sour, as she saw the infighting and stagnation of thought at both ends of the Capitol – the House and the Senate. She vowed never to campaign again.

Petite and slender, Shea was a ball of energy. Her enthusiasm for life and especially for what her husband and she were doing at their Lenoir Research Labs was contagious. She was blue-eyed with short, straight reddish hair, cut just above her shoulders. Shea had tried different hair colors and styles over the years, but at her present age of fifty-five, she had decided to go back to her natural color with a simple, easy-to-care-for style.

Yet, after those fifty-five years she was still in remarkable shape. She had been good about protecting herself from the sun, exercising, eating right, and limiting her alcohol. In that sense, she was a doctor's dream patient. The small mole above the left side of her full lips had always been a mark of distinction – something she had tried to cover with makeup when she was younger, but which she had grown to love about herself as she had gotten older. Being second generation Irish, Shea's fair complexion and rounded face was unmistakably from the land of "green." Ireland was a place where the two of them had talked about retiring one day. *Perhaps that day would not be too far off, now*, she thought. Financial success and security were almost within their grasp.

The turnoff to the company's building was a sudden, sharp bend, and the white sedan skidded slightly on the wet pavement as it rounded the corner. The car drove on autopilot without the need for Shea to oversee her progress, but all the same, she glanced up at the road to make sure the car was still tracking its course properly. Next to her, resting in an otherwise empty tan leather seat, were her two white, shopping-bag passengers contained 155 small, silver boxes and one larger gold box, all with matching bows -- presents she had gotten earlier in the day.

As her car pulled in between two yellow stripes in parking lot, it took the first available space as Shea usually did in the morning. Neither she nor her husband believed in reserved spots for owners or managers, except, that is, for the Employee of the Quarter, which was up front, next to the twelve handicapped spaces mandated by the state -- spaces that were never used. As she pushed through the glass front door emblazoned with the sapphire blue letters **LRL**, Shea could hear the music playing upstairs in the conference room, and she hurried past the receptionist desk marked by the Lenoir Labs name and logo, and scrambled up the main steel and glass staircase. By the time she had reached the door to the large conference room, Meghan Armstrong, her administrative assistant, had spotted her and cut her off at the entrance.

"You're late, you know," Meghan said, sternly. It was apparent she'd already had a glass or two of Chardonnay and was working hard on another. "Your husband's already here. He's over there in the corner making small talk, I imagine."

Shea smiled. She had known Meghan for twenty years, and they were good friends, both outside and inside the company's four walls. "Yeah, I got stuck at the office," quipped Shea, jokingly.

Meghan's intensity softened, but only slightly. "Right," she snorted. "Now get in there. Everyone's been asking about you."

Shea walked in through the window-paned, walnut double doors that led into the room where the party was well underway. In hand were her white shopping bags and feelings of excitement and joy. It was an exciting time – a time when she could relax and enjoy instead of worry and fret.

Instantly, she was surrounded by her staff and others telling her how stunning she looked and how glad they were to see her. Shea did look amazing that night, wearing light-gray slacks with a double-breasted, cream-colored jacket marked by wide, matching-gray chalk stripes. The coat was linen with a fine, tight-weave that gave it a rich, elegant appearance. Her three-inch pumps were also cream, with a narrow heal strap and open toes.

She approached an older man who was busy chatting within a circle of others, oblivious to all else around him. His appearance was meticulous, unlike what one would expect from an inventive genius. The only thing that resembled that of an eccentric scientist was his long, silver-gray hair and goatee. Tall and husky, his proportions set him apart in any crowd. More like a front lineman than a wide receiver, his stature was imposing with its size and girth. Yet, softening all of this was his affability – a smile that could soothe a demon, and a smoothness and regality that could impress any monarch of England.

"Shea, it is so good of you to come to your own party. I'm glad you could make it," said Patrick, kissing her tenderly on the cheek. They still had a deep bond after all their years together. They had seen their share of ups and downs, but in the end, their feelings for each other had only grown stronger.

Shea returned the affection, patting him lovingly on the back and answering, "I was told this was *your* party. That's why I'm so late."

Patrick laughed, his round belly jiggling at the comeback.

Patrick and Shea had started the company from nothing. He had been a young PhD doing electromagnetic superconducting experiments at the Massachusetts Institute of Technology (MIT) while Shea was studying law at Harvard, just across town in Cambridge. They said they had found each other at the local bar, but could rarely pull that explanation off with a straight face. In fact, they had met at the main library on the MIT campus. Shea had gone there to research technical information on a case she was studying in her law class when they literally ran into each other at the end of a carol. They had dated for a while, but then each of them setoff in different directions – she to Washington; he to an engineering design firm in Boston.

A few years later during Shea's first term in Congress, they saw each other again at a conference in Washington. Their romance was rekindled, and they were married within two years, when Shea had returned for her second stint in Washington. By then she was fed up with politics, as he was with the commuting back and forth from Boston to Washington for work. She moved to Boston to join him and strike out on their own to develop Lenoir Research Laboratories.

"Is everyone else here?" asked Shea, surprised at the number of people who had shown up. It was, after all, a Friday night – a night when most employees would have been glad to be out at dinner, the bars, a ballgame or anywhere except their place of employment.

"It seems like it," answered Patrick. "At least everyone from the lab is here. And, it seems like a lot from the front office made it as well."

Shea kissed him on the cheek, and Patrick wandered off to talk with other employees. He was good at that, even though he didn't often get the chance to mingle with others during the day at work. He considered time at work precious – that which should be dedicated to advancing the design and the cause, rather than socializing. So, most employees didn't know him very well – at least the softer side of him.

Shea took her glass of Pinot noir and made the rounds too. Unlike her husband who was terrible at names and remembering what each person's family members were doing, she was very good at it. He often remarked to people that if his wife had met them once, even within the last thirty years, she would remember their name, what they were wearing, their children's names, in what they were involved in school, and even what the family's pet's name was. It was exceptional, as was she.

"Hello, Annie," answered Shea, coming over to the chief financial officer of her company. "How are the girls -- Janet, Amy and Regan? Isn't Janet about ready to graduate from high school?"

Annie smiled warmly. "Oh, she's graduating from high school next month. Amy is starting singing lessons – she's got such a lovely voice. And, Regan, well you know about Regan. She's twelve going on twenty-two. If it were the nineteen seventies again, she's be wearing pink sunglasses and chanting *Flower Power!"*

Shea chuckled. Patrick and she had no children of their own, even though they had tried. The news from the doctor had been devastating to both of them. At first, they had considered adopting, but after the business took off, everything else just got set aside. Shea felt remorse about not adopting or, perhaps even getting artificially inseminated, but there had never been a right time. Other things just kept getting in the way.

The small talk continued for another ten minutes or so before Meghan came over to interrupt. "It's time," she said simply, still sipping on her wine. She pulled Shea away from her captive audience, dragging her to the front of the room.

Shea was comfortable at the center of attention – quite the contrary for her husband who enjoyed the behind-the-scenes approach. Patrick preferred knowing that his contribution was in the back of the store, in the warehouse or lab, so-to-speak, rather than in front with the customers. Therefore, it was up to Shea to start things off on the right foot and make the introductions. She gave the white shopping bags to Meghan while she began clanging her spoon against her wine glass, hoping to draw everyone's gaze.

"Good evening," she said as loudly as she could. "May I have everyone's attention?" After a few more clangs, she got most of the people to interrupt their conversations and look up at her.

"Thank you. Thank you all … I just want to say that we're glad all of you could make it tonight …" she said, then adding, "… not that any of you had a choice in the matter." There were several laughs scattered throughout the room.

"No, really, I … *we* are really glad you could join us to celebrate the great news of the company. We've all been working really hard these past many years to produce something that will prove to be beneficial to industry, the environment, and to the country. We have all believed in this project and, surprisingly, today it appears the government also believes in what we are doing. I won't spoil the news – I'll let Patrick tell you – but I will say that he and I both appreciate all of the effort you've put in for us, and we know that you will continue to help us over the next twenty … hell, fifty years or so to ensure that our technology is used to reduce our dependence on foreign energy and minimize the impact civilization on the planet."

To that, the group responded with appreciative applause.

"Anyway, I know Patrick is dying to talk with you. So, without further ado, here is my husband."

There was a groundswell of clapping that enveloped the room. The employees truly did love Patrick, even though he was more subdued during the workday. He was smart and engaging. Although he didn't stop to ask about their personal lives, he usually asked about how *they* were doing and showed sincere interest in knowing the truth. He would stop them in the hall and see how their day was going, or he would ask what he could do to make things easier for them. On a regular basis, he showed that he really cared about his employees, and they appreciated that.

As the company got bigger, he had impressed upon his managers that same importance of caring about their employees – just as he had when the company had been smaller. He had always said that if the company shows it cares about its employees, the employees would care about the company. It was a maxim that had been and, Patrick believed would be true for years to come.

"Thank you, Shea," said Patrick, giving her a peck on the cheek. "Thank you," he said again, this time raising his hand in appreciation. "First, I'd like to ask my wife why she thinks I'm still going to be toiling away in the back lab for the next fifty years. Heck, I'll be three hundred years old by then!"

Everyone in the room let out a laugh. It was quintessential Patrick.

"But seriously, *you* are the ones that Shea and I should be thanking tonight. You are the ones who have made this company possible. Without you and your commitment and energy, we could never have gotten to where we are now. You, and I mean *you*, have made this company a success."

There was another round of plaudits for his words, and Patrick reacted – his face beaming. He was proud – for himself, his wife, and for everyone in the room. They had done what others said couldn't be done, and still further, what others hoped he wouldn't be able to do – resurrect a dying industry. Alternative energies had been prematurely mandated by the government at a time when the efficiencies weren't there to sustain it. As regulations were heaped on oil and gas companies making it almost impossible to make and distribute fuels, energy prices soared. Businesses shut down, unemployment rose, and jobs were sent overseas where fossil fuels continued to be easily and cheaply produced. By creating a super-efficient engine, Patrick and Shea had hoped the government would reverse their decisions to cripple fossil fuels and let the markets sort out funding for and usage of alternative forms of energy based on their viability. It was common sense, but that didn't always surface in debates in Washington.

Patrick had been born in Springfield, Illinois, the capital of that state which had two distinctions – first, for being the home of a great president, Abraham Lincoln, and second, for being the first state of the Union ever to file for bankruptcy. Named Patrick G. Disone II, after his father, he was athletic and smart, excelling at almost everything he tried. President of the debate team, vice-president of the chess team, and student class treasurer, he had been well respected at his small, private high school of fewer than two hundred students. The fact that he was nearly six-foot four when he was a sophomore didn't hurt either. He'd tried out for the basketball team and made the varsity squad but was never good enough to be a starter. Still, he was voted co-captain of the team his senior year -- due mostly to his infectious positive attitude that gave the rest of the team the confidence they often needed to come from behind to win games.

Now, he was older and wiser but still just as popular. He'd grown a goatee when he was in his thirties and kept it ever since. It was part of him now – who he was and who he'd become. At his age, fifty-eight, he was only a few years away from when the law said he had to retire. He had developed more and more wrinkles around his blue eyes, going from one to several in the last year alone. With teeth pearly white and perfectly aligned by his orthodontist at age ten, his face and body were the epitome of what women thought

17

desirable for a man in his late fifties. But there was one mark of distinction that he'd had since he'd been born – a small, heart-shaped birthmark on the side of his face, just below his right ear. Shea often told him it was there for a reason for it and that it would help shape who he was as a person. And, she was right.

"With your patience, I'd like to take a moment to reminisce. Nearly thirty years ago, I remember sitting at Giuliano's Pub with my wife and Sergei ..." he said, pointing to their chief technology officer, who was sitting the corner in a rare scene of drinking a beer from a can, "... and Meghan here. We sat around until one in the morning discussing the future of this company. We talked about what it could become and what we thought we were capable of making it. I'm not sure we really believed that we could attain what we've now achieved. What we've developed is important and meaningful, and now with one hundred fifty-five employees, we can make it a reality for the rest of the world!"

People in the crowd, having had several drinks by this time, were clapping more loudly, adding whistles and chants.

"But in the very beginning, we grew slowly. Then, as the mathematics and technology began coming together, we were able to build prototypes that worked pretty well. These early models were only ten percent more efficient than existing ones, but that was enough to make a business out of it and begin marketing them in other countries around the world. We then faced-off with the government, which issued an embargo against our exporting them. However, we were able to fight that too and won. The courts issued orders getting them to lift their ban.

"But I digress ..." he said, chuckling to himself, "... Our goal was not yet met. It took another twenty years to create something truly revolutionary – something that would change the way we look at our natural resources. And, we call it the MB 12, after the inventor of the four-stroke engine, Wilhelm Maybach. The MB 12 is the most fuel efficient combustion engine ever made. Its efficiency rating is 280 percent greater than those engines made just a few years ago and the fuel efficiency is twenty-two times greater. Cars with the next generation of this engine will be able to run an entire year on a tank of about twenty-five gallons. Right now, we're working on jet engines that can fly from New York to Los Angeles, fully loaded with 250 passengers, on only 670 gallons of jet fuel, instead of 15,000. Costs to travel will fall precipitously. Airfare between New York and LA – now over 3,700 dollars one way – could fall to under 200 dollars ..." he paused and then added, "... plus another 135 in taxes."

The room broke out in laughter.

"No, seriously," he continued, "we have created something extraordinary that will make things more affordable for everyone, lower our consumption of precious oil reserves, and lead the way to other inventions never before thought possible."

There was pride in his voice and steadiness in his delivery. He glowed like he'd just won the spelling bee in his third-grade school room. This was his moment – but it was also a moment for Shea. She beamed too, standing right beside him.

"But the news of the day," said Patrick, "is that we received a long-awaited letter from the Patent Office ..." But he stopped abruptly when Shea leaned in and whispered in his ear. Patrick cleared his throat and said, "Sorry. I was just reminded that it's no longer the Patent Office. They used to call it that when I was younger, but it's now referred to as the ... what was that again?"

Instead of repeating it to him, Shea stepped in, holding up her wrist and pushing a button on her personal communication device (PCD) to project a holographic image into the room. "I'll let Patrick finish, but it's a letter we got from the Agency of Tangible and Intellectual Property Assessment and Rights Protection." Then she motioned back to her husband to continue.

"Yeah, that's much easier to say, I think," Patrick said, with chuckling in the crowd. "Anyway, we got the letter from the Patent Office," he said again to much more chuckling in the room, "and as of today, we have been granted thirty-four patents for the MB 12 series engine – what we call the SECE engine or super-high efficiency combustion engine. It's taken only six years to get this legal protection for our work, but it's something that is critical to the on-going success of this company and those who work here. Our plans are to begin manufacturing the SECE engines in eight plants around the country. This will create over 23,000 jobs in those plants alone and another 146,000 jobs in companies that will support our manufacturing process – providing parts, services and other resources needed to sell and distribute this marvelous engine throughout the world. As a result, we are not only contributing to a cleaner environment and reducing the usage of our natural resources, but we are employing thousands of people who will make a living from the wages we will be paying. I can't think of anything better! It is a very exciting time for all of us, but I want to save time for my better half. Shea, I know you wanted to say some things ..."

"Thanks, Patrick," said Shea, touching him lovingly on the arm. "There are those who argued that we couldn't do it ... that we shouldn't do it – that it would upset the 'fabric' of our economy. Yet, they were all wrong. Yes, there is no question that the technology will change things. Indeed, it will, but so did every other technology developed by mankind. Where would electricity be if we had decided that AC current was too dangerous to unleash upon the public? Where would autos be if we had squelched the idea because of the potential for putting buggy whip makers out of business? As a human race we must continue to furrow new ground, always searching for new places where innovations and creations may spring forth. It is all part of us; it's part of our DNA. We are all explorers or discoverers at some level. Whether it is creating a new recipe at home or painting something on a canvass. That is the very nature of humankind. It's also what makes entrepreneurship so special. Creativity is a gift. Not everyone has that. I certainly don't, but thank God I married someone who did!"

Everyone in the room smiled. They knew there was something special in the team of Patrick and Shea, and something extraordinary about the company they created. Patrick was the brilliant scientist and entrepreneur; Shea the smart mastermind behind the operation of the company. Together, they made it all work.

"Innovation and commerce have always gone hand-in-hand," continued Shea. "I don't want to bore you with history, but humor me for one moment." Shea had always loved history. As a young girl, eldest of four siblings, she had devoured biographies and history books in high school, and continued those studies in college. Graduating with honors with a triple major in history, economics and political science from Boston College, she was well situated for either a career as a university professor or a lawyer. She chose the latter.

"You only have to look at Spain during the fifteenth and sixteenth centuries, or the Dutch during the sixteenth and seventeenth centuries. Heck, even go back to the ancient cultures of Phoenicia or Corinth or other great realms – they all flourished on open commerce and free trade. They thrived on the entrepreneurial spirit of their people. But, we in America stand at a crossroads. We have prospered mightily from the capitalistic spirit that took us from a quaint colonial nation in 1789 to a superpower by 1942 when we sent our first ships and troops into battle in WWII. But, since then we have decayed as a nation, falling into the same crevasse as did Western Europe after the war. Socialism wrapped its cold, bony fingers around the neck of free commerce, pulling on the purse strings of its citizens and emptying them of everything of value. Shamed by their wealth, these nations redistributed the value created by their most productive people, and succeeding only in de-motivating the poor while nourishing their own cravings to be seen as *good* and *righteous*. Elitism was and is the word that cannot be spoken. Yet, it perfectly describes how the pin-heads from the elite universities believe they know better what's good for all of us than we do. As many of those pin-heads now work for the government, we have changed our motto from *In God We Trust* to *In Government We Trust*. And, as we have seen, that hasn't worked out very well."

At this point, Patrick moved close to his wife and whispered in her ear. She smiled and held up her glass. "My husband is telling me that while my *rant* is entertaining, we have a party to get back to. That's his way of telling me to shut up and let you get back to it." She laughed. "He's right, of course. So, I'll just say this. Twenty some years ago, we swore we would do something unique at the Lenoir Research Labs — something that would revolutionize the way commerce is done. It is true that services are done over the computer and SI-net these days, sending electrons over circuits to deliver information or instruct machines to produce products remotely. However, until a material transporter machine is developed, we will still travel via air, water or road, and we'll need an engine to do that. That engine is the SECE.

"And finally, I just want to say that Patrick and I will lead you to the top of the mountain where we want you to join us. We believe we can succeed on our own hard work and perseverance. Although we can't control what the government or other authorities do, we can control what we do. And, right now, I see no limits to what we can accomplish."

She got a rousing, boisterous round of applause.

Patrick stepped in one more time, smiling and raising his hand. "Now, if you'd like to cast your vote for our next Congresswoman from the state of Massachusetts," he quipped, garnering a laugh from everyone. "No, seriously, now we want to turn things over to our CFO, Annie Reynolds, for some other great news. Annie ..." Patrick said, motioning for the financial head to come to the front.

"I do have some good news," said Annie. "For almost all of you -- those who have stock options in our company -- it's a good day. With the patent confirmed, we will be selling part of the company in the public market within

21

the next few months. We don't have all the details right now, but we will notify you as we get closer to the time of the offering."

The Company had always offered stock options to employees who worked hard. It enabled them to purchase the company's stock at prices just below their value as an incentive to stay with the company and share in the wealth and value they were helping to create. As a result, all expected that over one hundred new multimillionaires were likely to be produced – from senior executives to administrative assistants.

Patrick stepped back to center stage. "So, we have a lot to celebrate tonight! We have plenty of food and drink – you all deserve it. And again, thank you for your tireless effort!" he said.

He turned and kissed Shea tenderly on the lips, mouthing the words *I love you*. She returned the affection, moving her arm around his waist and squeezing him tightly toward her.

The evening wore on with more drinking and more celebration. But, by two in the morning most had gone home to sleep off their overindulgences and recuperate for the weekend. As for Shea and Patrick, they had left the party earlier, going back to their modest home in Needham only a twenty-minute drive from the office when there was no traffic. Both were feeling little pain, having drunk more wine than they were accustomed. Shea ended up driving home, worried about how much Patrick had drunk during the evening.

Patrick pressed his finger to the biometric lock on the front door of their house and heard the shifting of the tumblers within the doorframe, while Shea pulled the car into the garage below and turned off the lights by voice activation. It had been a long day.

"Thank you for such a splendid evening," said Shea, coming in through the mudroom door next to the garage. She walked into the kitchen, opened a cabinet door and pulled a glass off the upper shelf.

"Haven't you had enough?" asked Patrick, raising an eyebrow.

"Just water," she answered. "I'm thirsty. Is that okay?" She turned and filled the glass under the spout on the refrigerator door before taking several gulps. "*Ooooh*, I was really thirsty," she said. There was a twinkle in her eye as she looked at Patrick. He was the love of her life. He always had been. There had been something from the start between them – a connection that seemed unbreakable. She couldn't fathom life without him any more than he could without her.

He picked up the same glass from the counter and took two quick sips. "I'm thirsty too," he said, with an entirely different connotation, staring into her eyes intently.

She knew what he meant and reached out to caress his hand. She took his fingers and pressed them up against her moist lips. She kissed them seductively, using her tongue to lick each finger and suck on its tip.

"So, I guess it's mutual," he said with a slight grin.

She paused only for a moment, interrupting her flirtation with his digits. "I guess you could say that," she said in reply, almost purring.

He began kissing her on the neck, pressing his soft lips against her cheeks and around her ear. She threw her head back and let him move over her gently, his warm breath making her pulse quicken. She trembled as he unzipped the back of her dress, and she felt the straps of her gown fall from her shoulders to the floor.

She was beautiful in his eyes – she always had been. And this evening she looked even more so.

Patrick put his hands on her tender and soft back as he worked his magic. He continued caressing her, kissing her shoulders and sliding his fingers effortlessly around to her breasts. She groaned again as he placed his hands on her nipples and began rubbing them gently. The rest of the evening was a long crescendo to ecstasy. And afterward, they both fell quickly asleep in each other's arms.

*****

CH 2 Deputy Secretary of Control

News of the patent approval and authorization for Lenoir Labs to begin marketing its new high-efficiency, SECE engine technology reached the Department of Technology Assessment and its Deputy Secretary's desk by an unusual route – a public news wire from the United Press Association or UPA. The article was intended to be scathing rebuke of the action, questioning the government's approval of what the president and his Administration had vilified for decades as an evil against society – that is, anything related to fossil-fuels. Even though marked as a news piece, the article was really an editorial with rehashed misstatements and untruths, railing against pollution and anthropomorphic generated carbon dioxide.

Most at the UPA were second-rate journalists who had given up any attempt at being impartial. Researching and investigating news stories was hard work. It took time, and most news agencies had neither the time nor money for it. News had become whatever you wanted it to be or, more precisely, whatever the editor wanted it to be. Simply put, it was whatever sold, regardless of the truth. Truth and the facts had long-since been sacrificed on the holy alter of humanism and political correctness.

For three years, Angel Ratner had been the head of the Department of Technology Assessment, a department that fell under the broader auspices of the Department of Fair Trade, formerly known as the Department of Commerce. As deputy secretary, she knew her job well and made sure she was in sync with the wishes of the President. She was politically savvy and understood the importance of aligning herself not only with her direct boss, the Secretary of Fair Trade, but also her boss's boss, President Jack Fourier.

Ratner was petite, but mighty. Her five foot, two inch body disguised a force that few in Washington could or were willing to confront. Cunningly creative, Ratner could hatch subtle and nefarious strategies, but she also felt no remorse about declaring outright war and coming out fighting, guns blazing. In fact, there was a story told that she had debated a prominent U.S. senator, destroying his arguments completely. When leaving the hearing, she had taken nine paces toward the exit doors before turning and, using her hand as a gun, had pointed back toward the senator, saying *"Bang!* Got you" -- all with a smile on her face.

With chestnut brown hair, highlighted by streaks of blonde, at forty-two Ratner looked unassuming enough. Shallow wrinkles had grown under and

24

around her dark eyes, and her eyelashes were prematurely thinning, making her otherwise cherubic face look more masculine. Many alleged her eyes had been blue before she'd come to Washington, but since she'd been there a while, they had turned coal black. Her voice was deep for a woman of her size, and she projected it well. There was never a question of when she had entered into a conversation, as her words cut through the air like a samurai sword through human flesh. When she battled those she considered enemies or threats, it was usually to the death, and her intent was always to leave them destroyed, if not politically mortally wounded.

At the same time, Ratner could be personable, even charming. She could make small talk with the best of them, especially if it involved a head of state or other important dignitary. Most would walk away from a conversation believing that she really empathized with what they were talking about – that she understood them and their plight or cause. However, it was only an act, and after years of practice, she had honed it well. In reality, she believed that she was special to the world – that she had a superior intelligence and way of thinking. After all, since she'd been a child, she had always been told she was brilliant. To her, she was one of only a handful who really *understood* what it was all about, and she felt it was unfortunate that there weren't more like her who understood the way things should be done.

No matter, she would tell herself boastfully. *They have me.*

"What the hell is this all about!" she screamed across the room, her voice carrying through the open door that led to her private secretary.

Quickly, a tall, prematurely-balding young man rushed through the doorway holding a computer tablet and pen. "Madam Secretary, did you need something?"

"I wasn't talking to you!" she snarled, motioning for him to go away.

"What's this crap about?" Ratner said to the person sitting on a low chair in front of her desk. "Who authorized the approval of this patent?"

Staring at her with a blank look on his face was her Vice-deputy Secretary of Intellectual Property, George Thomas. He was one of many vice deputies and one of hundreds of other lower level bureaucrats that ran the department under her. The hierarchy within the Executive Branch of government had gotten unruly and few could follow the arcane structure under which they were forced to function. Secretaries had deputy secretaries, who had vice-deputy secretaries, who then had senior vice-deputy secretaries and junior vice-deputy secretaries. However, below that were additional layers of senior assistant vice-deputy secretaries and junior assistant vice-deputy secretaries. The list was nearly endless, and the ability of constructing a meaningful organizational chart impossible.

Soft-spoken, but erudite, the young George was considered part of the "up-and-comers" of the People's Party. His hair was short-cropped and brownish-blonde, which he had cut every week to keep it perfect. Only twenty-six, he was pencil thin and somewhat gangly. In college, others had initially made fun of his awkwardness, but he made up for it with his ability to adapt. He was a chameleon, shaping his views and his associations as needed to get ahead. He quickly conformed with whatever group he was involved at the time. Even within the ranks of the school jocks, he was able to make friends. In government, he found the situation the same. There were those who were rabid activists, dogmatically adhering to their principles. Then, there were those who kept their heads down to do their jobs and survive. And lastly, there were those who blew with the wind; like willows, they bended as they needed to as tempests roiled around them – only emerging stronger and straighter afterward. George was a willow. He knew he needed to please all sides, but especially, his tough superior, Deputy-secretary Ratner.

His signature attire was a navy or dark-gray, chalk-stripe suit, blue-cotton, starched shirt with a white collar, and a paisley bow tie. Few people wore suits, but he was very fond of them and his bow ties. In fact, he had bow ties in just about every color combination imaginable. Coming from Princeton, he was Ivy League, and although he didn't really need glasses, he wore a pair of round-framed, black-wired lenses that made his blue eyes overtly larger. The entire package made him look smart.

"Madam Secretary, I'm sorry. I learned of this issue this morning when I came in. It was one of my senior staff who must have sent out the notice without my knowledge. I don't know why he let the patent go through. We've been fighting that company for years over their patent submissions. We know where the president stands on fossil fuels."

"That's right!" shouted Ratner. "He is *not* going to be happy!"

"We're investigating how it happened as we speak. But, Secretary Ratner, it's an easy matter to correct, though. I've already started the process of reversing the decision."

"And the senior staff person?"

"I will take care of him right away, Madam Secretary," said Thomas, shaking in front of his boss. He did not want to become a *persona non grata* – not just in Washington, but everywhere he might go. Ratner had the power to do just that if she disliked someone or she felt the person weren't loyal. Thomas felt there were few places on Earth where she had no influence, unless it was some remote region of New Guinea or the Republic of the Congo.

Ratner's face grew stone cold, frozen with anger. She pounded her fist on her desk. "How stupid are you?" she asked cruelly. "Lenoir makes *combustible* engines, for God's sake! *Combustible* engines! They use fossil fuels – and we don't like fossil fuels. Duh! Haven't you heard a *thing* the president has been saying on this? All of the scientific community is in full agreement that oil and coal are destroying our planet! They are killing us – all of us!" The tone in her voice only hardened. "Do I need to say anymore, G?" the nickname she'd given him, as she felt his surname, George, took too much effort for her to say.

"No, ma'am."

"And about that staffer of yours. You said you'd handle it – how?"

"I'm going to fire him, ma'am."

"Bull sh*t, G! I want that bastard in prison! Do you hear me?"

George's face drained. "Prison, ma'am? On what grounds would we ..."

"I don't give a crap what you come up with! I want him rotting in jail. Do you understand? Now, handle it!" She put her head back down to scroll through files on her computer screen. When he didn't move immediately, she looked up and glared at him. He immediately got out of his chair and rushed from her chamber without another word.

The next day, the official documents were issued, reversing the decision made earlier to approve the patent of the Lenoir Research Labs Company. George had come up with a reason. Although it was a lie, it was believable, and that was all that mattered. The reason cited for the reversal was that a new set of data had been presented by a competing firm – data that allegedly challenged the legitimacy of the company's patent claim. The competing firm protesting the patent was not named, but it didn't need to be. It was an old friend of the current president.

However, true to bureaucratic efficiency, the revocation documents were lost in the red-taped morass of the department building. Misfiled, the e-papers sat in a junior-assistant deputy secretary's computer inbox under *Urgent*, instead of *Extremely Urgent* or *Critical*. So, although the decision to deny the patent was official and in force, the communiqué to the company was not received by anyone at Lenoir for more than a month. In the meantime, Shea and Patrick continued to prepare to sell part of their company to raise money to begin manufacturing their SECE, unaware their fate had changed completely.

When Ratner received the re-filed revocation paperwork she was placated, at least for the moment. A crisis had been averted, and there would be no calls from the White House ordering her to appear and justify the patent to the president. But in her mind the crisis should never have happened in the first place. She had dealt with worse before. And usually if it meant finding someone else to blame, she would. If it meant lying through her teeth, she would do that too. If it meant doing something more ... well , it hadn't yet come to that. But, then again, only time would tell. She was never about to let anyone engrave her tombstone for her. If anyone tried, she would be there, chisel in hand, to write over it or better yet, to impale the chisel through their hand before they even had a chance to touch it.

***

"Honey, when do you think you'll be home?" asked Elise, George's wife.

Thomas was regularly late. Ratner kept him until all hours, sometimes as late as one or two in the morning, only requiring that he be on time at eight in the morning. She was unrealistic, but that didn't matter. It was the nature of the job he had now that she was now in charge.

"Uh, I should be home by eleven," he said, looking at the clock. "I just have two more analyses to do for the Secretary. She wants them on her desk first thing in the morning."

"George, you always say that. She never looks at any of it for weeks! Why do you have to bust your hump to get her things when she never looks at them?" asked Elise. "She's always doing this to you! It's just not fair!"

"I know. I know."

"You've been saying that! When will it change?"

"I don't know. But it will. I promise," said George. "I'll be home soon." He hung up, as frustrated as she was. He hated working seventy-hour weeks and getting berated and belittled for everything he did. He had children and a wife at home whom he didn't see often any more. That he regretted.

He opened the door as quietly as he could, trying not to awaken anyone. The townhouse was small, out in Annandale, and he had gotten on the last subway train from downtown Washington. Sometimes he'd been so tired that he'd slept through the entire Purple Line route and ended up in Fairfax. Tonight, he'd managed to stay awake and get off at the right station, staggering in weariness to his car in the parking lot and driving home. The roads were nearly abandoned at midnight on a workday, and it was easy for his car to navigate home on its own without a problem.

George tiptoed up the staircase and cracked the door on his eleven-year-old son, who was sleeping soundly. His cherubic face and dark hair reflected in the hallway light. He loved his kids and his Elise more than life itself, and it pained him to miss these important years of their lives. Still, he had to bring home the 'bacon' so they could live.

Quietly, he crossed the room and pulled the covers up closer to Nathan's face. He kissed him on the cheek and patted him on the head. Nathan didn't move, sleeping soundly without a stir.

George repeated the gesture in little Caroline's and Christian's rooms. They were a few years younger than Nathan, born twins, they shared a room next door. His younger ones were in second grade, and both were clamoring for their own rooms. "Next year, maybe," he would tell them. "We'll start looking for a bigger house."

They had the money to buy a new place, something bigger than what they'd been living in, but he just hadn't had the time to look. He had kept telling Elise that it would be 'soon' when they could look – that he would take the time off if he needed. But Ratner had never consented to the time off. It would have to wait, he had said.

Leaving the twin's room, Caroline had awakened. "Daddy?" she asked, half asleep.

"Yes, pumpkin," George said

"Are you home?"

"Yes, dear. I'm here. I'm here. Is there something you need?"

"No. I … I was just worried about you. You haven't been home. Why aren't you at home, Daddy?"

"I'm working. Things are really hard at work right now. But things will get better, Car. They will. I hope to be home more in the near future." He wasn't telling the truth, but he knew that's what she wanted to hear.

"Okay, Daddy. I love you," she said closing her eyes.

"I love you too pumpkin," he answered, stroking her blonde hair.

George turned off the light next to her bed and closed the door behind him as he left. His bedroom with Elise was just down the hall to the left, and he could hear her softly snoring inside. As soon as he cracked open the door, the slight creak awakened her.

"Honey? Is that you?"

"Yes, dear. I'm finally home," he answered

Elise rolled over and looked at the time that was projected onto the wall screen next to the bed. "It's nearly one in the morning, George!" she exclaimed.

"I know. It's late. I'm sorry," he answered, trying to comfort her. "Go back to sleep. You won't hear me in the morning. I'll be out of here before you wake up."

"This isn't good for your health. You're going to wear yourself out, you know."

"Yes, you're probably right, dear. But, just a little while longer. I'll get some time off or I'll transfer. I'll do something. I promise," said George.

Elise pulled up the covers. He kissed her softly on the forehead. "I love you, Elise," he said, looking at her sadly. He missed being with her and the family. He only hoped that what he had told them would come true.

*****

CH 3 GOVERNMENT, INC.

It was a beautiful, sunny afternoon in Redwood City, California, just south of San Francisco. This area along the bay had been a hotbed of technology back in the day, but because of increased intrusion by Congress and agencies of the Executive Branch, it now produced very little. These days, virtually all of the technological innovation came from overseas. High taxes, difficulty obtaining patent protection, rampant overseas copying of designs, extensive new testing requirements, and reams of mandated government forms and reports made the business more about keeping the government satisfied than keeping customers or shareholders happy. Most believed it's time had come and gone.

Of all the abandoned, hulking monoliths once dedicated to grand capitalistic ideals, there were only a handful of corporate buildings that remained occupied. All belonged to companies known as *government-aligned companies*, even though most people referred to them as GovCo's. These were huge corporations that lobbied themselves into bed with Congress and, in return, received the massive amounts of military and other government procurement contracts that came with it. Government contracts were lucrative, especially when one had high-level sponsors in Congress. It was a classic you-scratch-my-back-and-I'll-scratch-yours relationship. Congressmen got kickbacks and perks from the companies as well as money for their campaigns, and the companies got, well, rich. More importantly, the GovCo's got exempted from many laws passed that handicapped, outright crippled or even destroyed their competitors.

Yet, the leaders of these GovCo's defended their actions in private, arguing that their dealings with congressmen, hiring of lobbyists and creation of industry advocacy groups were only in response to the government's heavy hand in trying to regulate it. Some even pointed fingers at Theodore Roosevelt, the Trust Buster, for starting the vendetta against big business in 1902 with his lawsuit against JP Morgan's railroad trusts. Business, they claimed, was only trying to survive, and government's barrage of laws and regulations made that almost impossible. It was a chicken-and-egg conundrum, but however it began, the outcome was the same – these bedfellows were embraced in a symbiotic relationship that benefited themselves to the mutual exclusion of almost everyone else.

In the end, the group that suffered most was small business. They lacked the clout to hire the well-healed lobbyists and create advocacy groups with enough clout to matter. Even the U.S. Chamber of Commerce, which was supposed to look after the general business interests of both big and small, had long abandoned the pretext and now overtly defended GovCo's interests. Sadly, small business lay prostrate at the hands of government and their GovCo competitors.

And those in small business who held out hope that the friction between government and GovCo's may one day afford them an opportunity to break free of their chains would be disheartened. Power trumps money every time. For even though power begets money, money does not always beget power; and without both, one cannot be assured of success. So, the power of government office had become synonymous with total, absolute control over everyone and everything. After all, those in power were there for a reason – they were better educated and better intentioned than anyone else, especially the profiteers they liked to vilify as greedy capitalists.

But for now, since those in GovCo's flew them to Hawaii for conferences or to Europe for so-called fact finding trips, they would be spared and would continue to be exempted from deleterious laws. As long as the gravy train was running on time and the conductor was of the right mind, *status quo* was a good thing.

One of those GovCo's was EG, Inc., a conglomerate of many companies that spanned multiple industries worldwide. It had been founded back in the nineteenth century and during most of that time had succeeded by competing honestly in the marketplace. However, it had become huge, and like a black hole, had begun sucking everything around it into its swirling, insatiable vortex, including government politicians who enjoyed their "hospitality."

Kilby Thorne had been selected by a divided board of directors as CEO of EG after his predecessor unexpectedly died from a massive heart attack. Within a year, he had consolidated his power, getting those on the board who had opposed his appointment thrown off and replacing them with friends. Like Roman emperors of antiquity, Thorne was ambitious beyond measure. He had always dreamed of being the head of the largest company on Earth, not to mention one larger than most countries on the planet. By his third anniversary as CEO, he had built an organization in Washington that assured the interests of the company were looked after by the politicians who ran the two houses of Congress. He did so by entwining their political fates to the success of the company. Each politician had a weakness, and he was ruthless in finding out what it was and exploiting it. If he could find none, he would create one for them.

EG, Inc. generated significant cash – which would have been used for marketing and advertising; however, Thorne found that lobbyists and advocacy groups were better investments. It was about domination, and what better way to dominate one's market than to push through legislation that favored one's own company and punished its competitors. By creating new rules that favored EG's strengths and minimized its weaknesses, winning was all but ensured. It was a simple plan; it was an effective plan. And it worked.

Within a short time, EG, Inc. had become a multi-billion dollar global enterprise with branches and research facilities in seventy-six countries. Its work was confidential, but the shareholders' 10-K and annual report would cite technology and research and development as the major product lines, along with its original, primary business segment, heavy manufacturing. Its founder had built one of the first combustion engines during the nineteenth century. However, government grants had pushed them into alternative energy sources in the twenty-first. None of these were profitable on their own, except for the generous government subsidies that more than made up for the losses. Its primary customers were the Department of International Security – formerly named the Department of Defense -- and the Department of Eco-Transportation or DET. The DET had remained true to its mission, albeit working more closely with the Department of Energy Stewardship on new means of creating wind, solar, geothermal or other forms of clean, although not affordable, energy.

The mission of the Department of International Security had changed markedly during the previous decade. No longer was its purpose to defend the United States. With the continued impotence of the United Nations, which had become a cesspool of corruption, President Fourier, had ordered the department to be the worldwide peacekeeper in countries where he identified human rights abuses. Of course, this too had become political. Those countries that helped Fourier and the People's Party stay in power through backchannel campaign contributions were placed on a watch list to be evaluated by a hand-picked commission established by the president. However, for some "reason" they never moved off that listing. Instead, they continued to receive foreign aid and assurances of non-intervention by the U.S. government. Likewise, leaders of large countries with sizeable military threats would also be ignored. It was only those leaders of small, vulnerable nations who vowed to fight Fourier or challenge his authority that were infiltrated by U.S. special forces. There, Fourier could easily tally wins for his humanitarian image and his polling support at home.

These were the activities where EG could make the most in profits – long, sustained conflicts, without a defined goal or mission. Those were the best. And with those and other contracts, EG's ability to monopolize its markets and keep competitors out was made a whole lot easier. Thorne made sure that he serviced Fourier first, and in return, he and his company were well fed with taxpayer money.

The limousine sped onward, hustling toward the technology conference where Thorne was scheduled to speak. Given his stature in the world of business, everyone knew who he was. He had near rock-star status, and thousands had signed up and paid their ten thousand dollars to hear him speak.

Although the conference was in Paris, that city was now divided -- much as Berlin was at the end of WWII. France had been forced to divide into two separate countries by Islamic militants that took over the capital and the rest of the northern part of the country. Now, the north was called the Islamic Republic of Franconia, while the south was referred to as Vichy France, after its WWII name. Paris, like Berlin during half of the twentieth century, was an island with the Left Bank occupied by Vichy and the Right Bank controlled by the Muslims. Earlier, England had abandoned its parliamentary system and ousted the monarchy, replacing them with sharia law and appointing a supreme Islamic leader. The Ayatollah, who was unelected, could not be removed and would rule until his death. As result, Britain had become the Revolutionary Kingdom of Islam (RKI) almost overnight, and Islam had done what a thousand years of world conflict had been unable to do – destroy the once-mighty British Empire.

Together, the western European countries of England, Belgium, Netherlands, Northern France, Germany, Denmark, Austria, Finland, Sweden, and even Switzerland, were part of the Northern Union of Islamic States. The Southern Union of Islamic States was an arc of states spanning from Spain and Portugal through Southern Italy, Greece, Turkey, east to Syria and Jordan, and then back west through Egypt and Libya along the northern coast to Africa to Morocco.

There were few independent states left that were not ruled by an ayatollah or Russia in Europe and the Middle East. Only Germany, Austria, Switzerland and northern Italy, including Rome, had managed to survive the Persian onslaught. Likewise, Saudi Arabia and a fortified Israel, both with nuclear deterrents, had isolated their territories from a sharia overthrow or the claws of the Russian bear.

Meanwhile, Russia had taken advantage of America's weakness and the world's distraction with Islamists. Mobilizing their tanks, they had led a German-styled blitzkrieg to romp across Europe before anyone could offer resistance. Within two months, the Russians had subjugated all of the Eastern European countries they had controlled as satellites after WWII, plus Finland.

As the black Mercedes stopped in front of the gray, cement walls of the massive convention center, Thorne jumped out, not wishing to wait for his driver. He strode up to the entrance like a man who owned the place, but then again, perhaps he thought he did. Wearing an eighteen thousand dollar, tailored suit, Hermes tie and cuff links made of gold, Louis XVI French coins minted during the revolutionary period in 1792, he looked every bit the part of a business tycoon – one that had power and the backing of those in government who held even more.

He was ushered backstage where his bottled water, decanted into a rare 1934 Cire Perdue crystal pitcher and kept at exactly 20 degrees Celsius, awaited him. Ignoring the water, fresh fruit, Beluga caviar, smoked Chinook salmon and everything else he demanded be readied for him, he walked out on stage to thunderous applause.

"Welcome," began Thorne, standing at the mahogany podium and gripping the sides with his large-knuckled hands. He was a robust, stocky man, many times the girth his doctors had advised, but he was never one to take orders from others – doctors or not.

Thorne was a large man with several chins below the one with which he was born. His love of food was apparent, and did not shy from it, especially when it was at a two- or three-star Michelin restaurant with prices at a level most people paid for a new car. His skin held a bronze tan like a Greek god, but actually reflecting his pension for spending leisurely time at the beach. The brilliance of his blue eyes was framed by his very bushy and unruly gray eyebrows that seemed to spin off in all directions.

"I'd like to welcome you to this year's exposé on industrial technology," began Thorne, "and the achievements U.S. companies are making in different fields – from plasma conductors to super-cooling meta-compounds. As you know, my expertise is in energy and the technology that goes with creating machines and engines that utilize different sources of energy. We at EG also research and create new robotic devices that further the ability of mankind and womankind to endure physical adversity to a much greater extent than we ever thought possible. We are proud to be a major contributor to the American technology movement – pushing the envelope of science to improve lives throughout the world. Our artificial arms and legs are second-to-none, bringing normalization to millions of world citizens who have lost their ability to use limbs through birth, accident, or military service. Indeed, we have been successful in pioneering fully-functioning artificial eyes and, soon-to-be-released, auxiliary implantable devices that will replace damaged brain functions and return to the user full mental capability with even more rapid memory retrieval. Integration between the human cranium and machines has been well-established, but we at EG are accelerating this progress. We have a device that will seamlessly connect the brain with an implantable computer, allowing the person to have all the senses of a human, but all the benefits of data retrieval as well as direct access to information stored on the Super-Internet, or SI-net, as it was called, all over the world. All of these devices will be on the market within the year. "

None in the crowd knew, but in fact EG had done very little to develop anything new. In almost every case, any technology they had "developed" had been taken the old-fashioned way – strong-armed. It had paid politicians and judges to look the other way while it forced smaller companies to sell-out their technology to EG or face crippling litigation over trumped-up charges of stealing EG's technology – technology EG never had. In the end, EG won, and capitalism and free enterprise lost. It was a case of backs being scratched and pockets being lined – a *modus operandi* used for thousands of years.

"But none of it would be possible," said Thorne, "without a close partnership with a strong federal presence. And we have that. We at EG believe that what makes a strong company is a strong nation behind it – that's the foundation of capitalism. Our country was founded on the notion of democracy and capitalism working together. It was World War II that brought out the best in America. The industrial might of the country was transformed overnight on December 7, 1941, from commercial to military. It was President Roosevelt and his leadership that drove the machinery of the country to produce massive quantities of armaments and munitions for not only our troops but for those of our allies, including France. And, as a result, today the world is a better place for it." With this mention, he got a hearty applause.

Known for being long-winded, Thorne pressed on, but after thirty more minutes, even he grew tired of talking. Hastening his concluding remarks, he said, "Over the years, all nations that are democracies have evolved. They have moved toward socialism or some religiously-sponsored state. Both are higher levels of consciousness than that of pure democracy. They reflect improvements in humanity – our continued evolution to higher and greater beings. So too, capitalism has evolved. It has moved from the days when commerce was unbridled and unregulated to a state where it now works hand-and-glove with government. It is a more efficient system, with fewer casualties and greater efficiencies. Big companies have much greater economies of scale than small ones and can employ many more people. The impact of big companies on society is much greater, and we can give back much more through our philanthropic contributions.

"In conclusion, we have finally realized that competition is bad for society. It pits company against company, nation against nation, people against people. When we eliminate the creative destruction wrought by this raw and crude doctrine called capitalism, we get a smooth, well-oiled machine capable of doing great things. Socialism is the one true system that can marshal the resources needed to bring about innovation and change in this world. And when big companies work directly with governments, the resource pool is even larger, and so much more can be done.

"As for technology, we would not be where we are if it weren't for EG and those in Washington and other capitals around the world that fund important programs they believe to be vital to society. EG has used federal money to invest in such things as self-managed robotics, gene therapy, cold fusion, nano-scale machinery, and anti-gravitational transportation research. These represent the new frontiers of the world – these are the future for your children and their children."

Again, Thorne was a master of exaggerating or outright lying about reality to suit his ends. EG, in fact, had made no such investments in any of those programs, and none were any further along in finding answers than they had been thirty years earlier.

At this point, Thorne paused and basked in the audience's applause. Then, he took a sip of water from a small glass hidden just under his podium and continued. "In conclusion, let me say that EG will continue to work closely with the U.S. federal governments and those around the world, to ensure that we help countries meet their economic needs to grow and thrive in the years to come. In this way, we are servants of the world, generously giving our time and money to efforts that will better the lives of everyone on Earth. Thank you."

His speech drew cheers and plaudits, and he relished the moment. The sound of clapping hands was his reinforcement that he was somebody – he was important. His ego needed feeding, continuously, and this satisfied that need – at least for the day.

After the ovation subsided, there was a scheduled period of question and answer from those in attendance. Convention organizers had stationed microphones in the two aisles that divided the grand ballroom into three sections, and a queue began to form behind each one. The first few questions were from technical types, inquiring about the latest software programs that the company had been working on or other projects that were grossly over budget or delayed. Thorne was prepared for such questions and easily sidestepped them, describing the process of developing software, cures, machinery, or other such inventions as tedious. "These programs require billions of code lines," he said more than once, not really knowing the answer, or "the inventions required extensive trials, reviews and testing, which in many cases took years."

Then a wiry young man stepped to the mike. He was short with a thin frame. His long black hair appeared as though he hadn't washed or brushed it in weeks. The stubble on his face echoed the appearance of an unkempt individual who cared little about what others thought of him. Yet, there was an intelligence about him that shown through the messy facade. He appeared calm and poised, and his demeanor was inquisitive and non-threatening.

"Mr. Thorne, I wonder if you could tell us something about U.S. Senate Bill 601 and how your company was able to get a special exclusion for exporting military-grade robotic programming to Libya, Sudan, Iran and Pakistan? Would you care to comment?"

"I'm not familiar with what you are talking about," said Thorne, startled by the question. The expression on his face was one of mild shock, and the tenseness was obvious. "Let's go to the next questioner," he added, trying to extricate himself from the discomfort.

But the young man persisted. "I'm sorry, Mr. Thorne, but my research shows that a lobby group you paid two million dollars to last year, called Watson and Peters, has connections to Senator Milligan and Congressman Combs, sponsors of the bill. These two took trips to Australia, Brazil, and Europe – all paid by Watson & Peters. Milligan and Combs both pushed through the legislation. But on page 2,341 of that bill, there is a footnote that gives, quote a company based in Redwood City, California, incorporated in Delaware in 1932 that deals with technology, alternative energy and engines and machinery manufacturing, that has more than thirty-two thousand employees and offers its employees special benefits, as described in the regulations, sole rights to sell such intelligence to foreign entities, unquote. Do you know that EG is the only company in the entire country -- in fact the entire world -- that meets these requirements? Is this coincidental?"

Thorne twitched. "I really haven't read the bill, so I can't really comment," he said. "It's time to move on to ..."

"Did you realize that some of the countries listed as those EG can sell to were once on our Department of International Policing's list of terrorist states – that is *before* this law was passed. Now it allows sales like this to those countries. Is that a good thing?"

"I am not in the Congress, so I don't have any opinion as to what laws they pass or don't pass," said Thorne.

"But didn't you just say in your speech that companies and government should work hand-in-hand? Is this an example of what you meant?" asked the man.

Thorne's complexion changed from a bronzed tint to red, as anger flushed through his veins. He gritted his teeth and then relaxed his jaw. He'd been through testy confrontations before, and in his early days he would have lashed out at the man. However, now that he was CEO, he had learned to be much more careful about his response, especially since the media was there. Yet, he couldn't always count on their discretion when reporting on his appearances and at times had to make a call to their editor-in-chief to ensure his review was presented favorably regardless of what he had said.

"As I said before, I am not familiar with that matter. However, I will say that EG does not get involved with government policy, as you are inferring. We have a long history of working *with* government – not *against* it or the people of America. What is good for the country is good for EG. Now, next question."

That response had bought time for the security guards to close in on the man. He looked around nervously, watching as the building guards descended upon him. Dressed in dark suits, white shirts and plain, narrow black ties, two guards on a walky-talkies grabbed him and another pulled out a Stun unit, injecting the man with an instant paralyzing drug that left him unconscious.

His body fell the to the burgundy and blue paisley-patterned carpeting that lined the aisles and major thoroughfares in the hall. Within seconds, security had him by his armpits, dragging him from the crime scene -- his outdated, unpolished black loafers digging furrows into the carpeting behind him.

Thorne smiled, knowing that the man would be imprisoned for months for his imperiousness. "Next question," he said calmly, pointing to the next man in line. His face showed relief that the irritant had been addressed and removed from the premises.

Similar to the first man, the second also portrayed a look of disinterest in his appearance, and spoke quickly at the microphone, in anticipation of what was coming to him as well.

"That's not all," said the second man, obviously a co-conspirator with the first. "We also have information that EG got an exclusion from the Department of Taxation & Enforcement so that the company paid *no* taxes last year on profits of over 6.8 billion dollars worldwide. In fact, the U.S. government has given EG tax credits to be used to offset any future tax liability the company may generate for the next twenty years. Isn't that right?"

There was restlessness in the crowd. The fact that not one, but two men had been willing to stand up to Thorne was remarkable. Both knew what they were getting into, and that they would suffer in a barren, bleak prison cell for months before having any chance of parole or freedom. Since the Islamic revolution, prisons in the Islamic Republic sector of Paris had turned into virtual torture chambers, with stories of horror, including partial dismemberment and beheadings, not uncommon. For the most part, crimes in the Vichy section of Paris were still under sectarian law. However, prisoners there were easily forced to do whatever the Vichy government wanted of them; all the guards had to do was threatened them with a transfer to the Sharia Law side of town on the Right Bank. It was remarkable to what crimes they would confess.

Again, Thorne played dumb. "I sure you must be mistaken. These bills to which you and the former gentleman are referring do not reference EG in any component whatsoever. To imply that EG somehow was trying to curry favor and get breaks from the law is preposterous. It impugns the very dignity and integrity of EG and all of the people who work there and is completely unfair to them and their families. Their children will also have to face the ridicule and mistreatment from those around them due to your insensitivity. How dare you!" he finally thundered. "It is clear that you are part of some conspiracy group – probably anarchists – who threaten the very fabric of our society. You are the ones who seek to destroy everything we, as a people of Earth, have built. You are the types who would wish us to go back to living in caves and beating our clothes with rocks to clean them. *You* sir are a disgrace to humankind!"

But with all the bluster, the question had struck a nerve in the audience. Socialist and Islamic countries around the world desperately needed money, and there was only one good source -- taxes. As a result, the U.S. had agreed to a UN Resolution imposing a worldwide tax on all citizens. It was called the WW VAT or worldwide value added tax, which would be collected by the UN to fund its misguided and corrupt initiatives. Everyone knew where the money would go – to line diplomats' pockets. But that had come to be expected. To make matters worse, the U.S. Congress had tacked on additional taxes for its own needs. President Fourier had just announced an increase in the U.S. income tax rates for most Americans, going from 49 to 94 percent for the upper tier of society as well as hefty increases in the rates at every other level below that.

"So, it's okay for EG to get out of paying taxes when the top tax rate has been raised to ninety-four percent?" asked the man, bracing himself for the second wave of dark suits that were marching briskly toward him.

Thorne grinned again. "That's where your argument is idiotic!" he said. "It is a well-known fact that the U.S. economy prospered the most in its history during the 1950s when marginal tax rates were nine-one percent. There is your proof, sir! I need not have to say anymore!"

Ever since the rates had been dramatically increased, the media had pointed out that the president was only restoring tax rates to where they'd been in 1944 – 94 percent -- and through the boom years of the fifties when they were at 70 percent. "It was the greatest time in American history," the media had said. "A time of marvelous prosperity and growth." Unfortunately, facts were not to get in the way of a good story.

"I'm sorry sir, but your facts are wrong," countered the man, his eyes widening as he viewed the oncoming assault. "Facts are pesky things, I know. But the percent of income paid in taxes by the top three percent of earners *rose* from 2.7 percent to 4 percent from 1958 to 2010 even though tax rates dropped to thirty-five percent. As tax rates rose from 2020-2040, the percent of taxes paid dropped again. And as for the booming economy during the

1950s? It is hard to argue that a 3.1 percent growth rate, as adjusted for the Korean Conflict, was anything but, well, average. Are those the truths you were talking about?"

But without regard to what the man had said, Thorne's anger boiled over. "No! It is not right. You have your facts wrong," he snapped . "You're only trying to smear EG. That's all you and your kind do! EG is a reputable company. We treat our employees well, and we treat the people of the world well. We are a patriotic organization – all of us citizens of the earth. I won't let you slander the name of Elam-Grande – our founder," he said, stammering with rage.

The guards quickly grabbed the second man by the arms and not so gently hauled him from the room -- just as they had the first. The CEO adjusted his tie and took another sip from his glass before continuing, but the damage had been done. He was furious that he'd come unglued by a foe as unworthy as the punks who'd addressed him. *How dare they?* thought Thorne. *After all, didn't they understand who they were talking to?*

Outside the hallway, building security handed the men over to city gendarmes who cuffed them and threw them in the back of a black, unmarked police car – a steel grate separating those in the front seat from the criminals behind. The car sped off with two other standard police cars, sirens wailing, but these escorts dropped off, turning at the next intersection after they were outside the visual range of the convention center and any reporters' cameras. The unmarked car continued straight, turning off its blue and yellow flashing lights hidden in the grill before disappearing from sight.

Later, the young men's friends inquired with the police about their whereabouts, but they couldn't get any answers. They pressed their case with the Vichy Ministry of Justice too, but to no avail. They never saw or heard from their friends again.

*****

CH 4 UNION'S HEAVY HAND

Shea and Patrick were thrilled with the news that they'd finally gotten their patent approved after all those years of filling out paperwork and writing checks for legal fees. And, they were even more excited about the future than at any other time they could remember. *It was a good time to be alive*, Shea thought, sitting at her desk.

Shea looked at the long list of messages that had stacked up on her computer since they'd had their celebration and wondered when she'd be able to get through them. Since the company's press release, Lenoir Research Labs had been deluged by investment firms wanting to invest and people wanting jobs in a venture that was about ready to bust-out. Most were just opportunists, but a few people had solid track records of growing small companies into large ones. In those, Shea was particularly interested.

"Shea, there's a man here to see you," said Meghan, Shea's assistant. "He says he has an appointment, but I don't have him down for anything. Perhaps it was something you scheduled?"

"What is his name?" asked Shea.

"Marty Syms."

"I don't know a Marty Syms."

"I guess he's with the government. He showed me his card, but it was confusing. It looked real official, you know – government-like. I think he's with the Department of Technology or something," said Meghan.

"Okay. Then, just put him in the conference room. I'll be with him in a minute," Shea answered, finishing a few things she was working on in the computer.

Shea picked up her notebook computer and left her office, hurrying down the broad set of glass stairs that led to the main conference room where they had enjoyed their party only weeks earlier. She confidently pushed open the heavy, wooden door and held out her hand in a warm greeting. "Hello, I'm Shea Disone. I'm sorry I didn't have you on my appointment list today, but how may I help you?"

The man did not stand up and did not extend his hand in return. Instead, he sat in one of the black, leather conference room chairs and smiled at her disingenuously. The man appeared small in the chair, someone of slight build and minor stature. Yet, she never underestimated anyone with whom she met for the first time and about whom she knew nothing or very little.

Shea guessed his age to be somewhere in the late forties. He was dressed in a suit that hadn't been pressed in some time and wore an even more wrinkled, light blue button-down shirt, open at the top and without a tie. Even sitting down, he kept his coat fastened, which accentuated his rather obvious belly that protruded from under the jacket's bottom button.

Although Shea smiled, her guest did not return the sentiment. He was a stern-looking man, one hardened by his surroundings. And it didn't take any more time for Shea to sense that the visitor was not there on friendly terms. It was clear he was on a mission. What that mission was, she had no clue.

When the man didn't reply, Shea looked confused. "Again, I'm sorry, but is there something I can help you with?"

The man contorted his face as if he'd smelled a chunk of Camembert cheese. But, it only made the wrinkle lines around his eyes deeper and more pronounced. He cocked his head back and placed his arms folded behind his ears in a gesture of superiority that made Shea feel uncomfortable.

"Yes, I know who you are," he said smugly. "But, do you know who I am?" he asked, now smiling devilishly.

"Uh, I believe my assistant said your name is Marty Syms, correct?"

He laughed. "No, that's not my real name. My real name is Dusty Syms, and I'm a president too. I'm the president of the International Machinists Union, the largest union of laborers in America and the world. I represent the 13.6 million workers in the field of industrial machinery. People who work for companies like yours."

"I see," she said, cautiously, now understanding full well what he was after. "And, this 13.6 million – all of them are paying members of your union?"

"Not yet," he answered.

"So, what can I do for you, Mr. Syms?" she asked, now folding her arms as if to ward off any forthcoming assault.

"What do *you* think, Ms. Disone?" he said almost laughing. "I want you to unionize your labor force, of course."

"And why would I want to do that? My people are very happy here. I pay them a good wage, and offer them great benefits and working conditions."

"All that is well and good, but they still aren't union. That's what you're missing here."

"What will you offer them that they don't already get from me?" she asked, being careful in how she asked the questions. The government dealt harshly with those companies who gave even a hint of being anti-union. More recently, small business owners had been sent to prison for allegedly obstructing a worker's right to unionize. She knew of two such cases personally – friends of hers who had dared to take on the union bosses head-on. They had lost not only the union fight, but in one case, the government had awarded ownership of their company to the union as reparations.

"Leverage, Ms. Disone. You see that's the point of the union. To provide leverage for our workers. They have none now. Management runs the place as they deem fit. In any way they want. You can fire people for no good reason. You can put their families in desperate situations overnight. You can force their children to go hungry for days at a time. And you know what, Ms. Disone? You really don't give a damn about them, do you?"

"You don't know me," she said, firing back. "I care a great deal. That's why I have very few people leave from here."

"Oh, but I know your kind, Ms. Disone. You're all the same. You are the greedy owners at the top of the food chain. You rake in the millions and force your people to eat the scraps. It was always that way until we formed unions in this country. Thank God too! Now, workers have the voice and the power. It's the power of the masses, not the power of the few at the top. It's about workers' rights!"

Shea took a seat across from the man and pulled up her chair. She liked a good battle, and this was one she was more than willing to take on.

"The workers' rights, huh? Then, what do you actually know about my company?" she asked.

"I don't need to know anything about your company. It makes engines. That's all I need to know. Oh, and that you must use machines to do it. That's where I come in, you see. You must have technology staff and machinists who work their asses off for you, am I correct?"

"Go on."

"Sure, you have nice offices for them and a clean plant floor to make your engines on, but you wouldn't give them shit unless you *were* forced to by us or the government. And, since the government isn't doing enough, it's up to the unions to fill in the gap – to ensure the worker gets a fair shake. Because, in the end, you're certainly not going to. You're only going to screw him over. We've seen it time and time again throughout history. The little guy gets stepped on by the big guy. Well, that's changed, Ms. Disone. You can't run your business like that anymore."

"So, the union will come in and save my workers from the tyrannical forces of management within this company, is that it?" she asked.

"Not only that, but we'll force you to give everyone a job who comes lookin' for one. You'll have to keep everyone on and not fire them unless we say you can. And, you'll have to obey the union's standards for pay and make sure you're payin' all of your workers at a rate that we think is fair."

"And fair is … what, exactly?"

"Oh, that's easy. It's whatever it takes to meet their family's needs," said Syms.

He paused a moment only to see if he was getting under skin yet. That was his mission. If he could ruffle her and cause her to say something anti-union or better yet throw him out, he could bring charges against her with the Department of Justice. All he had to do was poke the stick and wait for a reaction.

But, to his agitation, she did not react. Shea remained cool and collected. "Mr. Syms, I think it's important that I record this conversation so there is no misunderstanding between us."

Syms immediately became uncomfortable. "I don't see why that would be necessary," he said, fidgeting in his chair.

"Oh, I think it is," she answered. Then she turned to the wall where the computer speaker was affixed. "Computer … begin recording. Shea Disone, August 18, 2047, meeting with a Mr. Dusty Syms of the International Machinists Union." She finished and sat down next to Syms at the long, high-glossed walnut conference table. "Now, as you were saying," she said. "I believe you were telling me that I had to unionize my workforce and were laying out the reasons."

"Yes, your workers will greatly benefit from a union, as I've stated," he said, squirming.

"But did you not also say that there would be demands on the company too – that we'd be forced to hire people you want, that we won't be able to fire anyone unless you approve, and that we have to pay what you tell us to pay."

"Those are broad generalizations, Ms. Disone. I did not say those things in that way. These are not demands and I never presented them as demands," said Syms, back peddling.

"As I told you, Mr. Syms. I have virtually no turnover in staff here. They are very happy. They get wages that are above the national average, they get more vacation and better working conditions."

It was Syms turn to be aggravated. "I know this is not what you believe, but the truth is you have slaves working for you," said the union boss. "They may say they're happy, but they're not. They just don't want to get fired and be without a job. But, this is what the American worker today is facing. He's facing starvation and poverty if he stands up to companies like yours. As a result he has to suffer under your ill treatment and oppression. He doesn't have a choice!"

"And you've talked with my employees?" she asked.

"Of course," said Syms, lying. "Since companies don't do it, unions have the obligation to provide hard working Americans who come to work every day and bust their asses for companies like yours a fair shake. That's all they want is a fair shake, Ms. Disone. And instead, you stiff them. You treat them like machines out there to be plugged into the wall and set in motion at eight in the morning until you unshackle them from their desks or their machines at five. We don't even treat our dogs like that!"

Shea was doing everything she could to contain her anger. So, she took a deep breath and leaned forward.

"Mr. Syms, I'm so glad you came to explain that to me. I sincerely see the error or my ways, and I shall repent."

"What?" he answered with surprise. He sat up and took his hands away from the back of his head. "You do?"

"Yes. Absolutely. You are right. And let me tell you why you are right."

"Ms. Disone, I know I'm right. You don't need to tell me …"

"Well, I think I should tell you anyway, just in case you missed this part of your economics class in school."

47

Now it was his turn to fold his arms and become defensive. It was immediately clear to him that she hadn't been persuaded after all.

"Yes, let's say that you are correct, and I mistreat my employees. Let's say we do all that you ask." She took a deep breath. "I guess that giving people a cheerful, supportive work environment is truly cruel and unusual punishment for being a laborer. I must admit that I do expect my people to put in a full, productive day of eight hours of work, not eight hours of clock time that produces only two or three hours of real work as many union members register. I'm sorry that I don't give workers twenty or thirty more chances after they screw things up and then give me an attitude of *so what are you going to do about it anyway*? I must admit that giving workers breaks during the day and a generous holiday and vacation schedule is abusive and something I shouldn't do. It's better that they be able to demand time off whenever they want without recourse. Our pay scale is at or above the industry norm, but we expect productivity from our people too. We don't pay for people to stand around all day talking about the football game the night before as in most union shops. Also, we value the opinions our people give us and make them feel important by involving them in decisions that affect them directly. And finally, we have ended up in the horrible position of employees actually liking to work here. That's really intolerable; don't you think Mr. Syms?"

Syms only growled at her.

"And as to the economics lesson you missed in high school or grade school if you didn't get that far. This is what would happen if I took your words of wisdom. It's all based on history, but I'm not sure how much you remember or even learned about that either," she said sarcastically.

"First, you want me to hire everyone who comes here looking for a job. So, let's say I have two hundred workers now, and two hundred show up and want to work here. Let's also assume that most are unskilled and don't have the abilities I need to do the job. My payroll just went up from twenty million per year to forty million per year. I also have to train those people who don't have the skills I need, so my training costs go up by three hundred thousand. I have to double my space and equipment add them, as I don't have enough room for two hundred more people, so the costs of renting space for me rises by one million dollars per year. And, thanks to the government requirements on health insurance and benefits, those costs go up by 1.2 million. In the end, I'll end up with those who make it and those who can't; yet, I can't fire those who can't if they're union. They can come in late, not work while they're here, or not even come in at all for periods of time. They can be drug addicts, alcoholics; you name it. The result is I have to eat their wages, benefits, and the rest without getting any more production out of them. Historically, about forty percent won't make it, so that's about eight million more in costs for me."

"That's right. You'll have to eat those costs, Ms. Disone. But, you have the money. You're rich; you should fund them, even if it comes out of your own pocket!" he said with renewed confidence.

"Okay, let's say I do that. We now have a total increase in costs of, what, over thirty million. First, I don't have thirty million dollars or even close to that. But then again, let's say I did. I will spend all of my savings and produce nothing more than I did before. Eventually, and quickly, I will run out of money?"

"*You* run out of money? You can't run out of money. You're rich! But, let's say you do. If you run low, you just get it from your bank. You borrow, Ms. Disone. I'm sure you have a bank you use to borrow money from to run your business. Everyone knows how that works. "

"I'll play along, Mr. Syms. So, you'd say I just drive up to the bank, talk with someone there, sign some papers and they will give me thirty million this year to fund my losses. Is that what you're saying?"

"Yeah."

"You think it works just like that?" she answered, snapping her fingers. "I tell the bank how much I want they just hand it over. Is that what you think?"

"Pretty much."

"Sorry there bud, but it doesn't. The bank asks, 'but what about these big losses? How will your business be able to pay us back what you borrow if you're losing money?' What do I say to that?"

"You have enough money yourself in case that happens."

"And if I don't?"

"Then, you tell the bank that you're providing for your workers – your hardworking employees who bust their ..."

"Yes, yes. Mr. Syms. I tell them that I have no plans to make any money and won't be able to make any money because I am providing for those less fortunate. Is that it?"

"Well, it's the banks that are also money grubbers. They need to be reformed too!"

"We're not talking about the bank now, are we? We're talking about my company. You do understand that if the bank says they will give me thirty million dollars, they will want that repaid plus interest? And, if I don't repay it, they will seize my home, my cars, my belongings -- everything."

"It's your responsibility to your fellow man," Syms replied.

"So what is *your* financial responsibility, Mr. Syms? What risks have you taken? What are you sacrificing financially or otherwise by bursting into my company and forcing *me* to sacrifice for my fellow man? It's always easier to make someone else give things up than for you to, isn't it?"

"It's your moral responsibility," said Syms. "You have the money to sacrifice. I don't."

"How much money do you make, Mr. Syms?" Shea asked, her jaw becoming even more rigid and stern.

"That's none of your business," Syms replied.

"And yet it's okay for you to make presumptions about how much I make? Why is that?"

"It's obvious. You own this company, so you must have a lot of money. I bet you make a million a year."

"So how much should I make so I'm not rich in your eyes?" she asked, her eyes narrowing.

"Anything over three hundred thousand dollars is unnecessary," he answered without batting an eye, truly confident in his opinion.

"Well, I think it's anything over fifty thousand. I'm sure you make more than that. So, you should give up anything over that to those less fortunate in my book."

"That's a ridiculous number," he answered.

"Why is mine any more ridiculous than yours? Because it's my opinion and not yours?"

"It's a fairness issue," he said again. "It's all about fairness."

"But I think mine is fair," she replied.

"Okay, fine. Fifty thou."

"Well, I changed my mind. My new opinion is seventy-five. I think it should be seventy-five thousand. Is that okay with you too? It seems to me that the right number for you is whatever is more than what you make. Is that right?"

Syms wasn't sure how to answer.

Shea laughed at how farcical the conversation was becoming. "Mr. Syms, I've got a better idea. Since we can't decide what the right number is – other than it's based on one's personal opinion -- why don't we use your money? That's right – *your* money! In fact, you need to use all of your savings and investment money and buy into my company in a few weeks at market value. You'll be putting it all at risk then. If the stock price goes up, you win; if it goes down, you lose. If we can't compete against other companies because of the union, then we both lose together. We'll be in it together. What do you say? Then, if I go bankrupt, so do you. Now, I'd say that's fair."

"Don't be ridiculous," he spat back.

"Why is that ridiculous? Tell me?"

"Because you -- management -- makes all the decisions and leaves out the worker. They have no choice."

"Not always. Like I said, we involve the workers here in decisions."

"Yeah, but not the big ones that matter," said Syms.

"Perhaps. So if that's true, the worker has the choice to leave and work someplace else, right? If the company goes under, the worker loses his job. But what do I lose? I lose my job, my career, and virtually everything I own."

"But you've also gotten rich at it," said Syms.

"Not for long. It seems that you'd like nothing better than to take all of that away from me so I may sacrifice and contribute it all to the greater good of mankind."

Syms stared at her.

"So, let me understand then, Mr. Syms. I'm rich because I make a profit at my company. Because I make a profit, I can afford to hire people and give them a working wage. Because I give people good jobs that they enjoy, I am a bad person. I think that's about it, don't you think."

"It always comes back to you; doesn't it?" Syms answered, finally finding a life preserver to grab onto. "Of course, it's always about you, isn't it? It's always about the rich, fat cats at the top."

"But if there is no incentive for me to try to form a company and make it profitable, why would I? If my only upside is being able to create unnecessary jobs for people who may or may not work, and my downside is bankruptcy, why should I try?" asked Shea. "It's human nature to want to succeed in life and have creature comforts. It's true of the worker too. But although some want to succeed in life, others want just to get by and have the government or someone else pay their way for them. It's called socialism and it's a course that has failed everywhere it's been tried."

"That's a lie."

"Explain that to me," she said, waiting to see what explanation he could possibly give. "Where has it succeeded?"

"Listen, I'm no historian. I just know it has!" he said belligerently.

"So, is there any room for profit in a corporation? And if not, then how does it expand its business so it can hire more people?" she inquired. "It has to reinvest something that's left over. If there's nothing left over, then it's stagnant – stuck where it is."

"I never said *all* profits are bad. Some profit is okay -- just not a lot of profit. *That's* the problem," he said.

"What's a lot of profit, then? Is a million a lot of profit?"

"Yes, that's way too much profit. That could be given to the workers."

"So, if I have a one hundred billion dollar company with one hundred thousand workers, one million in profit would be too much. That would be 0.001 percent of the total revenue of the company, and would result in each worker getting another ten dollars before taxes, but about five after taxes. That's too much profit?"

"Well, not for that size company, no."

"Then, what would your number be? Two million? Twenty million? Two hundred million? You realize that larger public companies would never attract any investors if they made a profit of less than three to five percent? They would put their money elsewhere. Without investors, the company would have no money to expand and grow."

"Not if we control how much return they can get in this country. No one should make more than five percent. If we made that law, then they'd be happy with five," he answered, smugly.

"There is no law to prevent them from investing outside the country and making more someplace else. That's where the money would go. It would go to Canada where they can get twice that."

"We'd pass laws preventing them from investing outside the country."

"Investors would simply leave the country and setup companies overseas, then," she answered.

"I'd make that illegal too," he said.

"So, you'd just pass a whole bunch of laws preventing people from exercising their free will to decide what to do with their money, where they can go, and with whom they can associate. Is that it?"

"Yes, if necessary."

"And if people left the country in order to find freedom?" she asked.

"I'd ban that too!" he said without thinking.

"So, you don't believe in the Constitution of the United States, I take it? You've just created a dictatorship like the Soviet Union or China during the twentieth century. Now you've destroyed democracy along with capitalism. Congratulations!"

"If that's what it takes," he said, having no other answer. "But, that's the whole problem – it starts with capitalism! It's a zero-sum game. Do you know what that means?"

"One person wins, and one loses. But, I ..."

"Yeah, you win and I lose. That's what it means. The poor guy starves, and the rich guy sits back and smokes his expensive cigar."

"I don't agree that it's zero sum. If I can make the entire pie larger, then everyone can have a bigger slice," she argued.

"It's funny how it never turns out that way. The CEOs and big bosses like you take it all in and the little guy gets the boot."

"Perhaps in big companies, like the GovCo's. But I'm not defending them. I can't and I won't. It's the small business person who creates the ideas and the growth these days – not the GovCo's."

53

"You're all the same," said Syms. "Business is business. It really doesn't matter. Capitalism is the root of the problem."

"If unions are the answer, what has your union done to improve things in the nation lately?"

"We help the worker – plain and simple," said Syms. "Our workers make more money. Then, they spend that money and the economy grows."

"This is what I know about your union. You've managed to kill productivity in the workplace with union jobs. Independent studies have shown that although there is equivalent production and quality between union and non-union groups, union labor costs twenty to thirty percent more. You've forced jobs overseas to places where it's less expensive to get the same work done. Sure, the workers here are more skilled, but when a union worker here makes eighty dollars per hour to make one hundred T-shirts and one overseas makes three dollars per hour but takes three hours to make those one hundred T-shirts, it's still eighty versus nine dollars to make those T-shirts. You can't compete against that. My company would have to sell those one hundred T-shirts for about two hundred dollars to cover production costs, delivery costs, storage and shipping costs. An overseas company would sell the same T-shirts here for thirty dollars. Which company are the people going to buy from? "

"Sending jobs overseas – that's traitorous! It's anti-American!" he shouted. "We should impose five hundred percent tariffs on all imports!" he shouted. "That way, those T-shirts would cost two hundred dollars whether they're bought here or from overseas. That's what we need to level the playing field!"

"Okay, so let's say we pass laws to raise tariffs on foreign T-shirts to increase the price of that T-shirt at the mall from thirty to two hundred dollars so people can only buy American-made. Now, we've created inflation by jacking up higher prices for *all* Americans. Now, they have to make enough to buy those T-shirts for two hundred instead of thirty – a 567 percent increase. So, a worker making, say fifty thousand per year, would now have to make over three hundred thirty thousand per year to have the same life-style. That's what you call inflation."

"No! With the tariff, we can bring those jobs home to America where they belong," said the union man. "We'll just pass the tariff laws to keep foreign products out of this country. That's the way it should be anyway. At the same time, workers get a big raise! You call it inflation; I call it prosperity."

"You do understand that you won't be able to export anything to any other part of the globe, right? Production of T-shirts in the U.S. will drop because you won't be able to compete against any other country making those T-shirts. They will continue to sell them for thirty dollars. Your market will only be America."

"Fine. We'll still have jobs for Americans," said Syms.

"For products we import, yes. But as for other products we export from America, those jobs would vanish."

"Why? People overseas would just continue to buy from us, like they always do. Our price on those products wouldn't change."

"Not in U.S. dollars. But in that country's currency, it would go up significantly. The exchange rate would change drastically, causing the dollar to lose value and make everything we produce more expensive overseas. And, in almost every case, whenever country A imposes a large tariff on country B's products, that country B retaliates with tariffs on country A's goods, blocking them from the market. The best example is the Smoot-Hawley Act of 1930 that raised tariffs on twenty-thousand items. Our trading partners retaliated and threw the entire world into a deeper depression than ever before. And I won't even begin to talk about our need to import critical raw material from outside the country, like gallium, cobalt, titanium, and chromium -- raw materials we have to import."

"We can figure it out," said the union boss, curtly.

"Not if you wall-off America. Even now, some say we've fallen so far behind the rest of the world in technology that it will be difficult for us to catch up. Us! The USA! ... but, I get it. Your answer is that you want to isolate America? Cut us off from the rest of the world in trade? And you're answer is to make just enough for ourselves, then, right? That didn't work out so well for China, which walled itself off from the rest of the world until Nixon opened doors in 1978. China lagged far behind the rest of the industrialized world then, and it took fifty years for them to catch up."

"But they passed us, so you're just wrong," said Syms, without an argument.

"They passed us because we let you and the government put governors on our capitalistic engine. Forced to put low octane fuel in the tank, what choice did we have?"

"Government understands the bigger picture. It can move the chess pieces where they need to be for the entire chessboard, not just the one pawn. Companies only look after themselves. They only have their own best interest in mind and don't care about the greater good of the nation. We, the Union, and the federal government care about everyone, not just the rich company owners."

"Is that why GovCo's get special breaks in the laws they pass? Is that why our country has lost GDP during the past three decades? Is that why the USA is now twelfth largest economy in the world, when throughout the 1900s and early 2000s we were first? Yes, I see your point. Unions and the government have brought our country to its knees. Bravo!"

"You don't understand," said Syms.

"Unfortunately, I do. And, unfortunately, you never will."

Syms could take no more. He got up and pulled his coat closed, trying to re-button the suit jacket that had popped open. Syms stormed out of the room, with parting words, "You haven't seen the last of me!"

"Sadly, probably not," she answered.

Syms was the first, but he wasn't the last to approach her with demands. Her company was now on the map, and it was under siege. Like most successful companies and people of the day, they were targets because they had what others wanted.

*****

CH 5 THE LURE OF RICHES

Tough times at the company forced Patrick and Shea to take out personal loans to fund the business. There were several times when Shea had been worried about meeting their payroll for the week, as the money was almost gone. But Patrick had been a rock, giving her comfort and reassuring her that everything would be okay. Somehow, they had always pulled through, and Patrick had made it all the easier. Whether it was his charm or his ingenuity, he was usually able to convince the bank to extend its credit when they were desperate or asked friends to loan him money, which he readily repaid. Over the years, they had done without vacations, new cars, nice clothes, new furniture for the house, and countless other things that would have made their lives better. However, almost everything they earned went back into the business. So, while friends bought nice things and planned for their retirement, the Disones' worked – sometimes as long as seventy hours per week. They were achievers and they wanted to make something for themselves – something they built and would provide for them in the later years.

But without a patent and the government's blessing, no one had been willing to take the risk with them. It had even been hard to get a bank to be interested to loan them money. Now, the award of the patent and their new-found ability to commercialize their efforts was going to make it all worthwhile. Patrick had many friends, and several had connected him with people interested in investing in their company. Sorting the wheat from the chaff was Shea's job -- the financial and legal wizard of the pair. Patrick relied on her, and he trusted her without question. In the end, they had decided to go public and issue shares over the publicly traded exchanges. It would, in the end, benefit them and the company the most of all the options being considering.

Shea entered the boardroom with her black, monogrammed Valais clutched in her hand. Dressed smartly, wearing a cream-colored, linen suit with rosette embroidery around the sleeves and faux ivory buttons, she put down her case and pulled out the chair at the head of the long, oval table, taking command of the meeting that was about to begin. Sitting next to her was Emery Lawson, her outside counsel, and across from her was Annie Reynolds, her financial officer. They had traveled to New York to visit with their investment bankers regarding the upcoming offering.

"Good morning, gentleman," she said with a broad smile, her countenance beaming with confidence. "I'm glad Emery here could arrange for us to meet. I want to start the meeting by saying that the Lenoir Research Labs has successfully obtained approval from the Department of Technology Assessment to promote and sell its now-patented SECE or Super-Efficient Combustion Engine, the MB 12 series. With that in hand, Lenoir's future is bright. My assistant is passing out our latest forecast for the next three years. It shows revenue growth of 168 percent next year and 97 percent average per year during the next three years. Profits are up as well, showing significant improvement over prior years as we will get several contracts from other large companies, educational institutes and government agencies. Our current production engine – the HECE 2, MB 11 will be replaced with the SECE 1 – MB 12. The Highly Efficient Combustion Engine has been a good start for us, but the quantum increase in efficiency of the MB 12 is really the breakthrough. The SECE 1 is nearly fifty percent more efficient than the HECE. Therefore, we're looking for a multiple of twenty-two times EBITDA earnings for a buy-in."

There was a gasp in the boardroom, but it wasn't unexpected. The value of twenty-two times earnings before interest, taxes, depreciation and amortization was steep. The anticipated opening price per share had gone up from thirteen to more than thirty-two dollars as word of the significance of their invention spread. Now that the patent was in hand, there was less risk in the stock, which caused the offering price to go up dramatically.

Gladwell Pincus was the first to speak up. As Managing Director for one of the largest funds in the country, Pincus had been around a long time. He had held dominant positions in many of the most prominent technology companies during the previous few years. "Ms. Disone, I understand that with the patent approval the stock price would likely rise, but I believe the amount is excessive. Your future earnings projections don't support the price you're asking for. Really – twenty-two times EBITDA earnings? That's twice what we see in other companies like yours with similar potential. Basically, we don't think you can support a price of any more than twenty-two per share, not thirty-two."

Shea moved closer to the table and rested her arms on the high-gloss, mahogany surface. "I disagree. If you follow the logic and the calculations, we believe we have undervalued the stock and given our current shareholders room to improve their gains once we sell shares to the general public. The thirty-two dollars is low and gives the company a market valuation of four hundred eighty million. You and I both know that every major auto maker, power equipment manufacturer and others will be beating a path to our doorstep. Those industries alone are worth billions. Therefore, the company's value should be closer to 1.7 billion! You know that. No, the approval by the government is huge, and the current price doesn't reflect that potential at all."

Pincus frowned. He began shaking his head before Shea spoke up again.

"Marcus, really," she said questioning him. "Based on your own projections of sales, our stock price should be closer to forty. So, can we compromise? Being able to make a car having a gas mileage of nearly five hundred miles per gallon? How valuable is that? Engines now are only about sixteen percent efficient. This one is eighty-seven percent. That's huge! There isn't anything like what we have – nothing! Companies and governments will pay handsomely for this. Am I right?"

Pincus stopped his grimacing and leaned in again toward the table, putting both hands face down in front of him. "Shea. I know you *think* you're product is worth a fortune. Every inventor and entrepreneur thinks that. And in some cases, I would agree with you. But in this case, we've got a problem."

Shea looked at him, perplexed. "What? I don't understand. What problem?"

"Fourier doesn't like your industry. It's hard to make a good market in a sector that is being assaulted by the powers in Washington. You're swimming upstream. Once the government finds out how good your product is and what it can do, you won't be as free about selling it as you would like."

"Why not?"

"They aren't going to let you. They'll put a whole bunch of restrictions on you and make it tough for you to make any money. You know the direction they've been going in the last ten or fifteen years. They won't let you just sell this to anybody in the U.S.. You're market will be limited to overseas, as it has been. And with their crack down on fossil fuel – the last thing they want is a fuel efficient gasoline engine. If it were solar or wind or, hell, rubber bands, then you might have something interesting. But not something that's oil-based. That's, well, completely antithetical to their cause! And, you know it's all about the cause!"

"But they gave us approval," said Shea, defensively.

"Yeah. I'm not sure I understand that either. But, for now ..."

Shea fumed. "I don't agree. And anyway, you can't make that assumption. It's illogical. You don't know what will happen, let alone that it's likely to happen. So, based on that, you can't ding our stock for it."

Pincus smiled and looked down at his folded hands. "Shea, you're right. I *don't* know. But, it's my job to have an opinion and to ensure that you and my shareholders benefit from this offering. Therefore ..." He paused and looked back up at her. "... I'm willing to compromise. What do you say to twenty-five per share?"

"Don't insult me, Pincus!" she said.

"The stock may not be worth anything in a few months, Shea. I'll go twenty-seven, but not a dime more," said Pincus, holding firm.

Shea looked at her CFO and legal counsel. Both were shaking their heads against it. But Shea understood Pincus's point. It had always been a battle against the government, and the patent had come as a surprise. She didn't want to push her luck.

Relenting, she stood up and extended her hand. "You drive a hard bargain, but we'll go with this."

Pincus returned the smile and shook her hand. "Ms. Disone – always a pleasure," he answered.

"This should bring you 135 million gross, before fees obviously."

"It's not what we were looking for, but it will have to do. I think that should get us through the next two years. Then, of course, we may need another round. But hopefully, we won't."

"We can do another tranche, if you need it, sure ... But, what will you do with the money that you and Patrick make from this?" asked Pincus.

"Repay debts and probably loan back to the company to expand the business," said Shea. "If there's anything left ... I'll probably ... well ... buy a new car. I've got almost two hundred thousand miles on mine now," said Shea.

She looked tired, the dark folds under her eyes were deep and noticeable, as the last few years had been tough. Applying for and finally getting government approval to sell their new engine had taken its toll on both Patrick and her. They were no longer young, naïve entrepreneurs who didn't know what they were getting into. Neither had been fully aware of the risks and rewards. They could have lost everything they had owned, including their marriage.

It was true that their venture had been a financial sacrifice as well. During the years, they had put in more than three million dollars of their own savings into the company, and there had been no guarantee it would be successful. The averages were against them, as eight of every ten businesses in America were failing. Instead of socking away that money for retirement, they put it in the company. Four times they had been required to put in more than half a million dollars to meet payroll, never knowing whether they would ever get it back. The chances of losing everything were high, yet they persevered.

The meeting with Pincus and his crew was over, but the work was just beginning. There was a lot to do before the offering could be solicited on what was once Wall Street. Everything now was electronic – Wall Street was only a metonym. But there was one thing that hadn't changed. There would be a lot of one hundred-hour weeks ahead of them, and with it, a lot of coffee, Chinese food, and late nights. The final sprint to the finish was on. But the finish line was not where she imagined it to be.

*****

CH 6 FAUSTIAN PACT

As deputy secretary, Angel Ratner's action to rescind the patent authorization to Lenoir Labs would normally have raised eyebrows and led to a legal filings. But as with all actions taken by the government, fighting them came at a price – requiring significant resources and a great deal of time, neither of which the Disones had. The only thing they had was courage.

It had taken years for them to get the patent, and only minutes for it to be revoked. It might take years yet again to have it reviewed and re-assessed for reinstatement, if it ever would be. Unless you knew someone high in the bureaucratic food chain, nothing could be done to move things any faster. In the meantime, the revocation would stand, and the company would be dead in its tracks, unable to sell any of its products.

To Shea and Patrick, it seemed like the departments in government were vying for the title of *most thuggish*. Few challenged those departments at the top of this list, and if it were done, consequences were usually paid. At the top of this list of thuggish behavior was the IRS with the Justice Department a close second. However, under Ratner, the Department of Technology Assessment had made the top three. Getting patents, trademarks, copyrights, or other protection from the department had become a nightmare unless you were a GovCo. Therefore, the granting of a patent to a non-GovCo entity was unusual. Yet, rescinding a patent was even more so.

It was the Department's responsibility to vet all possibilities before granting a patent to ensure the invention was not a copy of something already on the books. It was their obligation to validate the claim made and uphold the integrity of the entire system of intellectual property rights. But for Ratner, it wasn't about integrity – it was about finding a way that she could exert her power and expand her influence.

Even though the deputy secretary was firmly planted in the group of untouchable departments, there was always the possibility of some rogue company succeeding in their fight against her. But, she cared only about her power and influence – with that would come the money and access. If it were within her power to do something -- and there was little that wasn't -- she gladly did it, and if it hurt those greedy bastards - the capital markets -- then so much the better. So, stripping away a privilege given to a commercial business could only mean one thing - they'd had a *good* day.

Whatever it took, she would not be denied. As her power grew, so did her ego.

Growing up, Angel Ratner had competed against six other siblings. She was the third in the line, with two older and one younger sister and two younger brothers. Tormented by her older sisters and ignored by her parents, Angel grew up without the attention she craved. She was always trying to gain her parents' attention and approval, a sometimes went out of her way to get it. Whether it was upstaging her sister at her wedding by deep-kissing her husband at the alter or announcing that the Thanksgiving turkey contained botulism and faking throwing up at the family's extended gathering when she was in high school, she had to be in the limelight.

Yet, it was often deeper and more sinister than just practical jokes. In college she had framed her roommate for stealing two rare books from the restricted section of the library, getting her expelled. In another case, she stole a friend's thesis paper the day it was due in class, putting her own name on it. The friend failed the course and never knew who had done it. And, to ensure her application for a job with the Department of Technology Assessment was accepted, she falsified her resume, references, and experiences, saying she had mastered in technology from Princeton, when she had never attended. The department never checked, and she got the job.

But, so it was that her life was made easy by these slights-of-hand. She'd never been caught always believing she was just too smart to be discovered. The effect was cumulative, and eventually, it was uncovered in an off-handed way.

As a senior in college, she took a psychology test that assessed one's individual character. She was stunned by the result and ripped it to pieces when she'd gotten it back. It read:

Ms. Ratner shows a most unusual personality trait, which appears in fewer than 1 percent of the population.

Character Profile: NPD – Narcissistic Personality Disorder

Persons afflicted by NPD are those who are excessively preoccupied with personal adequacy, power, prestige and vanity, mentally unable to see the destructive damage they are causing to themselves and to others in the process. People with such a disorder are characterized by exaggerated feelings of self-importance. They have a sense of entitlement and demonstrate grandiosity in their beliefs and behavior. They have a strong need for admiration, but lack feelings of empathy.

The subject borders both the elitist and fanatic narcissism traits, clinically identified by the results of this study.

"It's bull sh*t!" she fumed, after receiving the results. It was then that she dropped her psychology major and, instead, spent the extra year to get a Public and Environmental Affairs (SPEA) degree. It would be the ovule from which would grow a distinguished government career, marked by few substantive accomplishments, but rather achieved through extortion and sociopathic manipulation of others to get what she wanted.

***

Taking out her computer wafer-tablet, Ratner jotted down some notes. She was in a particularly sinister mood and felt like inflicting as much pain as possible on someone or something. This day it was Lenoir Labs. *My boss would like that,* she thought. *And, perhaps it might get notice higher up – maybe even by the President.*

She penned out various alternative approaches to handling the issue and settled quickly on two in particular.

> **Note: Let Lenoir Labs exhaust time and money fighting our patent rescission notice, or ...**

She continued writing the second point but stopped, smiling to herself. *Yeah, that will cause them some big problems*, she thought to herself. *It will put a major hurt on them.* She put down her computer pen and dialed an old friend. The phone rang and rang. Finally, a young lady's image came across the screen. "Hello, Mr. Thorne's office. How may I help you?" the young woman asked robotically.

"Yes, this is Deputy Secretary Ratner at the Department of Technology Assessment. I need to speak to Kilby, please."

"I'm sorry, Madam Secretary, but he's in a meeting right now. May I take a message or have you register a voice message?"

"I'm sorry you didn't hear me clearly. Perhaps the visual line got distorted. Anyway, I'm a very busy person. My time is valuable. When I call, I expect the CEO to be available to me. I am a government secretary, after all! Now, would you *please* interrupt him and get him on the phone. It's important."

"Yes, ma'am," said the secretary, retreating into meek obedience. She'd been through the drill countless times before and knew that most government calls were unimportant, and the caller always demanded to speak to the person at the top. Most of the time, they had no idea to whom they were talking, and she could have patched them through to the mailroom for all it mattered. However, this time, there was no getting around it; she had no choice. Important or not, the maw of this government official had to be fed.

A few moments passed before someone picked-up the line. Ratner was pissed.

"Thorne here. What can I do for you today?" he said trying to be pleasant, but not knowing who was on the line. He had pulled out of an executive committee meeting to talk to some government bureaucrat.

"Is that the way to greet an officer of the federal government on the phone?" retorted Angel.

Thorne softened his tone. He recognized the voice. "I apologize for any disrespect, Angel. None was intended."

"I should hope so, Kilby! It hasn't been that long, has it?" she asked.

"No, Angel. It really hasn't. Time flies. I've been really busy the past many months with the merger in China and the environmental problems in India. I apologize. What is it that I can do for you today?"

"Well, have you heard of a company called Lenoir Research Labs?"

"Yes, of course. They make state-of-the-art combustion engines. Why?"

"We are on a secure line, correct?" she asked.

"Yes, of course."

"Good, I thought you'd want to know that I may have some information on some technology for you. Although they granted a patent for their SECE engine prototype, we will be rescinding that approval. It was a mistake made within my department. Of course we have all of the documentation they've filed to perfect their claim for a patent. I just thought that it might be a piece of valuable information, especially since they will not be the exclusive owners of it after tomorrow."

"Go on," said Thorne, waiting for the usual *quid pro quo* request.

"Well, again, I just thought it was a valuable piece of information."

She was goading him, and he knew it. If he asked her for her price first, he would be making an illicit offer to a government official, even on a secured line. If she asked for payment, then she was breaking the law. It was a waltz that had been perfected on both sides of the line for years.

"This patent," asked Thorne, "what does it deal with? That is, what does it cover? Does it have software programming?"

"Are you interested?" she asked, baiting him.

"Send me the information, and I'll …."

"Unfortunately, I can't do that, Thorne. You know the rules of the department and the patent process. It just wouldn't be …"

"All right, Angel. I can see where we're going. Yes, I'm interested. Let's meet at Bryce's Café in Bethesda tomorrow at one thirty. That should give me time to fly into Reagan National and get out there. I'll see you then."

Thorne didn't wait to hear her response. He knew she'd be there. He also knew what she was offering. It was only a matter of how much he was willing to pay that concerned him.

***

Ratner sat at in a red-cushioned booth at the back of the café. She'd taken the D.C. Metro rather than her chauffeured limousine so her whereabouts would be less easily tracked. The noon crowds had died down, and only a few people were still left, mulling over their latte coffee and dallying over their mud pie deserts. Based on their drab dress, she pegged them for state and local government types taking an extra half hour on the taxpayers' dime. She fit in well with them, wearing a non-descript navy suit with government-issue, low-heel blue pumps. She looked like the bureaucrat that she'd become.

The weather was unusually temperate, and the winds out of the northwest brought cooler than normal temperatures for that time of year. As a result, the café had rolled up its garage-like windows to let in the nice breeze. The sun streamed in, creating an almost tropical feeling about the place.

At one forty-five, Ratner began looking at her watch. By two, she had finished her second vodka martini and had turned around to summon the waiter to close out the bill. But, when she turned back, she was startled by Thorne sitting comfortably in the seat across from her. Dressed impeccably in a custom, gray pin-striped Canali suit and Zegna tie, he smiled. "Didn't you think I'd come?" he said, motioning for the waiting to come to the table.

"You bastard!" she said, clearly irate. "You scared the crap out of me!" She took a moment to catch her breath again and sucked down the last of her martini.

Thorne only chuckled. "Well, I guess we're even, since you scared the crap out of me when you called yesterday. I wasn't sure what to think."

"You're getting too good at this game, Thorne. You've played it far too long."

"I could say the same about you, Angel. Now, I don't suppose you're wearing a wire or anything like that, are you?"

"No! Of course not. This is not official government business," she answered.

Thorne raised his watch and moved it up and down near where Ratner was sitting, looking at the dial.

"What's that?" she asked.

"Nope, you're not wearing a wire," he said lowering his wrist. "Let's just say it's a little app that I use for moments like this. Now, what is it that you'd like to offer me?"

"I could ask you the same question, Thorne — about being wired. But I know it's not in your best interest. So, I'll just come out and tell you. I've got the blueprints and detailed technology specs on the SECE — the combustion engine the Lenoir group just developed. It's incredibly efficient. I just thought you and your company may have some interest."

"Let's say I am interested," said Thorne. "What keeps Lenoir from filing a lawsuit against me when I come out with the same design? They're going to know where we got it."

"Perhaps. But there won't be anything they can do about it. They won't have a patent, will they?"

"They could protest that too, and keep everything tied up in the courts for a long time."

Ratner waved to the waiter for another drink, and held up her fingers for two, pointing to Thorne as well. "Judge Thomas isn't presiding over your jurisdiction in Atlanta anymore, Kilby. You have nothing to worry about."

"I believe he retired last month," answered Thorne.

"Yeah, we kind of forced him out. Instead, we have a new judge in his place; her name is J. Anne Stewart. She's always been loyal to the president, and I expect that will continue. That's why he appointed her to replace Thomas. I recommended her to him. She's an old friend of mine, you see – really smart, pretty and driven. We've always gotten along great."

"How much will it cost me?" asked Thorne, his eyes narrowing and face tightening.

"How much will it cost you?" asked Ratner, chuckling. She was parroting Thorne, but for good reason. It was an intentionally ambiguous remark.

Thorne knew such information could be worth millions, if not billions when sold outside the U.S. And even though it would likely be banned from use in America, the engine would create thousands of manufacturing jobs for EG and billions in revenue. It would be a goldmine. But, without the blueprints and specifications Ratner could provide him, it would take enormous resources and a unique mind to create the software algorithms necessary to build it -- if they could do it at all. Even with all of that, it might take years more to implement everything successfully.

"Don't play games, Angel. I asked you a direct question."

"Thorne, Thorne."

"I would need that patent, though. You'd have to grant me that patent protection."

"How much are you willing to pay for it? It's worth a bloody fortune."

"Ten million," said Thorne. "I think I can get the board of directors to approve that much."

"Board approval? Come on Thorne. You're not talking to some novice here. We both know that you'll never take something like this to your board. They would never want to get involved in something like this, and you would never want to expose yourself like that. No, Thorne, I'm sure this would be a black-ops program at your firm. Would it not?"

"How much?" Thorne repeated one last time.

He was stuck. He had dealt with Ratner on smaller deals before and knew how she operated. She was tough and uncompromising. In this case, she held the cards. Both knew it. She was right about the board too. They would not want to be tainted by anything like this. The best solution for Thorne would be that they would be told that EG had developed them – just as they had all the other innovations he had stolen from others over the years. All the Board cared about was profits, and since Thorne could deliver them, they were happy with him as CEO.

"Five hundred mil," Ratner said flatly.

"What?" said Thorne, almost hyperventilating at the huge number. "You've got to be kidding me?"

Ratner didn't say a thing. She only sat there calmly and took another gulp from the newly delivered Y-shaped glass that had just appeared in front of her.

"For that, I should get sex on the table right here," he said to her, shaking his head. This time it was his turn to take a long gulp from his drink.

Ratner smiled and thought for a second. "Perhaps. You know, nothing is impossible, Thorne. But maybe we can do that as a bonus on the side. Who knows. It depends on how nicely you treat me." She reached across the table and put her hand on top of his.

She was attractive, and there was a certain allure to her – her power and drive -- that did excite him. She had always excited him in that way.

"Kilby, just think about having direct access to one of the most revolutionary and practical inventions in a long time – it's worth quite a bit, don't you think?" she asked.

"Twenty-five million," countered Thorne. "I only have discretion up to that amount without being questioned."

"Then do four tranches of twenty-five each. That will get us to, what, one hundred million. I'll come down that far."

Thorne shook his head. "I'll go thirty-five. No more."

"You'll go at least fifty mil there Thorne. I have others I can call."

"Okay, forty million. That's it, Angel."

Even Ratner knew when she was looking a gift-horse in the mouth. She extended her hand. "Glad to do business with you there, Mr. Big. And like I said, sex on the side is another option. But I won't tell you how much more that will cost you." She gave a mischievous grin.

Thorne shook her hand. It was a Faustian bargain, but one Thorne was willing to make. He'd done deals like this with Ratner and other ministers before, just not one this big. This was one that could very well bring lawsuits and a mess. But, if he had Judge Stewart and Ratner in his court, he figured his downside was limited. His only worry was that it wouldn't unravel on him before he could start cashing in on the SECE engine and cashing out as CEO.

***

Thomas was responsible for screening Ratner's electronic mail. It was a job that he hated, but she had insisted on it. However, when she gave it to him, her instructions were clear – "Whatever you read is confidential. If I ever find that you breathe a word of something inappropriate or outside the purview of your authority, I will have your head! Is that understood?" It didn't require a second lecture. The message was abundantly transparent.

It was mid-morning when Thomas was able to get to the mail. He sifted through it as he always did. Hundreds and hundreds of messages from people inside and outside the government. Most neither he nor his boss had ever heard of, and he quickly discarded them. Others, he wasn't so sure and forwarded to her in a special folder marked *Possible Junk*. It was a balance between efficiency and thoroughness. Ratner would have his ass if he deleted anything that was important, yet she wanted him to attend to a thousand other things during the day. He couldn't possibly do both, so he did the best he could.

"From Michael Gantry," said Thomas, reading the next mail in queue. "Hot bargains on Wall Street! Buy today! ... Nope." He told the computer to delete. "From Bras for America ... Oh, this should be good ... " he said out loud with a smile, "... Buy two, get two free! ... Nope!" But it did make him laugh. "From Kilby Thorne ... Confirming Our Deal ..." *what's this about?* thought Thomas. He told the computer to give him full details, but when the information came up, it looked corrupted, as though some parts were missing. There was no way to get an understanding of what the email was about.

Rather than delete it, Thomas thought he should follow-up with Thorne to get him to resend it. He replied to the message, but it kicked back as a bad address. Looking at the PCD number, he instructed the computer to dial and get a hold of Thorne. The line buzzed.

"Hello, this is EG Incorporated. How may I direct your call?" asked the automated attendant.

"Kilby Thorne, please," said Thomas.

One of Thorne's secretaries answered curtly, "Thorne's office, how may I assist you?"

"Yes, this is George Thomas from the Department of Technology Assessment calling for the Deputy Secretary Angel Ratner. I'd like to ask Mr. Thorne if he could resend his message to Ms. Ratner, dated yesterday. Would he be able to do that?"

"I don't know, but I will pass along your message." She hung up, and Thomas was left wondering whether he would hear anything more.

The next day, Thomas began to worry. He hadn't heard anything, and he figured it was just another message he could delete. Pulling up the message list, he highlighted the one from Thorne and began to say the *delete* word, when the office phone rang.

"Yes, this is Mr. Thorne's assistant. He said I should resend it, so it will be coming shortly."

Within moments, there was message from Thorne that showed up on Ratner's list.

Thomas opened it, but it looked different than the one he had seen the day before:

> *To: Angel Ratner*
> *From: Kilby Thorne*
> *RE: Deal*
>
> *I really had a good time last night. You're a tough nut sometimes, you know. But since we go back several years together, I can forgive you for your aggressiveness. Actually, it turns me on.*

Thomas blanched at the message. But, he was hooked. He continued reading.

> *So, it sounds like we agreed on $40M. I'll wire the money when I get the SECE blueprints and SW programming.*
>
> *As always, I luv doin' business with ya!*
>
> *Kilby*

There wasn't a lot left to the imagination. Thomas knew exactly what was going on, and he shivered, sitting in his chair. But what he saw next, shook him to the core.

> *Copy: George Thomas*

That was it. There was no denying that he had seen the email. All he could do now was delete it and hope it never came up in conversation with his boss. She couldn't know that he'd seen it. It didn't matter whether he'd pledged never to divulge the contents of emails. This was beyond even that.

*****

CH 7 HEALTHY ~~CHOICES~~

It had been a long Friday at work, and Patrick and Shea had made dinner reservations at a newly-opened Italian restaurant in town that was 'all-the-rage.' It had taken several months to get a table, but they had gotten in through a friend who knew the pastry chef. The time hadn't been great -- an early six o'clock -- but it had been better than nothing.

Following the hostess, Shea and Patrick found their table which was just outside the noisy, swinging kitchen door. Their waiter, who said his name was Antony, pulled out Shea's powder-blue cushioned chair and helped her cozy-up to the edge of the cream-colored, linen table.

"I'll be your waiter tonight," said the waiter, offering a disingenuous smile.

Patrick settled himself into the seat opposite his wife, and placed the thick, white cotton napkin that had been folded into the shape of a peacock, onto his lap. Then, he lifted his eyes to see the beautiful woman sitting across from him.

"God, Shea. Do you know how beautiful you look tonight?" he said earnestly.

Thirty years earlier, she would have blushed. However, after years of marriage, her reaction was different. She knew he was sincere, and that she loved him every bit as much as he loved her. Their devotion to each other had grown every day since they had exchanged there *I do's*. It had not always been easy, but she would not have done it any other way.

Shea laughed. "Yeah, you tell all the girls that," she answered, giving him her pat answer.

"Not too many," said Patrick, "I only know three or four whose name is Shea."

Shea laughed again, almost spitting out the gulp of water she had just taken in.

The waiter came back over to the table, dressed in a black tux and white, wing-collared shirt. "Good evening, Can I offer you a beverage ... perhaps wine or an aperitif of some kind?" His speech was precise and articulate, but had the touch of an Italian accent.

"Honey, do you want something?" asked Patrick, taking the wine list from the waiter.

"Typically, the sommelier would be assisting tonight, but he called off. So, I'm afraid your stuck with me," said the waiter with a grin.

"You'll do just fine," answered Patrick, looking up and down the list. "What would you recommend? Most likely, I will be having a beef dish and my wife will have a vegetable salad of some sort. Is that right, Shea?"

Shea nodded, tucking her napkin into her lap.

"Oh, I see," said the waiter. "Uh, well, you do realize that we are a vegetarian-only restaurant," said the waiter.

Patrick looked up with surprise and glanced over at his wife, startled. "Uh, of course, I knew that. My apologies. So, I'll probably have a salad of some sort too."

"Very good," answered the waiter. "Then, I would recommend, the 2047 Chardonnay Oak Cellars Reserve. It's excellent with the grilled vegetable salad."

"But it says that it's a low-alcohol wine," said Patrick. "Does that affect the flavor?"

"I'll be honest," said the waiter, "it does slightly, but low-alcoholic wines are all we are allowed to carry now."

"Why?"

"The new orders that were passed," answered the waiter.

"New orders?" asked Shea. "I didn't hear about any new orders."

"Yes, yes. Just last month, the White House issued immediate orders banning all but low-alcohol wines and other beverages. No drink may have more that 8% alcohol content. That's the law now. I suppose they just don't want Americans to get drunk. They said it was a matter of national security or something."

"National security my ass," replied Shea, annoyed.

"Now Shea, let's try to have a nice dinner, shall we?" urged Patrick, pleading with her.

"Ok, fine," said Shea, but obviously not fine with it. Yet, she carried on. "Then, can we get an order of *foie gras*?"

The waiter's face turned pale. It was as if she had shot him through the heart.

"No, that was banned nation-wide in 2045," he answered.

Patrick interrupted the exchange to cool things down. "Oh, okay. Well, than, we'll take an order of *bruschetta*." It was an Italian dish of toasted-bread, garlic and tomato – an appetizer that Patrick dearly loved.

"Very good sir. That will be with organic tomatoes, as those are the only ones we serve here."

"That will be alright."

"And, would you bring us some balsamic vinegar, salt and some butter?" asked Shea.

"I'm afraid not," said the waiter. "We can't serve salt or butter anymore. The president banned those from all restaurants. Apparently, you haven't been out to eat for some time, I'm assuming?"

"You've got to be f***ing ..." said Shea, becoming belligerent.

"Honey," admonished her husband.

Shea calmed down, taking a few deep breaths. "I just can't believe ..."

Each day there was something new, something more intrusive in the lives of average Americans than the day before. It seemed that every aspect of life was being regulated. At first, it was only salt and sugar; then, it crept into other things like portion size, fat content, and the like. Freedom of choice was fine as long as it comported with that by which those elites in the government believed Americans should be abiding.

When the wine was brought, the waiter showed Patrick the label for his approval before it was opened. Patrick nodded, and the waiter began the ritual of slicing off the foil top, twisting the corkscrew into the cork, applying the rocker arm to the lip, and extracting the cork. There was a distinct, but small *pop* as the cork was coaxed from its cozy place inside the bottle's neck.

"You do understand that this is the only bottle you may order tonight, right? We're required to tell you that at the beginning of the reservation."

It wasn't as if Patrick and Shea were drinkers, and it wasn't as if they would need another bottle. But it was the principle that aroused Patrick's ire.

"Why?" she asked. "Is there a new law against it?"

"Actually, yes. We're not allowed to serve more than two glasses of wine or beer to each patron, nor can we serve more than one liquor beverage. I'm sorry, but that's just the way it is now."

Even Patrick shook his head as he watched the waiter poured the white wine into the tall-stemmed glasses in front of them.

"Thanks," said Shea disingenuously, as the waiter finished filling her glass halfway.

"I just can't take this anymore," said Shea, scowling after their attendant left. "This is really ridiculous!"

"Shea. Calm down," said Patrick soothingly. "Let's just forget all of that and have a nice dinner, okay?"

Shea took a deep breath. The tension in her face began to relax and fall away. She gave him a faint smile and reached out to take his hand. "You're right. I know I get all worked up. I guess there's really nothing I can do about it."

"It's okay. It's just me. We're here now. We haven't had a nice dinner out in … well, ages. So, let's just put all this aside," he said, comforting her. "So, what good movies have you seen lately?"

Shea laughed. Both hadn't seen a movie in over a year. There were no outside movie theaters anymore. Everything was virtual reality, and they didn't even own a pair of VR goggles needed to watch any movies at home.

The dinner passed with conversations they hadn't been able to have in months. Their lives had become so busy and complicated, trying to hold what they had together, that they'd forgotten how important it was to reconnect once in a while.

Although there were no deserts with sugar permitted, they did manage to have a bowl of fresh fruit for their final course. Coffee regulations also only allowed for decaffeinated types, so each ordered a decaf cappuccino as their final night's treat.

On the screen at their table, the bill popped up, showing what they had ordered and the prices. Patrick perused it …

Salads – Roasted Vegetable	2 @ $45.00	$ 90.00
Wine	1 @ $85.00	85.00
Fresh Fruit	2 @ $12.00	24.00
Coffee	2 @ $15.00	30.00

Subtotal	
$229.00	
Wine Health Surcharge (100%)	*85.00*
Coffee Health Surcharge (100%)	*30.00*
Children's Foundation Federal Tax (12%)	*27.48*
Luxury Tax (20%)	*45.80*
Food Wastage Charge (local fee)	*50.00*
Tourism Tax (state tax 15%)	*34.35*
VAT Sales Tax (20% + 5% restaurant)	*57.25*
Total	*$ 558.88*
Required Gratuity (45%)	*103.05*
Grand Total	*$ 661.93*
Rounding	*$ 662.00*

"There must be some mistake," said Patrick, calling the waiter over. "It was two hundred twenty-nine dollars for the meal. How could it come to six sixty-two?"

"How long has it been since you've been out to a restaurant, sir?" said the waiter, curtly.

Shea fumed at the comment.

"It's all standard, sir," continued the waiter. "The surcharges are for your unhealthy choices of wine and coffee. The penalty on those is one hundred percent. The Children's Foundation is obvious – it goes to help the children. The other taxes are local, state and federal."

"Why is there a luxury tax and what's this forty-five percent gratuity?" asked Shea, pointing to the screen.

"Anytime you go to a restaurant, it's considered a luxury service. Many don't have the money you rich people have to go out to dinner every night. As for the required gratuity – Congress passed that with the fifty dollar per hour minimum wage law last year. All restaurants charge a minimum of forty-five percent gratuity for services, but you can give more if you like," said the man, knowing his remark would just add salt to the wound.

"This is insane!" shouted Shea, loud enough that made others in the restaurant turn their heads. The restaurant was not full, and now he knew why.

"Just scan in your EID chip and your account will be debited, sir. That's all you need to do," said the waiter, curtly.

"We don't use EID chips," said Shea. "We don't believe in them."

EID chips were embedded identification chips that were mandated by law, but not everyone had them implanted. They acted as markers to confirm someone's identity but were also used to control various gadgets, deduct money from bank accounts and other activities. It was getting harder and harder to live in the country without it, but many had not wanted to be "marked" by the government. They felt it was an intrusion into their lives and potentially dangerous, if some agency decided to use them to track your movements. Trust was the key, and fewer and fewer people held that opinion with their elected officials. There were millions who had refused the mandate, and it had become impossible to enforce. Eventually, the agencies gave up trying.

"But you have to have an EID!" said the waiter in disgust. "It's the law!"

"Everything is the law these days!" Shea shot back. She held out her wrists. "Go ahead, you can arrest me here and now, if you want. But then again, I guess you won't get a tip then, will you?"

The waiter walked away from the table and pushed through the rotating door to the back of the restaurant. Within minutes, the manager walked out to their table. He was not smiling. "I understand you do not have an EID," he said.

"That's true," said Shea. "We will pay for our dinner, however."

"And how do you wish to do that?" said the manager, his hands folded behind his back.

"The old fashion way – digital scanning," said Shea.

The manager huffed, but left, returning ten minutes later with a small, black cube with a glass surface. "Here, scan your print, then," he said.

Shea put her finger on the box, and a thin, red line passed beneath it, sliding across the underside of the surface. When it had finished, Shea's image appeared in the same glassy rectangle, confirming her identity. She didn't like the fact that the authorities had everyone's fingerprints, but that was something that had been done years earlier. Done was done – there wasn't anything she could do about that. But an embedded EID – that was something else.

"Very well. It's all confirmed. And thanks for coming in," said the manager, turning on his heels and walking briskly away before he had to hear another word from their table.

Shea pushed the *Scan* button on the table's electronic tablets, which had given them the menu and the bill.

"What are you doing now?" Patrick asked with a sigh.

She scanned-in an image of her middle finger and smiled.

Patrick shook his head. "You're really a piece of work sometimes, you know?"

Shea laughed. "Yeah, I know. I can be sophomoric, can't I?"

Now it was Patrick's turn to laugh. Then, he laughed even harder when he read the screen, following Shea's high school prank. The table screen read:

Accepted.
Thanks for coming in!

"Let's get out of here before they charge us a meter fee for overstaying our welcome," said Patrick, helping Shea with her coat.

They both left, only to face a one hundred fifty dollar parking fee outside.

*****

CH 8 G

It was late. There was a cool drizzle coming down, blanketing not only buildings, splintered park benches, checkered cabs, and Type-A commuters and their standard-issue, black umbrellas. The sun, tired from the day's efforts to illuminate and warm half the earth, sank below the horizon, plummeting the city into darkness. However, Washington had begun the slide into darkness many decades earlier.

Thomas's eyes burned, red and stinging from fatigue, he rubbed them with his thumb and forefinger. It had been a long day, but then again, everyday working for Deputy Secretary Ratner was a challenge. Ever since she had been appointed to her post, she had run roughshod over all in the department. Those who had not already left were thinking about it; however, some felt trapped, having made the department their career. Thomas had gone almost directly into the service of the state. His father and mother had both found positions in administrations of previous People's Party presidents. They had experienced fruitful professional paths, retiring at fifty and having lifetime pensions that took care of them until they died.

For Thomas, things had started well. He had moved up the ranks quickly in the Federal Trade Commission and then been transferred to the renamed Department of Fair Trade. His empathy and understanding of the issues had landed him positions in management and overseeing vital programs funded by the government to improve trade relations with the increasingly antagonistic countries of the East. However, after twenty years, he had found himself in the Department of Technology Assessment – Deputy Secretary Ratner's department. It was also known outside of the building as *The Gulag*.

He waited until the light turned and the pedestrian indicator told him he could cross. He hated nights like this. The cold chill and dampness was a prelude of the winter to come, and although not as beastly in Washington as it was elsewhere, it still was cold to him. He pulled his navy, double-breasted coat closer to him and held on tightly to his black umbrella. He had no briefcase, as most everything was electronic. Those things he needed to work on, he would access over SI-net at home; otherwise, he would use his data stick, which he carried only if there were confidential files he needed to review.

One of the hydrogen-powered, double-accordion buses sped past him, splashing water onto his coat and soaking his pants.

"Sh*t!" he exclaimed, using his gloved hand to brush off any water that had beaded on the surface of his jacket. He was in no mood for additional abuse after his long day at the office. Ratner had already berated him earlier in the week for letting one of his subordinates issue a patent license to the Lenoir Labs. She had been particularly mean and cruel, following up with him several times later to ensure that he was bringing criminal charges against the employee. He had resisted, as it was a ten-year veteran with a wife and family, but to Ratner it made no difference. That day, she had threatened him verbally, telling him that if he didn't file charges by the end of the week, she would take matters into her own hands. She was vengeful; he knew that. And he didn't want to push his luck. Against his conscience, he was going to contact the Department of Justice to start the proceedings the next day.

The Purple Line Station was four blocks from the Department of Technology Assessment building. The escalator was one of the deepest in Washington, and it took several minutes to ride it down to the bottom. Getting off, Thomas recognized several faces of people with whom he often rode home at that late hour but was too tired to engage them, other than to smile and nod. The Orange Line and Blue Lines ran through the same station, and it was the Orange Line that stopped first. The silver cars passed, one-by-one, and the shortened commuter slowly ground to a halt, opening its doors and heralding to all who boarded that it was headed to Vienna, Virginia. The ding-dong sound of the closing doors hurried stragglers coming down the escalator and the train sped off into the black tunnel to deliver it's human packages.

Thomas looked at his PCD and the time. It's got to be here any minute he thought. Sure enough, the 11:54 came into the station bearing the purple badge of the line. "Purple Line to Fairfax" said a cheerful woman's voice, synthesized for the masses. Thomas hopped on and took a seat on the obnoxious tangerine orange and canary yellow, vinyl seats. He flipped his wrist to show his PCD and pushed some buttons to show messages and video recordings of day's events in the world. There had been no earth-shattering events, other than the financial crisis in South America, the on-going war between the Shia's and the Sunni's in the Middle East, and the uprising that was starting to take place again in India.

Six stops later, the Purple Line came into the station marked *Annandale* and slowed to a stop. The station was outside, and the drizzle had increased to a steady rain, making the walkways slick. Thomas strolled out to the abandoned area of the parking lot where earlier in the day the cars had been parked three and four layers deep. It would only be a few more hours before they parade of cars would reappear and repopulate the spaces within.

Without the congestion, Thomas spoke into his PCD to summon his car to the curb. Usually, the car obeyed within minutes and would appear, pulling over and opening the driver's side door for him to get in. This night, there was a problem with the communication to the car's computer, and the message did not register as having been received. Thomas exhaled deeply. *The day just keeps getting better and better*, he thought. Soon it would be over though, and he would be home in bed – at least for a few hours before he'd have to do it all over again.

Thomas found his car and pushed the buttons on his PCD to start it. The car's engine roared to life and the headlights turned on. It moved toward him, like a dog called by its master, slowly at first and then faster. Suddenly, it jolted forward and raced at him at high speed. Before he could jump out of the way, it hit him, throwing him over the hood and up and over the roof. The car continued forward, running into a light pole and snapping it in two before crashing into the side of the station itself. At that point, all the lights in the lot went dark.

Thomas's body lay on the ground, writhing in pain. Both legs were broken as was his neck and back. He could feel the pain shooting throughout his upper body, but he was helpless to move, paralyzed from the waist down. Opening his eyes, he saw the car in the distance, its hood crumpled and hydrogen leaking out of the tank in back.

What happened? he thought, wincing with discomfort. *I've never had the car do that before.*

He looked down at his PCD, but it was shattered, its display cracked and pieces falling out of the side. Out of the corner of his eye, he saw another set of headlights come on and another engine start. Thomas put his hand up to his face to shield it from the light and try to make out who it was. The black sedan squealed its tires, as if it were in a drag race, and it began barreling down on him.

What the ...? thought Thomas, but those were the last thoughts he had.

The car ran over him, crushing his chest and killing him instantly. Just to be sure, it stopped and ran back over his body to silence him forever.

"I think he's dead," said one of the men in the car.

"Yeah, I'm sure he is. Let's go. The secretary will be pleased that it was so clean. It's too bad you can't depend on your own car anymore to get you home safely," said the second man laughing.

The black sedan pulled out of the lot and vanished into the stillness of the night.

*****

CH 9 SECE

"Are you f***ing kidding me!" shouted Patrick, growling at the screen in front of him. Every morning he would pull up the latest news on the *Drudge Underground Report* to see what was happening in the world. Usually, the news only caused his blood to boil and sometimes even a flurry of expletives to spew forth from his mouth. "What the hell has happened to this country? What happened to the rule of law and to our Constitution?"

Outbursts like this one only happened when he was alone talking to himself, which he did often. In public, he liked to get along with others even if they were on the opposite side with their opinions. But that didn't change the way he felt about things. He felt as passionately as Shea; he just had a different way of expressing it. By yelling at a computer monitor, he didn't offend anyone else. And, the way he saw it, the fact that there was no one else in the room to hear him was a fitting metaphor for the way most people felt – that there was no one in the world listening to the grass roots public in the country anymore. People felt they just didn't matter.

Born of English and Scottish immigrants, Patrick had always had a feisty spirit – but one he kept well under control. Where he did use it was in his perseverance. He had fought through the maze of bureaucratic red tape and naysayers to achieve what he had in life. Nothing had been given to him. He had fought hard for what he'd earned, sometimes working two shifts a day at the same job every week. He often reminisced about the good-ole' days when he would kiss Shea goodbye at five in the morning as she lay in bed and drive an hour to the engineering lab at the office – a rundown, old two-story building that had cockroaches scurrying mindlessly about in the darkness before they were interrupted by Patrick turning on the lights. By seven that night, he would call her and say he would be late. She was used to that, but it still bothered her. She knew he was doing it for them, yet she wanted him home with her.

During the day, Shea worked in the front office, running the rest of the company's affairs. It, too, required long hours, but some could be done at home at night either in her home office or on the couch in front of the media screen. She would work until her eyes burned and her eyelids felt like they had ten-pound weights glued to them. By ten o'clock, the day would have taken its toll on her, and she would trudge upstairs to bed, often leaving on her computer screen, eerily flickering its maze of numbers and spreadsheets behind her like some sci-fi horror movie. By eleven or so, she would hear the tumblers turn in the lock downstairs, and her husband come in through the door, pushing it open to make a familiar, yet annoying, creaking noise she'd heard thousands of times before. Then, to top it off, would come a sharp, cracking sound as he'd throw his data stick and money card on the small, iron table in the entryway. She'd told him time and again not to, but it was of no use. He would then shuffle up the stairs, come across the room to kiss her on the cheek and then go into the bathroom. By the time he would come out, she would be fast asleep again, snoring softly beside him.

But the work days were quite different. They were busy – almost frenetically so. Juggling many things at the same time, Patrick tried to take care of his own work and assist others in theirs. It was exhausting, yet rewarding – especially when he and his team toiled together to solve a problem and succeeded. It was a level of satisfaction of which he couldn't get enough.

"What's wrong, boss?" asked Sergei, his chief technology officer who always made Patrick's office his first stop in the morning. Sergei would buy donuts in before coming in and tempt Patrick with them before climbing the stairs to the wing of the building where all the research and development was done. It was there that they did the hard work to convert theory into reality – taking computer images and mathematical formulae and molding them into a working model of a high-efficiency combustion engine.

"Nothing we can do anything about, Sergei," Patrick answered, putting on his smiley mask. "The only thing I know to do is what I'm doing – what we're doing. Beyond that, I couldn't tell you."

Sergei grinned. The corners of his mouth turned up as they always did when he asked the same question of his boss just about every morning at just about the same time. It was a routine they had – something they'd done for over twenty years. However, one thing the CTO had noticed was that Patrick's bouts of rage had only worsened during those twenty-odd years, as the business climate in America had steadily deteriorated.

"Oh, cheer up, Patrick," answered Sergei with his thick, Russian accent. "I have that special chocolate-glazed donut you love."

Patrick was a sucker for the chocolate-glaze. It was his favorite, and Sergei knew he could never resist.

Patrick waved him over and reached in to pull out his prize. "You're awful," he said to his CTO.

"I know, but you love me for it."

"Where the hell do you get these things anyway? I thought donuts were banned?" asked Patrick, biting into the soft, sugary dough.

"They are. I have a place where I get them. It's on the black market."

"You must have to pay through the nose, then."

"Yeah, but it's worth it. You can't find these things just anywhere, you know," answered Sergei. "So, Patrick, my friend, what's eating you?"

"It seems like everything," said Patrick, trying to chew and talk at the same time. "There are so many things beyond my control – our control. And, I think they've only gotten worse -- spinning quickly away from all of us, like galaxies in the universe."

"Kind of like the Hubble Red Shift," Sergei said.

"Yeah, exactly," said Patrick knowing his tech guy was referring to the red shift of light shown by galaxies at the outer limits of the known universe. "But I hope you're not working on astronomy projects today – just combustion engines."

"For now," Sergei answered, wryly. "I just hope you're working on the manufacturing of our little baby here, the SECE. Now that we've gotten our patent, we can start producing it. By the way, when will you have the first production lines up and running?"

"We should have the first ones in nine-to-twelve months, unless the Department of Environmental Protection gets in the way. We're in the process of finalizing our financing now."

"Ah, come on, Patrick! Where's your fighting spirit? You're not going to let that little EPA group get in your way? Are you becoming a pessimist on me?" asked Sergei, jokingly.

"Nah, of course not. It's just … well … not the America it used to be."

"Things change. That's the nature of life," said Sergei, trying to re-instill some modicum of optimism in his boss. "What seems bad today will become good tomorrow. As they say, there's always a, how do you say, a silver lining at the end of the rainbow. Right?"

The mixed metaphor made Patrick laugh. Coming from Sergei, it was comical. He was a brilliant technician. Computers were his thing, and he'd grown up loving the exactness of computer language and its potential. At the age of seven, he'd built his own computer from parts, and by thirteen had developed a complex computer algorithm to analyze the impact of changing sunspot activity on Earth's climate.

Patrick had seen in Sergei an intelligence that could transition easily from one mode of thinking to another. In this case, it was moving from the world of bits and bytes to the world of injectors and fuel compression. But, in many ways the two were inseparable, particularly in the modern era of technology.

Tall, thin and angular, Sergei had a traditional Russian profile – strong, square jawed, small narrow eyes, thin lips, and a blonde crew-cut with long sideburns down below his earlobes. At forty-three, he had decided not to succumb to vision correction and instead of the surgery had opted for a pair of thick, black-rimmed glasses that dominated his face. It wasn't often that he shaved, and the stubble that turned into a short, untrimmed beard was the way he usually presented himself.

"Yeah, you're right," said Patrick, responding to Sergei's wise words. "Bad things can turn into good."

"Absolutely," said Sergei, smiling. "But sometimes you just have to chip away at it. You know, a little bit at a time. We'll get there in the end."

Patrick grinned and nodded. "Spoken like a philosopher, there Sergei. You should have been a professor."

"Ah, perhaps. Or a psychoanalyst. But then you wouldn't have been blessed by my words of wisdom, then, would you?"

Together, they spent the rest of the morning reviewing the progress they were making on refining the engine design, making it simpler and more responsive to the changing engine additives that were made throughout the seasons – from winter to summer blends – as well as the demands from the manufacturing engineers who had to produce it in large quantities.

All of the modifications required complex computer programming, which was right up Sergei's alley. Not only was he a master of software engineering, he reveled in the challenges of mechanical engineering, molding the two disciplines seamlessly into something that would move cars, trucks, planes, trains and other modes of transportation.

At its core, Patrick, Sergei and the rest of the scientists at the Lenoir Labs had created an engine that was extraordinary. It was a remarkable achievement, and one that had not been duplicated by anyone else since the original HECE engine had debuted. The design was simple, the motion of the parts inside minimal, and the computer straightforward. What was complicated was the software and the unique way each of these simple things was integrated to make a combustion engine that was inexpensive, easy to maintain, fast to produce, and required resources that were easily procured within the confines of the continental USA.

But therein lay the problem; few believed it could be done. Other scientists had scoffed at the premise. They believed that such breakthroughs could only come about through highly complex systems, not-yet-formulated metals or compounds, specialty fuel products or a workforce made up entirely of PhDs.

When first filed, the patent application was ignored by government officials who preferred to think it was some sort of hoax. However, Patrick and Shea had persisted. Eventually, they found a *friendly*, as they called her, in the Department of Technology Assessment. Although not high-ranking, the woman had taken the time to review the findings and the lab work. Surprisingly, she had managed to convince her boss that it was sound work and should be given consideration.

However, they had not yet won the battle. Rebuffed several more times, the Disones fought long and hard with higher-level officials before, finally, the department relented and sent the application through the standard channels for review and approval. Their long nightmare ended when they received the patent notification only months earlier... or so they thought.

There was a greater, darker force at work. It was one of which they were aware, but one they thought they could surmount idealistically. In the end, it was simple. It was all about money, and who was feeding at its trough.

The potential of such a high-efficiency combustion engine threatened the money trough of green energy. Billions had been invested in alternative energy, and laws had been written favoring their development over all others. There were few combustion engines left in America, as gasoline had been taxed to the point no one could afford a gas-powered engine. The fact that electric engines were also extremely expensive and didn't last as long, only added to the cost burden for the average American. Even natural gas engines were frowned upon. Instead, people were forced to buy solar powered cars that didn't work well, delivering only enough power to reach about eighty kilometers per hour (about fifty miles per hour) and giving very little acceleration. The basic premise for President Fourier's approach to the economy and business, at large, had been that fossil fuels were bad – bad for the economy, bad for the ecology, and bad for America. His Administration had immediately launched an anti-oil, anti-coal, anti-gas campaign after being in the White House for only one week. The advent of a super-highly efficient gas-burning engine would be a serious threat to those beliefs.

Patrick was well aware of the negative political implications for such a technology. He knew that once he and Sergei began to produce it, he would be wearing a target on his back. Both competitors and environmental activists would be working diligently to undermine him, or worse yet, to destroy him.

As a result, he had installed guards and security systems in and around Lenoir Labs during the early years. Access to the technology and its secrets was limited to a very few, and only those few knew how all the pieces fit together to make the engine work – Patrick and Sergei. They gave others access only to those portions of the technology for which they were directly responsible. It was a segmentation strategy that worked well in most highly-creative, invention-driven companies. You knew what you needed to know – no more and no less.

"Are you ready for your presentation tomorrow, Sergei?" Patrick asked, as they reviewed the latest changes to the software code. "We have to impress the media and our financial backers, you know."

"What? Why me?" questioned Sergei, beginning to click his tongue in nervous anticipation. "It's only a bunch of financial geeks. What do they know about combustion engines? I could roll out an old Chevy L88 Corvette engine – you know, the 427. They wouldn't know the difference between that and a Slant Six dual quad Hemi from a '69 Charger."

"Don't get too uppity, my friend. I understand they are bringing engine specialists with them, like Gunter Muntz."

Sergei's nervousness turned to a rigid frigidity, almost instantly. "Muntz? He's a hack."

"You hate him, I know. But, we'll have to deal with him tomorrow just the same."

"After that circus he put together a few years ago, trying to discredit our work. It's hard to forgive him. He's an a**hole. We both know that."

"Yes, Sergei, we've all known a lot of a**holes during our lifetimes. Most of the time, we have to suffer through it, as intolerable as they may be. In this case, we need the investment community to love our company so we have a good sale at a public offering or with private equity. The higher the stock price, the more money we'll have to further our research and built-up our production capacity. He could be a fulcrum to help us leverage what we need out of these Wall Street people. We can't let personal feelings get in the way. We have to look at the long term here. You understand that, right?"

Sergei shook his head. "But I disagree. He won't be on our side – no matter what. Whatever he does, it won't be good for the company. I guarantee that," said Sergei. He was not good at acting, but he would do the best he could for the sake of Patrick and his company.

***

The next day came, and Patrick gathered his top scientists to choreograph the demonstration of the SECE engine that they had recently perfected. It was as much an unveiling to the media and the transportation industry as it was for the investment bankers and private equity firms who were courting the company.

Held at the company's headquarters, the meeting scene was chaotic with media reporters and photographers jostling for a better angle to get pictures and position themselves to ask the first questions of the chief executive and his scientific team of experts. New to the game, Shea had not realized the security problems with such a public spectacle, but it was too late. Amid the chaos, no one had required validation of anyone's press credentials, even though she had posted a check-in desk for guests to register. Meghan had only checked off their names and handed out badges, which were summarily stuffed into coat pockets or thrown into the nearest trash basket.

Patrick glanced at his watch and noted it was time to start the session. Walking to the small, portable podium, he thumped the mike both to test it and to gather everyone's attention.

"Good morning," he said, the upturned corners of his mouth giving away the pleasure he was having of unveiling his latest *baby*. "First of all, I'd like to welcome all of you to the Lenoir Research Labs facility. As I'm sure all of you know since you've all done your homework before coming here today …" he smiled as most others in the room chuckled, "… the lab was named after Étienne Lenoir, the nineteenth century inventor who was instrumental in creating the first commercial combustion engine. His work resulted in the development of the single-stroke engine in 1859 using coal gas and air. Of course, others copied and improved on his work, which led to the creation of Daimler Benz and other world-class auto makers.

"My wife Shea and I have spent most of our careers growing this company. Our aim was to develop a highly efficient gasoline engine that would reduce the country's dependence on oil imports, lessen the impact of emissions on the environment, and lighten the financial burden that commuters bear traveling to work and that long and short-haul truckers have in transporting goods. Overall, a reduction in the cost of transportation and polluting emissions would be a tremendous benefit to the country and the world as a whole. I also hope that the federal government will reassess its position on the matter and eventually permit the sale of this engine within this country. At present, we will only be allowed to sell this engine overseas.

"The SECE engine, which stands for Super-Efficient Combustion Engine – a technical phrase that my head scientist came up with …" again he smiled, and the crowd chortled, "… supersedes the HECE engine, or just the Highly-Efficient Combustion Engine that we developed nearly ten years ago. Whereas, the HECE was thirty-five percent efficient, the SECE is eighty-seven percent efficient. This compares with the standard combustible engine, which, when it was in use, was about sixteen percent efficient.

"Today, we have the pleasure and pride of demonstrating the new SECE engine. We have linked it to the monitors you see before you, which will record and report the efficiency levels, emissions, and other statistics regarding the engine's performance. Of course, you will be able to verify all of these data on your own. Our patent was approved by the Department of Technology Assessment just a few months ago, so we will be ready to roll-out and produce of this very special and, we believe, society-changing invention very soon.

"And now I'd like to introduce my chief technologist who has been with me for, well, as long as I can remember, Dr. Sergei Navarov."

Patrick yielded the dais to his friend and colleague. Sergei moved toward the podium and gave a slight, but awkward wave to the group in front of him. Patrick could tell he was about to start his nervous tick of tongue clicking, when he caught himself and cleared his throat instead.

"Hello," he said with his heavy Russian accent. "I'm Sergei Navarov, and I'm going to be showing you the performance and efficiencies of our SECE Model MB12, Series 3.5 engine." He nodded to Shea, who was standing beside a white, sheet-draped object, conspicuously resting in a cordoned-off circle in the center of the floor. Shea pulled off the sheet to reveal the revolutionary invention. To the surprise of nearly everyone, the engine looked much like any other engine. Perhaps more similar to the 1970s version of the rotary engine called the Wankel, after its German inventor. That engine had discs that revolved inside a chamber to compress the gasses instead of the standard valve heads, cam shafts, and pistons of the straight, inline engines and V-shaped V-8 and V-6 engines that had been popular through most of the latter twentieth and early twenty-first centuries.

Sergei spent the next thirty minutes describing the technical aspects of the engine without giving away any particulars that were secret and patented. He discussed the standard pieces of information in which the car magazines and, more importantly, the uninformed reporters were interested, such as the displacement, brake horsepower, torque capability, and other attributes. Then, he turned on the engine, which was remarkably quiet, while tapping out some keys on his computer. The technical readings of the engine's performance displayed on a holographic chamber overhead, complete with an animated version of what the engine was actually doing on the inside. As the engine roared to life, the simulated needle on the tachometer jumped, showing the increasing revolutions of the crankshaft. Another simulated dial showed the efficiency reading, which rose markedly in tandem with the tachometer.

"As you can see," Sergei said, "the engine runs very quietly. The display overhead shows the brake-horsepower and compression ratios. Based on the performance levels, at this RPM, we should expect to get about three hundred miles per gallon. Of course, this will vary based on the RPM's. Current modifications to the software should raise this number to around five hundred mpg when they are completed."

A bar chart tracked the progress of the demonstration, illustrating the engine efficiency level, estimated miles per gallon, RPM, brake horsepower, compression averages, and other critical data. The first numbers shown for engine efficiency started just above mid-way up the bar graph and showing a color of orange to the 50 percent level, then changing to yellow between 50 and 65. As the revolutions or RPMs rose, the efficiency also increased, and the bar graph climbed into the seventies, then eighties, changing color again to powder blue and gradually to a yellow, mossy green. Once the RPMs reached ten thousand, the engine was humming calmly, the horsepower output showed nearly 465 on the screen, with an efficiency bar a solid, bright green – 84 percent. This was quite the opposite of most combustion engines, which gave lower gas mileage the higher the RPMs.

There were gasps of disbelief in the group, and photographers were busy snapping pictures. Most had 4-D cameras that required multiple angle shots, but this had been solved by technology that allowed the reflecting of an image off other objects in the room. Even though the cameras had gotten smaller, the aggressiveness of the photographers had only worsened in recent years, and knocking over fellow journalists in pursuit of a story or picture was no longer a unique event.

"Well, I do apologize for this," said Sergei, clearly disappointed. "I promised you eighty-seven percent efficiency, and we're getting eighty-four this morning. It is most likely due to the humidity levels in the room, or some other small anomaly. This is easily corrected." He fidgeted uncomfortably, even though no one else in the room seemed to be particularly bothered by the discrepancy.

Patrick retook the podium. "Thank you, Sergei. Now, if you would please retake your positions so we may proceed, I'd like to take any questions."

The reporters were all over each other vying for the first question. Several blurted out questions in hopes of catching Patrick's attention. But it was during a split-second moment of awkward silence that one young enthusiast was able to insert his question. Patrick listened and smiled benevolently. "Let me repeat what I think your question is. You asked how the engine will be manufactured and by whom? Yes, we are working with an automobile company at the moment, although I can't disclose their name. We expect the engines to be in cars overseas within the next two years."

At that point, someone from Patrick's office crossed the stage and approached Sergei, whispering into his ear. He didn't say a word and left out the side door. Patrick continued to answer questions, most of which were nontechnical and easily addressed. Others were more in-depth, and although he could handle them, he wished Sergei had been there to give a more complete response.

After the event was over, reporters and photographers left the room, leaving behind the investment bankers to scrounge for more information -- most financially related. So, Patrick motioned for Shea to step in for the second phase of the program.

After he left the stage, Patrick walked over to Meghan and lightly took her by the arm, pulling her closer. "Where did Sergei go?" he asked, whispering to her.

"I was told to give him a message that there was someone outside who urgently needed to speak with him. At first he protested, but then when I told him the name, he left."

"Who was it?"

"It was a guy by the name of Muntz. I think," she answered.

"Where is Sergei now?" Patrick asked, suddenly concerned.

"I don't know. He didn't come back after the session was over."

Patrick flipped on his PCD. "Dial Sergei," he commanded. He waited as the ring tones buzzed in his ear. One, two, three, four … There was no answer. Then, Sergei's his video message popped up. "This is Sergei Navarov, please leave a message … "

"He's probably just gone out to lunch with him or something," said Meghan, unaware of the acrimony between the two men.

"In the middle of the most important meeting of our lives?" exclaimed Patrick. "Did anyone see them?"

"I didn't see them leave, no. But I spoke to the visitor who was waiting for him. He was over six feet tall, probably in his early forties. Brownish-blonde hair and no eyebrows to speak of."

"No eyebrows?" asked Patrick. Acting startled.

"Yeah."

"Then, it *was* Muntz," said Patrick under his breath. "Gunter Muntz."

"Is that someone I should know?" Meghan asked.

"Not necessarily. But, he's a problem," Patrick answered, with worry in his voice. He looked at his PCD, it was only ten o'clock. It had already been a long morning, and it was about to get longer.

Patrick ran down to the lobby, scanning all of the reporters who were still mingling there. There was no sign of Sergei or Muntz. So, he pushed his way out the front, glass doors into the curved pandus or semicircular drive that adjoined the building. Looking up and down, he saw a row of cars leaving the parking lot, heading out to the main highway just down the street. It would be impossible to stop them at that point, and by the time the police would arrive, they would all be gone.

Helpless, Patrick watched as the black and gray solar-powered vehicles followed the metallic traffic rails that were embedded into the pavement while their owners comfortably watched messages on their PCD's or listened to their music, the cars driving themselves off the premises.

How could this happen? he wondered, as his thoughts immediately conjured the worst-case scenario. *Would Muntz really do something this bad? Perhaps he was overreacting. Sergei had told him earlier that he needed to be more optimistic. Perhaps he was right. Maybe he just needed to see what looked like bad things as possibly good ones.* Yet there was something about the whole thing that dug into his subconscious and caused him to feel differently. That proverbial pit in his stomach would not go away.

*****

CH 10 CONGRESSMAN SUMNER

Wyoming had two Congressional delegates – Clara Wrangle and JC Sumner. While Sumner had remained loyal to the Constitution Party from which he had been elected, Wrangle had deserted it. Instead, she had seen the power shift early on and had chosen to give up her principles and follow the orders issued by her new party leader, House Speaker Preston Brooks of the People's Party. Earlier in his career, Brooks was the lieutenant governor under then-Governor Fourier of the state of Illinois. Fourier had encouraged him to run for Congress when Fourier had been elected to the U.S. Senate. Both men had done well, and both had fed off each other's success. Over the years, Brooks and the president had consolidated their power to suppress dissent and ensure they got what they wanted. If they didn't, they made sure there would be hell to pay. And even if that didn't work, the president would use the magic pen of executive order to get what he wanted anyway. Yet, there were still some willing to fight against them and risk everything to do so.

JC Sumner was frustrated. He was one of the few in his own minority party who had been brave enough to stand up to the controlling People's Party. He, and only he, had challenged the president publicly to debate states' rights after Fourier had made a comment that the Founding Fathers – corrected to be the Founders as he had insisted -- had never supported states' rights over federal government control. Re-writing history had become commonplace, not only with the Administration and in the media, but more damagingly, in public and private schools.

Sometimes outrageous, other times astute and serious, JC was an unusual politician in many ways. As shown by his relentless attack on the government departments, he had an unwavering sense of principle – right versus wrong. To him, things were black and white – no gray allowed. Some said it was naiveté; others said it was ignorance or just blindness to the reality of things around him. Whichever way, he suffered in his position in Congress – ostracized and often scorned by his so-called constitutionalist colleagues. However, the people he represented, his constituents, loved him. He reflected their beliefs and their values, and he spoke for them as no other Congressman spoke for his or her district in that hallowed body on Capitol Hill.

In front of Congressman Sumner sat a stack of paper nearly a foot high. He had intentionally printed out the 5,304-page House Bill, HR-2148-551, a monstrosity of legislation with references to hundreds of other laws scattered throughout. It was like a secret code embedded into war-time battle plans and was intentionally constructed that way by the House Speaker to make it difficult to understand. As with most bills Congress passed, the document was so complicated that no one really knew what it contained; but that didn't matter. The Executive Branch, with all of its departments, would interpret it the way they wanted anyway. After it was all said and done, the issued interpretations of the bill would expand the overall law to hundreds of times that in the original language – in this case, over 8.3 million pages. Virtually no congressional staff even bothered to read them anymore, and to be sure, no congressman did either– except Sumner.

Sumner could read and comprehend at over ten thousand words per minute. It didn't take him long to read documents, although a five thousand page one would take him a bit more time. But, he would also have his staff work around the clock to understand it too because the House had only been given seventy-two hours to read it before the vote. Speaker Brooks was pushing hard for its passage, as was the president. The only thing known for certain was that it was supposedly to reform the electoral process and simplify the way officials were to be elected. However, Sumner had found it to be quite the opposite.

Buried in the thousands of pages of the legislation were provisions that required every challenging opponent undergo a thorough background check, including one for mental stability. The definition of mental stability was subjective. Existing members of Congress were grandfathered, as they were for most laws they passed. As a result, the law exempted them from any such evaluations.

In addition, the law permitted exemptions from elections in districts or states where the incumbent candidate had garnered more than 60 percent of the vote during the previous election. The law explained that this was merely a cost-saving measure, as it assumed that another election would only produce the same result. And finally, all Congressional and Senate candidates had to pay an entrance fee of two hundred thousand dollars to enter a race to defray the costs incurred by the newly renamed *Free* Federal Elections Commission to monitor the races. This made it nearly impossible for all but the wealthy to run for public office.

As for the office of president, the law was intended to clarify the 22nd Amendment to the *Constitution*, which restricted the number of terms that the office holder could assume. Instead, it held that the amendment never intended to put the country at risk in times of a national crisis. The law stated that in times of national crisis, Article II, Section II, which 'designated the president as Commander in Chief of all armed forces,' would preempt the Amendment, and that the president's role as Commander in Chief would thereby supersede the role as president in those circumstances. This, it went on to say,

> '... would ensure the strength of the Union in times of instability and unrest. The importance of this provision cannot be lost to the misinterpretation of the 22nd Amendment. The Amendment was not intended to weaken the state by attempting to transition power from one commander to another in the middle of a crisis. Military strategy would never accept nor endorse changing generals, save the Commander in Chief, in the middle of a battle. That an officer of the armed forces would be replaced by another due to some well-intentioned, but misguided law would be viewed as grossly negligent. Therefore, the responsibilities and authority of the position as Commander in Chief preempt those of the standing position of president at that time and must continue until such time as the crisis has passed or such action or actions have been taken to minimize the threat to a level deemed necessary to permit free elections. The determination of a crisis shall be made by the Executive Branch, with concurrence by the Judicial Branch.'

Sumner was more than uncomfortable with the language and the new powers given to the president. It was a ticket to a dictatorship. A crisis could easily be manufactured, thereby enabling the incumbent to remain in power indefinitely.

Why, he wondered, *would the other politicians not see this? Why would the media not question this?*

He already knew the answer -- self-preservation. No one was willing to sacrifice his or her careers to speak out against it. Anyone daring to do so, would certainly be jettisoned from key committees and instantly lose all influence, together with the perks and money schemes that came with them. No, the gig on Capitol Hill was too good, and with the new laws, their positions were almost certainly guaranteed for life. So why rock the boat?

"Randy?" said Sumner, summoning his chief of staff. "Do you see this law working any other way but as a means to dictatorship? It looks to me like

Fourier can keep his office indefinitely if he deems a situation a crisis and cajoles the Supremes into agreeing with him. He could determine that his hangnail this morning is a crisis, couldn't he?"

Randy slowly trudged over to JC, his blue silk, paisley tie drooping down below its proper perch, his shirt's top button unfastened, and his white shirt sleeves rolled up. He'd been up all night, and it showed. "I don't see any other way it would work. It's just an automatic *Get-out-of-jail Card* for him. The way things are setup in this bill, it's not hard for him to declare a crisis any time he likes. The requirements aren't that tough. But I think it could be even worse than that."

Sumner looked at him with surprise.

"Even though the concurrence of the Supreme Court is required, there's another provision buried on page 1,454," said Randy, continuing his analysis, "it says that:

> *'In the event the Supreme Court is unable to concur with the president's decision on the definition of crisis as it may apply to a current or ongoing situation, other measures to determine the nature of the situation shall be undertaken. These measures shall be determined solely by a simple majority of the House of Representatives.'*

"Crap!" said Sumner. "That means …"

"Yeah. All the president needs to do is get his buddies in Congress to agree with him – cut them some deals. You know, the usual. Then, he can make up his own rules and stay in power … indefinitely."

Sumner sat back in his thick, leather chair and folded his hands behind his head, interlocking his fingers like a web. "Boy, I just don't understand how people can just turn over their freedom like this!" he exclaimed.

"Those that see it will either get something in return or are too afraid to say anything. Those that don't – well, they're too stupid or out of touch to ever get it. And by the time they do, it will be too late."

"Is there anything else in here we should be afraid of?" asked Sumner.

"Perhaps, JC. There's another provision that could force you out of office too."

"What? I didn't see that. Where is that in here?" Sumner asked, flipping the pages.

"Page 4,382, sir. It talks about having special elections for any legislator from a state that is on the *wrong* side of issues more than sixty percent of the time. It states that,

> '... *those lawmakers who are found to vote 60 percent or more of the time in the minority on legislative matters that pass both the House of Representatives and the Senate are subject to recall by their district's or state's voters. Such history of votes is indicative of the legislator's inability to grasp the concepts put forth in the legislative chamber or a chronic failure to vote as a successful lawmaker. Such members of Congress shall have their rights to cast votes on the floor of their respective houses suspended until a free and fair election is held to replace them.'*

JC was stunned. "Oh my God! Do you think that was written with a footnote, like 'We wrote this just for JC Sumner, as he's first on our *hit-list!*'"

Randy laughed. "It sure sounds like it. Doesn't it?"

Randy Marston had been Sumner's chief of staff for twelve years. They had gotten to know each other well – almost like father and son. After Sumner's son had died in an auto accident years earlier he had taken Randy under his wing.

Randy had graduated *cum laude* from Wharton, and although he'd planned to go to Wall Street and be in finance, that career was abruptly halted when the capital markets were virtually shut down by Fourier and his executive orders. The first requiring all market makers to pay a hefty fee to the Securities and Exchange Commission (SEC) to be able to trade. The second, forcing all trades to be registered with the Bursars Office of the Treasury Department. The third, making the executives of all companies registered on an exchange file personal guarantees pledging all of their assets – homes, cars, investments, everything, -- attesting to the validity of the financial information provided to the marketplace. And the last, imposing a tax, which ordinarily could only come from Congress, on all trades executed. It had killed the markets, and only the largest of trades were, any longer, being executed. There had been a mini-crash in the marketplace after those orders were released, so Randy had to find other work. He eventually found work with Sumner, but in the process of it all, he had learned valuable lessons about the effects of government interference in everyday life.

Their first meeting was unplanned and unscheduled. It was at a coffee shop on Capitol Hill, called Neb's Java. There the two had struck up a conversation about what was happening in Congress and in the world in general as they sipped their decaf espressos and read the morning news. The next thing Randy knew, he was in Sumner's office – low man on the totem pole, helping with the mail and sorting the Congressman's correspondence. He quickly rose through the ranks and became Sumner's trusted right-hand man – his chief of staff.

"What do we do?" asked Randy.

With Sumner's reticence, Randy looked worried. He glanced pensively at the Congressman, waiting for a response. But there was no glimmer of hope in Sumner's face or gesture of uplifting words. It was something Randy hadn't seen before in his boss. Usually the tireless and persistent embodiment of motivation and optimism, Sumner now looked tired, gaunt and just plain worn out. He'd been fighting the establishment for years, and it looked like he was losing.

Sumner saw the angst in Randy's face and realized he'd seen that same look in countless other faces across the country. It was the look of discouragement and despair, a look he couldn't stand to see in Americans. A once-great nation, much like the British empire, had ground its citizenry down to this. Known for their fierce independence and fighting spirit, these Americans and their ancestors were the ones who had fought back ruthless dictators in foreign lands, fought economic hardship on a grand scale, fought disease and contagion that had once dominated the planet Earth, and had resisted the darkness of radical Islam and communism. Now, they coward in fear or jumped for a handout.

The people needed a leader – someone they could turn to for inspiration. They needed a general who could command an army of patrons. They needed the old, full-of-grit-and-fire, Sumner.

"We have to fight it," said Sumner, trying to regain his voice.

"How?" asked Randy.

"I don't know yet, but we have to fight it."

"What if you go directly to the press?" asked Randy.

"What press? You're not talking about the *independent* press are you? It doesn't exist," quipped Sumner. "The main stream media hasn't been independent in years. Anyway, if I call a press conference, none of them would show up."

Randy was quiet for a moment. "What about the new service everyone's using on the SI-net? I think it's called *rasping*? I'm not sure how it works, but it by-passes the censors somehow. They have a tool you can use where you type in what you want to say, and it spits out a phrase with double meaning – you know, like a code. Then, what shows up on the site gets past the censors, but it has a deeper, more hard-edged meaning. Everyone who's used the site knows how to read the postings. They get it -- what the person really means, that is."

"Write something up," said Sumner. "I want it on the site - the rasping site -- within an hour."

"Got it sir," answered Randy, with a smile. He could feel a sudden surge of energy in the room. Was it possible that his old boss was back? Only time would tell.

*****

CH 11 MIA

"Any word?" It was Patrick talking to his private security team. There were only four on the team, but they were indispensable, especially given the new value of their invention. He spoke cautiously and deliberately, making sure they understood every word. "I need to know what happened to Sergei! We need to find him, you know! Now!"

"We don't know Patrick," came the hesitant answer from his security chief.

All on the team were embarrassed by what had happened. It made them look bad, and unless they found Sergei quickly, they worried they may never find him.

"I'm becoming disappointed in you," said Patrick, his angst rising. It was unusual for Patrick to be harsh. He was usually more even-keeled, but the pressures were starting to get to him – piercing his tough outer shell of armor. He pounded his fist on the table and then sat back and collected himself. Taking a deep breath, he stood up and put on his suit jacket, pulling the sleeves of the coat over his shirt cuffs. "Sorry, guys," he said. "I know you're doing everything you can. But, you really *have* to find him," he said again, more calmly.

Sergei had been extremely loyal during his tenure with the company. Patrick had relied heavily on him extensively, especially when there were seemingly insurmountable, technical problems. Now, he was relying on him to finish what they had started together – to ready the SECE engine for production.

But days passed without any word. His security team had no leads. All they knew was that Sergei had gotten a message to meet someone in the lobby. The person appeared to have been Gunter Muntz, a nemesis of Sergei's going back years. They had known he was coming to the demonstration, but thought he was only representing one of the financing groups, which was looking to invest in the company. Surveillance cameras around the facility showed Sergei speaking with a man with his back turned toward the camera. He was seen nodding and then going outside to get into a black Cadillac sedan that was parked out front. He went voluntarily, without any indication of coercion or force. Close-ups of his face did not reveal any signs of duress either. It was very puzzling for Patrick and his security team. Meaghan had told Patrick about the description of the man, and Patrick was certain it was, indeed, Muntz.

"This is Detective Morris," said the voice at the other end of the telephone line. The call had been forwarded to Patrick, after the receptionist had told him it sounded important.

"How can I assist you, detective?" answered Patrick, accustomed to the continual calls from the police seeking easy clues and information from the security team the company had already deployed to look into the matter.

Patrick took a deep breath. He was tired of the fishing, but felt he had little choice but to provide all he had. *It doesn't matter,* he thought, *as long as someone, somehow, figures it all out and they find him.*

"Dr. Disone, we continue to look into the whereabouts of your missing employee. Have you or your team come across anything?" asked the detective.

"Nothing today, detective. We got a call from your lieutenant earlier today on it, and we told him the same thing. The last time we saw him was at the presentation. You have the video footage, the same as what we have. Has your lab been able to identify the man with his back turned to the camera? Have you been able to enhance the audio or find another angle from cameras in other buildings nearby?"

"We do have video from a satellite overhead, but it's classified and we can't use it," said the detective.

"You can't use it? Why?" asked Patrick, incredulously.

"The feds. It's their policy not to permit any state or local group to have access to it."

"But it could help find Sergei?"

"Sir, that's not my responsibility. I really don't care about the why's, sir. I just do my job. That's all I'm supposed to do."

"Then find Sergei!" said Patrick, nearly shouting into the phone.

"Yes, sir. Of course," said the detective, dismissively. "But there's one other thing we need to know. This fellow Muntz. What can you tell me about him?"

The feud between Muntz and Sergei was not a secret, but little was known outside certain circles within the profession.

"It's a long story, detective. Is it really relevant?"

"Yes," the detective said coldly.

Patrick took a breath and began filling in the sordid details of the events that had transpired between the two men during the previous twenty years.

"... so their relationship – after rooming together in college – went south, quickly. They had always competed against each other in school – you know, who got the better grades, the prettiest girls, and all. But after they graduated, they maintained their quote friendship, filling each other in on their latest and greatest achievements and exaggerating every step of the way. Yet, although both knew what they were doing to each other, deep down, they probably resented the other's accomplishments."

"Did their jealously continue until recent times, then?" asked the detective.

Patrick stopped, but then thought he should tell everything he knew.

"Yes. I think so. Sergei told me that the cover story in *Technology & Mechanics Today.com* was something that sent Muntz into a frenzy. It was all over the media, oh, about four years ago after we had perfected the HECE engine. The news group wanted to do a story on the technology behind it. Obviously, it was Sergei who had developed most of it, and he was the one they interviewed for the article. His photo was on the front of the website, and it was picked-up by many other technical publications throughout the world. He got his fifteen minutes of fame and ..."

"And what?"

"... and, it apparently pissed off Muntz. Sergei got a nasty-gram from him the day it came out, telling him that he was a fraud and that he had stolen all of his ideas from Muntz himself. Sergei was shaken by the note and didn't know how to respond. I told him not to."

"Did he?" asked the detective.

"No, and that was the last time he heard from Muntz ... that is, until the press conference on the SECE engine. It appears that Muntz made an appearance."

"I see. Well, this had been most helpful, Dr. Disone. I do wish you would have disclosed this information to us earlier, but it is good to have it now."

"I didn't know if it would be important, so I waited for you to ask," he said, rather defensively.

"Oh, it's important all right. Dr. Disone, thank you. We'll be in touch."

"But, detective!" said Patrick, stopping him before he could hang up. "You need to get those satellite photos from the feds. There must be someone at some department some place who can get that video for you."

"As I said before, that's not my job. I can only use the tools and information I'm able – the department's able to get. Local law enforcement has largely been defunded you know. You're lucky that anybody here is working on the case. It's only because you paid us extra that we've spent so much time on it."

Indeed, Patrick had paid the detective some on the side. It smelled like a bribe, but he didn't see it that way. He saw it as a way to find Sergei, and in some ways it was just like they did business in other parts of the world – greasing the palms of government to get things done.

"I have my own security and investigative team too, detective. I paid you because I thought you could help me, and you implied that the only way to get your assistance was to *facilitate* it. Am I right?"

"I never said any such thing," answered the detective, "and I don't know what you're talking about." He knew full well what Patrick was saying but amnesia was always the best policy when involved in corruption. "Your attitude is not helpful. If you don't have any new information, then we're done here. Call me if you come up with anything."

The line went dead.

"Sh*t!" exclaimed Patrick, slamming his finger down on the disconnect button. "What the hell good are the police anymore. They take your money and then ditch you! Who are the criminals anyway? I can't tell anymore."

What Patrick didn't know was that all city police departments were *required* to communicate all of their cases to the federal government Department of Homeland Security regardless of the severity. It was never just a local or state issue anymore, but always involved the feds. The department consolidated all police matters nationwide into a vast, central database so that the U.S. government could piece together potential terrorist threats – or at least that was the excuse given. The government had decided that even a jaywalker could be someone on its *Top 10 Most Wanted List*.

So, in the end, it had been a power grab by the Administration, and it had worked. All criminal data was funneled to the NSA, the National Security Administration. The department had built a complex of buildings in Utah that dwarfed all other government facilities. They had started the project over fifty years earlier, and it had only continued to grow. Although still top secret, it was reported to be so large and house so many computer storage devices, that all the data since the beginning of human history could be housed there – one hundred-odd yottabytes or one hundred trillion terabytes.

Detective Morris typed into his antiquated laptop computer the information he'd gotten from Disone and his investigation team. It was business as usual, and when he finished the report he pressed the Enter button. A few seconds later, the information was transmitted and logged into the servers in the NSA. But it didn't end there. The name Disone immediately flagged the case in the system, and it was copied and forwarded automatically to the highest level of review in Utah. The first supervisor just glanced at it and started to push the Delete button – something he routinely did; however, he stopped. He had seen that name before, but he couldn't recall where. He motioned for a second supervisor to come over and take a look.

"Wait a minute," said the second supervisor. "I've seen that name before too." He grabbed his thick, black data binder and opened it to the last page where he kept the most recent notices from Washington. There had been problems with the electronic transmission of notices, as the system was old and in need of repairs. They had been sending and filing paper documents for months, waiting for the fixes to be applied. They were still waiting.

There on the last page was a picture of Patrick and Shea with a full narrative of their patent application and revocation. At the top were the bold words: **POTENTIAL FOR VIOLENCE**. He showed the page to his colleague, who stopped and took his finger off the *Delete* key.

"Looks like we need to escalate this one, huh?" said the first sup. Instead of deleting, he typed several more key strokes into the computer and then hit the Send button. The computer made a *swishing* sound as if the message were being carried off on a gust of air currents. "There. That ought'a take care of it," he said. "Now, can get back to reading my *Sports Illustrated?*" He propped-up his feet on the desk and grabbed his thin-set computer tablet, scrolling back to the page he'd been reading.

Of all people, it was Angel Ratner, herself, who received the message. It was handed to her by her new assistant deputy secretary, Margola Vasilik, who had inherited the horrific hours of her predecessor, George Thomas. Ratner was working late, and no one else was around except the two of them. Although she wasn't supposed to get copied on such messages bound for the NSA, she had demanded that her technology staff hack into various systems of other departments to gain inside intelligence – mainly, any dirt that she could use against others either inside or outside the government. She kept a book of who had done what. It was something she knew would come in handy one day.

"So, what do we have here," she said with a smile, reading the name Disone at the top of the message. "It looks like the Disones are trying to track down their lost companion. We don't get many NSA messages diverted our way. We were lucky with this one."

Margola stood behind her looking at the communiqué. "Potential for violence?" she asked, reading the bulletin. "Why do they think that? We only sent them a notice of rejection of their patent request. How is that a potential for violence?"

Ratner laughed. There was a touch of evil that edged the sound that came from her mouth. "It's not, you idiot!" she said sarcastically. "But when people like the Disones try to make you look stupid and jeopardize your career, you have to send a message – 'Don't f**k with me!'"

"I see," said Margola, cringing, never used to the drunken-sailor swearing of her boss, "but it was *our* mistake that the patent was approved in the first place."

Ratner looked at her assistant with a scowl. "I don't make mistakes!" she fumed. "You and Thomas were the ones who f**ked this up. And secondly, if the Disones hadn't continued to push and push and *push* for their stupid patent, none of this would have happened in the first place. They are the type of people who always get what they want. They push until they get it. I'm sure they're filthy rich, spoiled, self-indulged elitists who need to be taught a lesson. And that's exactly what I'm doing."

Leaving nothing to chance, she made sure her message got to the highest desk possible.

"Yes, this is Attorney General Prescott, what is it?"

"Attorney General, this is Angel Ratner at Technology Assessment. We have two potential terrorists in the country I thought you should know about. We believe they're part of a sleeper cell that's been operating out of a research lab in Boston."

The conversation was short, but consequential. The U.S. Attorney General knew what to do, and it wouldn't take long for his orders to trickle down to the staff within his department. The only thing certain was that the issue of the missing scientist from Lenoir Labs would take a backburner to the bigger threat. That threat – terrorists -- would have to be neutralized.

*****

CH 12 REGULATION

With his good looks, tall stature, charm and sexual magnetism, Fourier was a natural politician. His opponent in the presidential race had been a well-intentioned, government career man, who had come up through the ranks from state senator, to U.S. Congressman and then U.S. Senator. He had been the ambassador to China and had a long list of accomplishments, both foreign and domestic. However, he lacked the warmth and allure of his rival, and the landslide defeat reflected his inability to connect with the voters.

President Fourier had really never known adult life without politics. Just out of Tulane law school, he had applied to several high-profile law firms in New York, Chicago and Boston, but had been rejected. His father had been a U.S. Congressman and had funded his first state senate campaign while he was lawyering for a political action committee that supported the then U.S. Senator Mathews from his home state of Illinois. He won with the help of his father's connections and served two terms in Springfield before running for the Congressional seat his father was vacating for retirement. From there, it was only a short hop to the U.S. Senate. However, after one term, his father advised him that it was a far easier path to the White House if he were governor of Illinois. Few from the Senate made it into the Oval Office, as compared with the Governor's mansion.

Following his father's advice, Fourier elected not to run for a second term and chose the governor's chair, which he won handily. However, his sights were already set on the brass ring – the bigger prize of the presidency.

Thus, without an understanding of business, the U.S. economy or international affairs, Fourier was promoted to the highest rank in the country. It was there where he could exert his brute force to change the landscape of America toward his biases and illusions. He won the election against the Constitution Party candidate, Natalie Williams, by a wide margin, as the media ensured that the negative reporting of Ms. Williams's deeds from the time of birth were registered, recorded and widely circulated – whether true or not.

Therefore, it was easy for Fourier to read the election results as a mandate for him to do whatever he felt was needed to put the country back on its feet. And it didn't take him long. Within his honeymoon period of the first one hundred days, Fourier pushed several major bills through Congress. They were all consistent with the progressive agenda he had outlined during his campaign. The legislation was innocuous enough, but portended a direction of greater control and oppressiveness than the denizens had experienced since the days of King George III just prior to the Civil War. The first legislation from Fourier's Congress had largely been health-directed, coercing Americans by fiat to change their living habits to follow a more salubrious lifestyle. Years spending billions on advertising, forcing manufacturers to give more and more labeling information, and offering federal subsidies for low-calorie, low-salt, low-fat products, all proved to be futile government efforts to change behavior. But that would not stop those who knew better.

More and more bills came fast and furious, covering restrictions on all foodstuffs with sodium or salt content above certain levels. Fats could not exceed other percentages depending on the nature of the food, and nearly all foods had to be packed with vitamins from A to E.

However, despite the food police actions, the Alcohol Reform Act annoyed people the most. This was the final bill passed by the 130th Congress during its 2047 session. While the Election Bill had gotten people upset, the Alcohol Reform Act had created a firestorm, and it was all Congress could do to dampen the flames. The Alcohol Reform Act put a cap on the proof level of all alcohol sold in America. As proof levels reflected twice the alcohol content of a beverage – so a liquid of 20 percent alcohol would be labeled **40-proof** – the president pushed to have Congress enact a bill banning all liquids with a proof more than forty. As most vodka, tequila, whiskey and rum had strength of twice that -- eighty proof or more -- all of these liquors exceeded the mandate.

The outcry to the ban was quick and vociferous. But those in Congress, including the House Speaker, Preston Brooks, urged calm. "This is only a temporary measure," he said, trying to placate the masses. "We're only doing this to lower the level of anxiety within society. There are too many people right now dependent upon liquor as a solution to their problems. We must do something to reduce the number of alcoholics in society. It creates broken families, high healthcare costs, and fractured communities. It is government's responsibility to the rest of the country to protect it from this evil. Once we reduce the levels of dependency, we will reverse the law and let companies make such substances for popular consumption – if people still want to buy it."

But the legislation ended there, as Congress got significant pushback from its constituents. The phones lit up when the Alcohol Reform Act passed. Congress's back-peddling did not settle well at the White House, and the president became extremely upset and indignant. "How dare they shrink from this fight!" he was heard yelling. "I'll have every head of those who vote to repeal the law!"

Congress held firm and did not retract the law; however, there was violence in the streets. Small riots broke out in many places, and signs appeared bearing the words *No Repeat of the 18th* and *1920 is Ancient History,* referring to the date of passage of the Eighteenth Amendment establishing prohibition.

A flurry of executive orders followed, as Congress began to drag its feet on other health initiatives. President Fourier proclaimed all MSG in foods and all pesticides for crops be banned from use in agriculture. Only organically-grown produce was permitted. Additionally, all genetically engineered plants were to be destroyed in the field, even though they had been very successful worldwide in reducing starvation and production costs and improving yields.

"Why can't we get more meaningful legislation passed?" Fourier said, pressing his Chief of Staff, Trevor Allen. "What's holding us up?"

Fourier was a giant of a man. At six foot-seven, he towered over the rest of his staff. By his high school freshman year, he had only stood five feet nine. Both of his parents had been of average height. So, when his stature exploded during the next four years, they were equally surprised. It was his stockiness that had remained unchanged. As one critic once wrote of him during his gubernatorial race, "he is as thick as a sequoia and as tall as one too." Fourier's face was long and square-jawed. The lines around his eyes had always been more pronounced than normal, aging him more than was necessary. His eyes were inky blue, and his stare intense. Yet, his presence was softened by a pre-mature graying of his sideburns that was creeping into his short-cropped hair above his ears. His mellow, tenor voice was comforting, and with a slow, deliberate delivery, his speeches had a reassuring air about them.

By the time he was a junior in high school, he had taken all of the requisite courses to graduate and had breezed through all of them, except for Anthropology, which he found boring and uninspiring. However, he easily received scholarships to the major universities and eventually chose to matriculate to Brandeis University, going on to study law at UC Berkeley. He was smart, charismatic and good-looking – all the elements necessary to manipulate voter opinion and quietly take control of a once-mighty nation.

Still relatively young for a leader of an industrialized nation, at forty-five he had the maturity and poise of someone with twenty more years. But this grace was equally matched by his brilliant, analytical mind. Capable of deciphering the most complex problems quickly, he stunned most with his grasp of facts and figures, reciting them with effortless aplomb. Even without his cloaked use of contact-lens, SI-net streaming technology (he had refused implants), Fourier had a natural gift for numbers and could -- and did -- manipulate them at will.

"We've accomplished a lot in a very short time, Mr. President," answered Allen. "I think you've done remarkably well, and so does the press."

"It's not good enough!" shouted Fourier. "I want the rest of my one hundred day program enacted within the next two weeks. If it isn't, then I'll just have to do it myself."

"Yourself?"

"Yes. I'll do what I have to do to get this country to where I think it should be," said Fourier.

"But Congress does take a little longer to move on some issues. They've been very sympathetic to your requests. If we just stay the course with them and ..."

"No! They're not engaged in this. And if they don't engage, I'll do it without them."

"But, sir, we control both houses of Congress now. We've got an overwhelming majority in the House and in the Senate; we have just shy of the sixty percent we need for a supermajority. We can pretty much do what we need to do."

"Things happen, Allen," snapped the president. "My honeymoon is over. People are starting to catch on as to what we're doing. They're too *stupid* to see that this is all good for them. They'd rather live their pathetic lives in misery and poor health. No, it's better that we push everything through now on our own. I don't care how many eggs you have to break."

"Yes, sir," Allen responded, leaving the Oval Office.

Two weeks passed, and the remaining measures of the president were still stuck in committee on the Hill. As a result, the president's press secretary went before the media in the press room at the White House and announced a new series of executive orders. Some were small and seemingly inconsequential; others were more significant and raised eyebrows.

These edicts, as his critics called them, included an assault on energy consumption. Electricity usage was to be rationed, as was natural gas and gasoline. There were no shortages of any of these products, but they were deemed anti-ecological, and further damage to the planet was considered un-American and unpatriotic as a world citizen. Water was heavily taxed, and all non-essential usage was prohibited. Of course, this rule did not apply to Congressional golf courses and well-connected contributors who needed their gigantic lawns kept groomed and green.

It was at a press conference that Fourier's Press Secretary, Kenneth Beister, got a drubbing.

"Ken, why does the president feel it necessary to issue executive orders for all of these lifestyle mandates?" asked one reporter. "Why doesn't he go through Congress? His party controls both houses."

Beister, a young addition to the president's staff, was only thirty-two. A graduate of Princeton, or the College of New Jersey as he liked to say, Beister was down-to-earth, yet able to spin stories and fables with the best of them. Smart, but not as creative as he needed to be in his position, Ken struggled with his on-going defense of the president's actions, particularly when they were questionably outside the parameters of the Constitution.

"The president believes that Congress is not doing its job," said Beister. "As a legislative body, it has the responsibility to pass legislation that the people of this country believe in. They elected this president to do a job, and the Congress has stopped fulfilling its role in executing the will of the president. We have a lot to do in this Administration, and if the Congress won't make sure things get done, then the president will."

"But isn't the Constitution clear that it is Congress that passes the laws and the president who administers them? Isn't the president overstepping his power to legislate from the White House?" asked another reporter.

Another reporter also chimed in. "Yes, and I'm confused about Congress's role. You say it's to execute the will of the president? I thought it was the will of the people?"

Beister was taken aback by the temerity of the group that morning. Normally, they were compliant and easily manipulated to retell the talking points outlined for them by the Administration. Such apostasy was rare, and this development was alarming.

Beister looked down at his reporter roster. "I see that you are – your name is Claire Magneson – and you're from the *Detroit Herald*," he said threateningly. "It's understandable that your editors didn't get the summary papers on what the president is trying to do. I'll make sure that he or she gets them, since it's apparent that you're ill-informed on the matter."

The reporter shrank back into her chair, intimidated by the suggestion.

"Now, are there any other questions?"

Essentially, that killed-off any further questioning, and Beister stopped the press conference abruptly. "Thank you. Time's up," he said and left the room.

However, it seemed that the White House had dodged a bullet. The headlines of most news outlets read:

President expresses concern for Americans' health – takes action to help.

Yet, blogs running under the radar screen took it ten levels deeper – closer to the heart of the real issue.

White House dictates what we eat, drink and drive. How soon until they tells us what to think?

Oh, yeah. They already do.

*****

CH 13 TORTUROUS INTENT

Sergei wasn't sure where he was when he woke up. His eyes were burning, and his vision was blurred. The last thing he remembered was sitting in the backseat of a black Mercedes sedan. He was talking to Gunter Muntz about the combustible engine, when he felt a sharp pain in his thigh and then nothing.

He waited a few moments for his eyesight to clear and his hearing to return, but they weren't coming back quickly. He felt as if he were underwater, trying to navigate in slow motion across the bottom of a pool to get to the other side without a mask or snorkel. Fatigued from trying, he just closed his eyes.

When he came-to the second time, he was more lucid and aware of his surroundings. He raised his head to see that he was strapped into a narrow, hospital gurney in a dimly lit room. There were dull, stainless steel vats on one side up against a non-descript, beige wall, pallets of aluminum cans just below his feet, and what appeared to be some sort of processing machine on the other wall - probably used to can food of some type. A few yards away, a lone florescent light hung from a pair of chains from the ceiling, illuminating a stack of flattened shipping boxes. The light wasn't enough to give much detail but was sufficient to help him make-out the dark shadow of someone with a rifle, possibly an old AK-47 machine gun first used during the twentieth century. It was guarding a door painted the same color as the wall.

But at the same time, he felt the intense throbbing of his head, like someone had pushed a hot poker through his skull and forgotten to take it out. He tried to pull his arms up, but the leather restraints cut into his wrists causing pain as he squirmed. Likewise, his feet were bound to the steel bars at the bottom of the make-shift bed. Giving up on the idea of tearing himself away from his restraints, Sergei threw his head back into the gurney in disgust. But it wasn't long until he did get more company. The footsteps of someone coming down the hall just outside the guarded door were barely audible. As they got louder, he raised his head again in the direction of the sound, waiting with trepidation for their owner to appear. But just as the door was about to open, the entire area inside the room was flooded with bright lights coming from unseen banks of bulbs deeper in the ceiling. Instinctively, he recoiled in pain, turning his head away and squinting to keep out the searing whiteness.

He heard the door open but couldn't see who or what came in.

"Dr. Navarov. It's so good of you to come back to the living. We were beginning to wonder whether we'd given you too much sedative. You need to cut back on your personal prescriptions you know," said a soft, melodic voice standing behind him. It was female and young; yet, there was an air of authority and intelligence in it.

Sergei's mouth was dry and parched to the point he could barely speak. However, he was able to mumble a few words. "Where am I?" he asked, mumbling.

"Oh, Dr. Navarov. You're in a very safe place – in fact, it's one of the most protected places on Earth. We're in New Mexico. We're at a top-secret laboratory. It's where all of the good stuff is done for the Department of Defense or the NSA. In fact, you're sixteen levels below the surface in a bunker we call *The Cavern*. There isn't much to do down here in the Cavern. We don't have Saturday matinees or pool parties. No, we're much more serious about life than that. You see, Dr. Navarov, we have a replica of the engine that you've designed. We were able to manufacture most of it from your patent filing. It's taken many years, of course." Then she laughed and added, "I thought it was strange that you never wondered why we kept asking for more and more information about your filing. Didn't you ever question that? Heck, it took, what, seven-eight years or so?"

Sergei turned his head slightly, moaning; the pain was palpable. To the side of the gurney, coming into view was something that resembled the SECE engine. But, to his trained eye and intimate knowledge of the engine, there were differences that he saw immediately – differences that suggested they had merely adapted the previous version, the HECE, to work like the more advanced SECE engine. Beyond that, he could only imagine the variations in the software they were using.

"Yes, Dr. Navarov, we have re-created your SECE engine. It's your baby – or at least 99% of it. But you know what?" asked the woman, rhetorically, "That last one percent is a real bitch."

Sergei smiled. He knew that the last percent was always the hardest and took the longest time to perfect. But that was why they had perfected it, and no one else had.

"We've gone over all the blueprints available from your filing and made our own modifications to obvious red herrings that would undermine most anyone else trying to copy it. We've also analyzed all of the codes in the software we believe you've used. It's really ingenious what you've come up

117

with. It's really quite something." She leaned in closer, just above him so he could finally see her. "But, there's only one problem, Dr. Navarov."

He was in no mood to be questioned. His head ached and now his wrists were beginning to sting from trying to pry them loose from their restraints. So, he closed his eyes, hoping to re-open them to a whole new surrounding – preferably back in his lab at Lenoir or, better, back in his queen-sized bed at home.

"Dr. Navarov? Dr. Navarov?" said the woman, slapping him on the face.

Sergei opened his eyes, and unfortunately, the scenery hadn't changed. "Why are you doing this?" he asked.

The young woman grinned. "Why? Do I look stupid to you?"

Sergei noticed the upside-down badge worn by the woman. The name read: **Janice Polikowski**. However, her face was Asian. "How did you get in here?" he asked her.

"What do you mean?" asked the woman, startled.

"Somehow you got your badge, but it isn't yours. You must have surreptitious means to pull that off, I guess."

The woman was irritated. "It's not your concern," she answered, smugly. "What is your concern is the information we need."

"How much do you want?" he asked.

She smiled again, pushing the long strings of black hair back behind her ear. "You don't have enough for me," she said.

"Seriously. How much?"

"It's not up to me, you see. It's ultimately up to my employer. He's the one who ordered us to get the secrets behind your engine. It is worth billions to him, and he will pay us handsomely for getting them out of you."

"Us?"

At that point, another face appeared in front of Sergei. This was a face he recognized immediately. "Yes, old chap, us." It was Gunter Muntz.

"How did I know," said Sergei, shaking his head. Things were clearing in his head, and he was better able to sort out his thoughts. "So, who is the girl?" he asked, nodding toward the woman who'd been peppering him with questions.

"Oh, she's just our lawyer. You always said they could be sharks, right? Well, you can find out first-hand for yourself. She's good at what she does, and, of course, she's here to make sure that we don't get ourselves into *legal* trouble. It's one of those equal opportunity things, I think," he said, laughing loudly.

"Really?" Sergei said, skeptically.

"No, not really. But it sounded good," said the woman. "I am an attorney, but I really don't give a rat's ass about you or what is done to you. All I care about is getting the information."

"Who's your employer?" Sergei asked again.

"We can't say, and it's not important," said Muntz. "Right now, what *is* important is that we get that information. If you won't cooperate, we'll have to … well … make it uncomfortable for you. Will you cooperate?" asked Gunter.

"No."

"We know you're loyal to your boss. But, everyone has their breaking point, and we know what yours is."

Sergei stared at them, saying nothing.

The young woman leaned forward. She was slim and wore a tight, black-leather jumpsuit that hugged her like hot breath on a cold window. Her fingernails were painted bright red to match her lipstick, creating a vivid contrast with her pale, white skin. "I understand that you can't swim. In fact, that you're afraid of the water. Is that true?"

Again, Sergei just stared at her.

"I think the only thing we have time for is a little underwater exploration."

"I don't know what you mean," Sergei answered, nervously.

"Yes you do. You know exactly what I mean," said the woman. Then, she nodded to Gunter who was standing next to the head of the gurney. Gunter pulled out a black strap and viciously smacked it down across Sergei's forehead, tightening it until it dug into his skin. "You know what to do," the woman said to Gunter before walking away. All Sergei could hear was the pitter-patter of her shoes going out the door and back down the corridor outside.

Sergei saw a dark-brown, plastic bucket dangling a less than a meter over his head before a white towel brutally came down over his face. The towel tore

119

at the sides of his mouth, ripping the flesh away from its corners. He struggled, but in vain. He could hardly breathe as the cloth clawed into his mouth and gums. Throwing his head from side to side to catch a breath, Sergei fought it.

Muntz tipped the bucket, and water started pouring onto the towel, drenching it and Sergei's face. Instantly, the water bore through the porous towel and rushed down his throat and up into his nose. Panicking, he gasped for air but only sucked in more water. He could feel the deluge rushing into his lungs and forcing him to gag. Sergei struggled to find some molecule of oxygen to take in – anything that would keep him from drowning. He coughed, strangling as more water inundated his throat and his chest. His brain, normally calm and calculating, was in full arrest. Convulsing, his body jerked, and he felt parts of his consciousness dying. *I'm going to die!* he thought to himself. It was his worst nightmare.

Abruptly, the water stopped flowing, but he kept coughing, his body doing everything it could to purge it from his lungs. His brain couldn't push past the trauma – past surviving. His body fought back, searching for air, searching for something to fill his lungs so they would stop convulsing.

"So, do you have anything you want to tell us?" Muntz asked. There was no sympathy in his voice.

"Why are you doing this? Who do you work for?" asked Sergei, between gasps and coughs.

"What are the details to the software codes?"

 "And what if I tell you? You'll kill me anyway," Sergei answered.

"Maybe. If we do, it will be a lot less painful than if you don't tell us. How's that?" answered Muntz.

"You're evil," said Sergei in a low voice.

"I'm not trying to be. We just want some answers, Sergei. That's all. Just give us some answers on the software code."

Sergei knew that they had made small mistakes in the engine design itself too. So, even with the right software code, they still wouldn't have the SECE engine."

"If I tell you, will you release me?" Sergei asked.

"Sure," said Muntz. "Here's a pencil. Now, write down the software codes for the intake ports, fuel-air measurements, compression timing, spark ignition, and settings for the converter solenoid. Those are the things we really need."

Sergei started to reach for the pencil, but stopped. "I don't believe you. Why should I trust that you'll keep your promise?"

Muntz smiled. "I don't think you have much of a choice, now do you."

"Go to hell!" Sergei replied, throwing the pencil across the room. It hit the linoleum floor and bounced several times before coming to a stop by the canning machine.

"So, you're not going to tell us?" Muntz asked, with an edge to his voice.

Sergei turned his eyes, looking away from his adversary.

"You were always jealous, Muntz. You always wanted what I had, and now, you want it again," said Sergei, still not looking at the one torturing him.

Muntz didn't say anything, but instead forced the towel back across Sergei's face. The water again cascaded over his head. He gurgled and shook as he struggled to breathe. *This time, I'm going to die,* he thought. *There is no other way out, but to die.*

Sergei coughed and gasped. His eyes rolled to the back of his head and then forward again. It was horrific, an experience he'd never faced before and never wanted to again. Every thought and effort from his body struggled to breathe. Something he took for granted all his life now became more precious than gold. With it, he lived. Without it, he died.

"Come on, Sergei. Don't make this any harder than it has to be. Just tell us what we want to know. Then, we'll let you go."

"Bull sh*t," he answered, spitting water into Muntz's face. "You'll kill me after you get what you want. There's nothing in it for me. I know I'm a dead man." Now, he stared at Muntz with pure hatred in his eyes.

"But, dear chap, why would I sacrifice you? It's true that we don't like each other, but is that a reason to kill you? I think not. But, I do need for you to talk to us," Muntz commented casually, as if he were chatting with his old friend at a coffee shop.

Sergei looked at him. His face was unmoved. Then, when Muntz started again with the towel, Sergei recoiled.

"So you *will* tell us?" he asked, pulling the towel away.

Sergei shook his head again. "If *you* don't kill me, your employer will, won't he?"

"Unless I *do* decide to kill you first!" said Muntz, growing more agitated. "Maybe I should save him the trouble."

"You're not authorized to kill me, are you?" said Sergei, reading into what Muntz was both saying and not saying at the same time. "I can tell now that you can't. You're not high up enough in your organization to make that call, are you?" Now he was taunting him, hoping Muntz would make a mistake that might let him get free. "You never did amount to anything, did you?"

"Don't try me, Sergei!" said Muntz, getting angry.

"Who do you work for, Muntz?" Sergei asked, pressing. "A foreign government? A foreign company? Someone here in the states, maybe?"

"It doesn't matter," said Muntz.

"Is it someone in our own government?"

"If I told you, I would have to kill you anyway," was the answer.

"Just as I thought, Muntz. You're a nobody. You're nothing – like a gnat on an elephant's ass. That's what you are. You always thought you were better than me. But you knew differently. I beat you in college. I beat you at the National Physics contest in high school. I beat you in developing this combustion engine. I've always beaten you, and I always will!"

Muntz's temper was flaring. "Shut up! Shut up, Sergei!" he said trembling, as he held the bucket.

"You're a loser. You always have been. You've always been second best. That's right! Second best! Muntz, I will always be better than you, regardless of what you do to me! That's a fact and that's something you'll never be able to overcome – whether I'm alive or dead!"

Without letting Sergei say anything more, Muntz slapped the white towel down again, but this time the water came in torrents. He poured freely, angered by the implication that he was nothing – a nobody. *I am somebody!* he thought. *And of all people, Sergei is going to be the last person I take it from!*

Again Sergei began gagging, but Muntz kept pouring. The water kept coming and coming. Sergei flailed and shook violently trying to cope with the inundation. He continued to gurgle and froth, but then the coughing stopped.

Sergei's body went limp. He had stopped fighting, and, worse yet, he had stopped breathing. Muntz tipped the bucket upright and set it down, watching for Sergei to revive. But there was no sign. "Sergei, wake up!" he shouted, ripping the towel from his victim's mouth. But Sergei's eyes were fixed and dilated – his face, still and frozen.

"Grab the AED!" he shouted to the guard, still standing by the doorway.

Frantically, they tried to revive him, pumping electricity through his body to restart his heart.

"Again!" shouted Muntz, knowing he'd made a big mistake. Still no pulse. "Again!" he yelled, putting the paddles back down on Sergei's chest. The electricity went in and Sergei's chest heaved, but there was still no heartbeat.

The Asian woman came running back into the room, her tiny feet chattering along the tile floor. "What have you done?" she shouted, pushing Muntz away from the gurney. "We were supposed to get answers from him, not kill him!"

Repeatedly, they tried to shock his heart back into a rhythm. After each pulse, they listened for a heartbeat. But after twenty minutes, they put down the paddles. Sergei was dead.

"What do we tell the boss?" asked Muntz, shaking and looking ashen. He stared down at the newly-minted corpse.

The Asian woman glared back at Muntz in disbelief. "I ... I'm not really sure. You've really f**ked up this time."

Muntz hesitated, and then said. "He died of a heart attack as we were questioning him. There was nothing we could do. It was over before it started."

"Our boss won't buy it," she answered, shaking her head.

"We have to try. Otherwise, we'll look as cold and blue as our friend here."

"Let me know how that works out," she said, closing the door behind her.

Muntz looked down at his life-long nemesis. He'd hated Sergei all his life; but now it was over, and he felt no satisfaction. He was empty. He realized that he hadn't hated Sergei for Sergei. He'd hated him for what he'd represented – his own failures. Now, he had to face his latest one with someone who would be less sympathetic to his screw-ups. His boss.

*****

123

CH 14 RASPING

The message went out through the Rasping network, explaining the potential impact of the proposed election law to those wonks who were dedicated followers of the site. There was little time before the bill would be brought before the House for a vote. HR 2048-551 would be passed within two days and sent to the Senate for its stamp. It was still common to have some small disagreements on legislative matters that required a Conference Committee to work through the differences, but in this particular piece of law, those disparities had long since been resolved. The president's signature was all but assured.

"Where are we?" asked Sumner, watching the blogs and news outlets for some indication that the story had been picked up.

Randy shook his head. "Unless we get a spark someplace, it doesn't look good. I was right that the Rasping network would get it through to our target audience, but it appears we just won't have enough time for it to take off."

"What about a video?" asked Sumner.

"What do you mean?"

"Some sort of video that will catch on. If we do a video – a parody, a song, a comical sketch or farcical vignette – something that has the chance to go viral. That's what we need!"

"We don't have time now," said Randy. "It would take a month or more to write it, film it, produce it, ..."

"Not if we filmed it here in my office. We'll use our PCDs right now. You go get three or four of the younger people in the office and bring them in here. I have an idea," said Sumner.

It only took about ten minutes before the door to Sumner's congressional office opened and in marched many of his new and younger staff members.

"Have a seat," said Sumner, motioning for them to find a place wherever they could.

"As you know we have a problem in getting out the word that this election bill could very well destroy our democratic system of government. This is serious stuff – it doesn't get any more grave than this. So, we put out the message on Rasping – you know the site many of you use – but it hasn't caught on quickly enough to spread to the general population. We're running out of time. The House bill will pass the day after tomorrow. If we do anything more, I think we have to do some sort of video and hope it goes viral. What do you think?" Sumner watched their faces closely to see if any had a positive reaction to his plan.

It was DeAnthony who chimed in. "I heard you were thinking of a comedy or something, but I think that would just dilute the message. This is serious, and a farce would negate that message."

"Yeah, I agree," said Samantha, another staffer. "I think if you do anything it would have to be a satire. You know, something so far off the edge that people have to sit-up and take notice."

"How far can we take it?" Randy asked, interjecting. "Where do you think the line would be?"

"It's got to have shock value, yet be funny," said DeAnthony.

"Any ideas?" asked Sumner.

"I may have one," said Trish, a demur first-year staffer. She was quiet and unassuming, but recognized as one of the brightest new faces on the Hill.

After listening to her, Sumner did not hesitate. "Let's go. Get whatever you need. You have …" he looked at the time, "… three hours. No more."

The skit was impromptu with extemporaneous lines and serious interplay between the three main characters. It centered on a Congressman at his desk, shocked at what he was reading in a stack of paper that represented the House bill. He tells the audience about the onerous parts of the legislation and the potential for a dictatorship. Suddenly, the doors to his office burst open and two men in plain clothes come in with guns drawn, yelling for Sumner to put his pen down before he does any more damage. Sumner begins to protest, but the men slam his face into his desk and tell him he is a traitor to his own people. They yell that he will be executed for his crimes against humanity for voting against the president. Then the skit goes black, and shots are heard.

It was provocative, and it caused the stir intended.

The video was seen by nearly five million viewers, and it was growing exponentially every hour. The phones in Congress began ringing, and SI-net was alive with banter and outrage. It was the first time in memory that the people were taking a stand against what was happening in Washington. As all communication with any federal agency or branch of government was catalogued, tracked and subject to investigation, each patriot brave enough to make contact was putting something at risk.

When the day of the vote came, every member of the House had gotten inundated with angry voters. They were indeed rattled.

The bill was brought up for the vote, despite urging by those under Speaker Brooks to postpone it. The chamber was noticeably absent many members, most probably fearful of casting any vote at all. But what was essential was that there was a quorum, or enough members present to make the vote count.

"After calling for a roll count, Mr. Speaker, there is a quorum. Therefore, we will proceed with the vote," said the Clerk of the House. "Before the House is HR 2048-551. According to rules now in place, there will be no debate or amendments permitted. Please cast your votes. The balloting begins now."

The floor was open for electronic voting for the next thirty minutes, and when it was over, the Clerk reviewed the results.

Sumner sat nervously at his desk, watching the tallies go up on the board. However, just before the vote was closed, the tally screen at the front of the chamber flickered and went black. Sumner leaned forward and glanced around when the screen faded. "What's going on?" he asked. "What's wrong with the screen?"

He got up quickly and walked to the front of the chamber, where the Clerk sat. "What's with the screen?" he asked, both concerned and angry.

"We don't know, Congressman. But it doesn't matter. We have the numbers right here," she said sweetly. Then, she turned to address the body.

"The results of the vote on HR 2048-551 are – the Yeas 179; the Nays 130; and Abstentions 16. There were 110 not voting. Mr. Speaker, the bill passes."

Sumner hung his head. He knew it would only be a matter of time before he was cited as a problem lawmaker and banned from the floor.

"It has begun," he said to himself, shaking his head.

*****

CH 15 "GET IT DONE!"

The message was sent encrypted. It was from an annex near Los Alamos and ready simply,

> **Working to get answers. But there may be an issue. Will keep informed.**

"I don't understand," said a voice in the room. "How could it take so long to beat it out of him?"

"I'm not sure," said another. "We've been planning this for months. We had the right people, the right place, the right time – it was all planned out. This should have only taken a few hours."

"Well, I'm not happy. You have to find out what's happening. Why haven't they gotten the information? We have to have that to make this thing work!"

"I ... I don't know. But, I'll find out," said the assistant.

"Who was it again? Who did you employ to get this done?"

"It was Chou and Muntz. Chou is an attorney – someone inside who can keep things above board and yet tough enough to make sure we get what we need. Muntz is ... well ... close to the subject. He knows him well. He can dig into areas that should pry things out of him. He's got a personal investment in this as well as a financial one."

"What's our exposure at this point? Who else knows about the mission?" the woman asked.

"Just a handful of people. They're all working for us – off the books, of course."

"Then why aren't they getting results!" said the woman, more agitated. "Am I supposed to wait forever? I've got an engine that doesn't work right and what at this point looks like two morons who can't get the information we need. Worse yet, they can leak what we've done to the authorities. That's not a good place to be." She paused. "Why didn't you use professionals like I told you?"

"We did, ma'am. We used professionals to extract him, but we thought it best to use someone he knew in that part of it – someone who could easily get to him."

"And why Cho?"

"Cho knew Muntz. She is also tied-in to EG, so we could have information on both sides for our dealings with Thorne."

The woman's anger grew. Her face became more and more contorted with the corners of her mouth tightening and her eyes narrowing to the point that only her nearly black pupils showed. "I want it handled! Do you hear me?" she said, growling like a wild beast. "I want the whole thing either finished like we planned or handled so there's no trail. If this fails, no one is to know this took place – no one!" she shouted.

"I'll take care of things."

"You'd better, Margie," said the woman, using the nickname she gave her new assistant. Or you won't have a pot to piss in either."

"Yes, Madam Secretary. Is there anything else?"

"No. Now get out of here."

Ratner thought about her next moves. The SECE engine was almost fully developed in her secret lab not far from Los Alamos. She'd siphoned off all the information from the patent filings submitted by Lenoir Labs over the years to develop her own version. Realizing the billions at stake, she had found it easy to justify stealing the secrets and being in a position of power to kill Lenoir's patent application had made it all the easier. She'd also been shrewd enough to offer the plans she had, albeit incomplete, to the highest bidder – Kilby Thorne of EG. That was her backup plan in the event she couldn't make the engine work on her own. A cool forty million would be enough, but billions would be better.

As of now, she didn't have the answers she needed to finish it, nor did she have any easy way of getting them if Sergei didn't cough them up. She wouldn't be able to hold off the EG CEO forever, and she wanted the rest of the money he promised her. She had never been a patient woman. Waiting was hard on her, but nothing compared to the toll it usually took on everyone else around her.

*****

CH 16 PEJORATIVE PROFITS

The numbers did not look good, and Carson Stevens was nervous. As chief financial officer of EG, it had been his responsibility to ensure the company made profits to sustain the business, keep its shareholders happy and attract new investment money. But, recent federal mandates had made that virtually impossible.

To that point, GovCo's had been spared the wrath of the Administration's punitive measures against business. Their cozy ties on Capitol Hill had greased the tracks for them to chug past the red tape that was crushing smaller businesses. Yet, even now, the need for more money to run the government was superseding that precedent. Therefore, Stevens's responsibilities as CFO had changed – no longer was he to maximize company profits. Now, he was to ensure the company made just enough money to operate, but no more. Excess profits would create problems for the company, its officers and its board of directors. And if profits became really excessive – as defined by the government – then all of the officers, from the chief executive down to the vice presidents, would be thrown in prison and their property confiscated. It was draconian, but President Fourier felt it was the only way to bring capitalism to its knees and usher in his view of a utopian society – one based on equality for ... most. For EG, profits had become excessive under the new definitions -- very excessive -- and Stevens, therefore, had a problem.

The term *profit* had been unpopular for decades, but only more recently had it been made a crime. Lawmakers campaigned against it, and many companies had to move out of the country when their profits exceeded acceptable limits. No company trying to do business in America wanted to be known for making money. In fact, several shareholder meetings had gotten out-of-hand when union protestors stormed the halls, demanding the companies payout all of their profits to the union. At the same time, communist party members demanded that Congress pass laws requiring companies give at least 90 percent of their profits away to inner city neighborhoods based on their need. Of course, their proposal required that these profits be funneled through local communist party committees because they knew best which neighborhoods were most in need; *they* would ensure that the truly needy people got them. The White House came out in strong support for these ideas, saying that it was time the workers and the poor had a greater say in what went on in business and where their profits were spent.

Fourier argued that since it was the workers who created the wealth, that they should both share in it and decide how it should be distributed.

The president got Congress to pass these initiatives, and many on the Left believed that their utopia was almost within view. But after the president signed them into law, the stock market collapsed, causing a rippling effect throughout the world. Fearing that the death knell of American capitalism had begun, companies began fleeing the country in droves. Fourier watched as the economy began to disintegrate before his very eyes. It was no longer a matter of how severe the recession would be; rather, it was how long the depression would last.

To save the economy, the Fourier Administration had issued emergency orders to have the federal government take over the venerable New York Stock Exchange, the NASDAQ, the INet Market and the ECOGreen stock exchange. But under new regulations issued ostensibly to control and better manage those markets, they froze-up entirely. No one dared buy anything. There were only sellers. The all-time high of the DOW Industrials Average of 48,745 was reached more than twelve years earlier; it hadn't seen that level since. Now, the average hovered just above 19,000 but was expected to fall further. In fact, there were few companies left that had once made up the Standard & Poor's or S&P 500 – the largest five hundred companies in the country. Of those on the list fifty years earlier, only forty-two remained incorporated in America.

As for Stevens, he had to show some profit to his board and his shareholders - - just not very much. Anything over 0.05 percent of sales was considered obscene, at least according to the president's Executive Order, number 15332. Profits in excess of that were subject to full taxation plus penalties. Those profits in excess of 1 percent would result in federal charges filed personally against the officers and board members.

EG's profits were closer to 18 percent. The lobbying and bribing of Congressmen and Senators over the years had paid off handsomely. So did offering department secretaries things like 'exploratory' trips to such places as the Italian island of Capri or the beaches of Monaco, allegedly to develop business for American companies there. Such efforts had also gotten them special dispensation for taxes, buried deeply inside several laws that were well over ten thousand pages in length. Now, all Stevens could do was petition his Congressmen and Senators to get a special exemption for his GovCo. This was something that used to be easily effectuated for a GovCo., but not anymore.

Even with a waiver for some of the profit, EG was so far above the limit, punitive action by the IRS was inevitable. It was looking at profits in excess of $21 billion on sales of nearly $120 billion worldwide. That was not acceptable – no matter how many payoffs were made. This was unsettling to the board of directors and Thorne, the CEO, who wanted to show their support for the president's initiatives, yet be rich and live well. To be sure, it was all a masquerade – a thespian game to show equality and fairness to the audience of politicians and the uninformed American people.

"How are we going to spin this?" Stevens asked, looking over the shoulder of his Director of Finance, Parker Donahue.

"Twenty-one billion. That's a lot of money, Carson," said Donahue, his thick, gray eyebrows curling over his eyelids. "It's one thing to make, say seven or eight. But twenty-one?"

"We can't get by with that!" said Stevens excoriating his subordinate. "How could you mess up like that? We have enough global subsidiaries that you could have dumped off the profits overseas or something. You could have buried them in some captive insurance company in Bermuda – anything but this!"

Donahue shook his head. "Yeah. I know. I've been expecting things to turn on us in Russia and in South America. Currencies were going against us, and we thought we would have massive inventory write-offs from product that we were discontinuing. However, in the end, one of our crack sales reps landed a multi-billion deal with China to sell older versions. So, we didn't get the expenses I was counting on. Instead we got a bunch of profits I can't use!"

It was an odd conversation – a CFO and his finance director complaining about earning too much money.

"It's too much to give away as bonuses, I suppose," said the director with a smile.

"Nice try," said Stevens.

"Do you have any ideas? I suppose we could give it all to charity."

"And you really think the board would go for that?"

"No, of course not. Our shareholders would bail too as our stock price crashed. We'd be out of business," answered Donahue.

"Yep, and thirty thousand employees would be out of jobs."

"Thorne wouldn't do any of that anyway," answered Donahue. "He's too tied-up with the b-craps to do something like that." *B-craps* was the word he used instead of bureaucrats. "We have to do something else."

"What?" asked the CFO. "The IRS granted us a special exemption from taxes twenty years ago because we told Congress we wouldn't make much money on their contracts. They let us off the hook when we created a bunch of well-paying but meaningless jobs in their states and districts – especially for Committee chairmen Schooner and Reim. Those jobs cost us hundreds of millions,"

"Yeah, but they've helped us keep down profits," said Donahue.

"This time, it's just not enough, though. I need more."

"The only thing I can do it divert about ten billion to an offshore company. I set several up last year, just in case we needed to move some money around. I've got this one in the Maldives, one in Prince Edward Island, and one in the Isle of Man. Take your pick."

Stevens thought for a moment. "Take the ten and bury it on one of the islands. Get it off the books. That's about all we can do. For the rest of it, we'll have to find another way." He knew how to play the game; he'd been doing it for decades.

"You know, the Deputy Secretary of Taxation, Scott Pearson, is a friend of mine. I can talk to him. Maybe he can fix things so that our problem is 'overlooked.'"

"What will it cost?"

"Well, how much is it worth to you?" asked Donahue, bluntly. He sat back in his plush, cordovan, leather chair.

Stevens grimaced. "How much do you think it will take?"

"Well, direct deposits into foreign accounts would help."

"Accounts – plural? More than one?"

"Oh, yeah," said Donahue. "You're going to have to grease several palms to get this by."

"Fine. Do it. But nothing that's traceable back to us, you hear?" warned Stevens.

"Are we going to tell Thorne?"

"What do you think?" the CFO said dismissively.

Donahue got up and left the room. He needed to access an IP address that wasn't connected with the company's network to make the call.

It was little more than two days later when Donahue called Stevens. It was on a private line. "I just heard back from my guy who knows someone who knows someone. The person told me it is only 22.5 million US dollars to various accounts ... in Mongolia."

"Mongolia?"

"Yeah, that's what I was told. Account numbers are AZRC458 801838298, ..."

"Whoa, hold on," said Stevens. "Read them slowly."

Donahue read off the accounts, SWIFT2X numbers, and others required to make the exchange.

"Isn't Mongolia part of China now?" asked Stevens. "And if I just send money there, how am I guaranteed anything? I have nothing but someone's word?"

"Do you know Bailey Griffin?" asked Parker.

"Yes, of course. He's the Secretary of Taxation. Why?"

"Hold on a second."

The voice on the phone changed. It was much lower and coarse. There was an air of authority about it, and it certainly was not afraid of speaking its mind.

"Stevens, this is Griffin."

Stevens sat up in his chair. "Secretary Griffin. It's been a while."

"Probably about two years," said Griffin, seemingly in a jocular mood.

"Yep, that's about right. We were attending that symposium in Istanbul."

"Yeah, really tough assignment," said Griffin, laughing at his own joke. "I'd never been there before ... well, anyway. Donahue here was just filling me in on the issue with EG."

"Yes, sir," answered Stevens, haltingly. He knew that next to the president, Griffin wielded about as much power as anyone else could in Washington. The previous president had raised the top taxing position from a commissioner-level to Cabinet-level. The office and its taxing power was frequently used by the White House to destroy political enemies. Of all the people in Washington, Griffin was one guy you didn't want to piss off.

"This is a secure line, so I'll get right to the point," Griffin said directly.

"Uh, yes sir. It is sir."

"Okay, well, if you make a donation north of sixteen to my cause, we can make this happen. It sounds like your company is doing very well these days too. Congratulations on that."

"Thank you sir, uh, I ..." Stevens was unsure whether he could handle a sixteen million dollar payment without eyebrows being raised. It was a capital offense to bribe a government official, even though it happened all the time. You just had to make sure you got far enough up the food chain that it didn't come back to bite you later. "We'll handle it, sir," said Stevens, nervously. "And the other 6.5 million?" he asked, wondering how Donahue had gotten to 22.5.

"Oh, the other accounts are my grandkids' trusts. I always want to be sure they have enough for their education." Griffin laughed again, and Stevens parroted him disingenuously.

The wire was sent. The money was received in an obscure bank in Ulaanbaatar, Mongolia. A total of 22.55 million U.S. – the extra fifty thousand going to the bank to keep things quiet. The proper amounts were recorded into the four accounts and exchanged immediately into silver bullion. The next day, the company made its tax filing to the IRS. It totaled 1,764 pages, but the electronic filing was swift and painless. They heard nothing back from the IRS and received no notification of a problem. Stevens kept his fingers crossed. Dealing with high-ups in government was always unpredictable. It was not unusual for "payments" to be lost and requested to be re-processed. Of course, none were lost, and the payments became multiples of that originally agreed.

Weeks later, Stevens got a call.

"Boss," said the voice on the other end of the phone line. It was Donahue.

"Yeah, what's up?"

"I just heard back from our accountants. They said our tax filing was accepted. There won't be an audit. You can sleep again."

"So, we're all good?"

"We're good, my friend," said Donahue.

"Good job. I hope you understand. I am friends with Griffin, but it is best if I let you handle things. Less messy that way."

"I understand, sir."

"Stevens, you'll find a little envelope in your office when you get in. I thought you and Dora wouldn't mind going on a little holiday for a while. You deserve it."

"Thanks. She'll be thrilled."

Stevens hung up the phone. They had avoided paying twenty-one billion dollars in taxes plus another five billion in penalties. Worse yet, they could have all gone to prison. Instead, for only 22.55 million, they'd skated through another year. He just had to make sure it didn't happen again. They couldn't make money like that again. No, it was his job as CFO to make sure they didn't.

*****

CH 17 RESCINDED

Meghan Armstrong signed for the certified letter and brought it directly to her boss. She walked directly into the executive office even though she saw Shea was on the phone. Shea looked up and motioned for her to come in, but then put her finger to her lips. "Patty, it's been good talking with you. I'll have my assistant Meghan follow-up to schedule a meeting. Thanks again."

Meghan waited patiently until she disconnected before speaking.

Shea pressed the *Off* button on her desktop, and the image of Patty vanished into thin air. "What do you have for me, Meghan?" she asked, looking at the envelope her assistant was holding. She reached out to accept the suspicious envelope and turned it over in her hand. "What's this?" she asked. "We haven't gotten a piece of paper like this in a long time. I didn't even know anyone delivered these things anymore."

"When it's certified, I guess they want to be damn sure that someone physically gets it," said Meghan. "I signed for it. Usually when we get things like this from the government it's not good news."

Shea tore open the letter that held the seal of the Department of Technology Assessment and yanked two cream-colored pages from the inside. She unfolded them and held them up to read.

> *Dear Registrant:*
>
> *We regret to inform you that there has been an administrative miscommunication from the Department of Technology Assessment. We inadvertently sent you a notification indicating that we had approved your patent application for the commercialization of your product. Unfortunately, the application has, in fact, been denied.*
>
> *You will not be able to manufacture, produce, sell, promote, distribute, bestow, transfer, create, generate, advertise, develop or otherwise commercialize the product for which you submitted your application. It was determined that another inventor has a patent on your idea.*
>
> *This is a final determination that is not subject to appeal or change.*

If you have any questions, you may email them to: technologyassessment@departmentfairtrade.gov.

Most sincerely,

A Ratner

Angel Ratner
Deputy Secretary
Department of Technology Assessment

"This must be a mistake," said Shea, partly to Meghan and partly to herself. Quickly, she told her computer to dial the number at the bottom of the page and waited. She heard a pre-recorded message indicating that her wait time would be no more than ninety-three minutes. *I'm not waiting that long!* she said to herself. She knew the times were grossly understated anyway, and it was not unusual for callers to wait six or seven hours to speak to a human, if they got through at all. Most often, they were just disconnected at some point and had to call back and get back in queue.

But Shea rethought her predicament and decided to call back anyway. So, she redialed the number and put the line on hold while she waited for someone to pick-up ... three hours later, that someone or something answered. It was a robot made to look like an attractive woman that appeared on the screen in front of Shea. With big, blue eyes, long dark hair and perfectly proportioned face, the robot tried to smile and deliver a message she had delivered thousands of times before – one with the same empty, dispassionate voice used every time.

"Yes, this is the Department of Technology Assessment. How may I direct your call?" said the robot, blinking periodically to assume some element of realism.

"This is Shea Disone. I'm with Lenoir Research Labs, and I just received a ..."

"Ma'am, I have calls waiting. I can't help you directly. I'll forward you to the party who may be able to assist you. Please repeat your issue."

"Uh, I got this rejection notice on our submission for ..."

"Hold please." The screen changed to images of a dense green forest with birds chirping in the background. The computer simulation was replete with white-tailed deer wandering off in the distance and small, gray squirrels scurrying up two tall Ponderosa pine trees closest to the viewer. It was a futile attempt to calm those who had waited so long on the other end of the line.

Then, the image disappeared, replaced by a black screen with the words **404 Error**. Shea was about to come unglued when a harsh voice said, "Say *one* for assistance with a notification you received; say *two* for payment of a bill; say *three* for ..." This went on for several minutes, until she heard "... say *twenty-six* if this issue has to do with a patent submission; say ..."

Shea shouted twenty-six loud enough for the squirrels to fall out of the pines she'd just seen. She rued the decision she'd made to make the call in the first place. The line rang and was answered by another automated robot. "You have reached the patent submission office," said the handsome, deep-voiced, male attendant. "Say *one* if you want to know the status of your submission; say *two* to see if the office received your submission; say *three* if you received a rejection letter ..."

Almost ready to throw something at the screen, Shea yelled the number *three* into the microphone.

The forest video came back on and played for five more minutes before a real woman appeared -- a chubby, pale-faced woman in her late twenties. She was chewing gum and twisting her stringy, black hair with her fat fingers. She was quite a contrast to the comely images that had come before her.

"Hello, this is Ms. Pritchart. How may I help you?" said the woman, looking bored and disinterested.

"This is Shea Disone," she answered, trying to be professional and regain her composure. "We just got a notice of rejection from the department regarding our patent submission, and ..."

"What is the number on your letter please?"

"Number?"

"Yes, the application number on your letter. It starts with a PAT prefix."

Shea glanced at the first page. In the upper left corner was the number PAT 19898332345. She rattled off the number to the woman and waited for a response.

"Yes, I have that submission. How many I help?" said the woman.

"Well, we received an approval letter, dated October 14 from your office. That letter clearly states that our patent application was approved. Then, today, we received this letter, dated January 5, stating that our patent was rejected. I don't understand. It must be some sort of mistake. It's now June 8 – how could it take five months to ..."

"No, the letter dated January 5 is correct. Your patent was rejected alright. It says it here in my official files. I guess the earlier one was a mistake."

"That can't be. There is no one else out there who has anything remotely like what we are trying to patent," said Shea.

"Not according to my records. It shows that there is someone else, and they already have a patent for it."

"Can you tell me who it is?"

"No, I'm afraid I can't."

"Who else can I talk to there to get more answers about ..."

"I'm afraid we're out of time. I must move on to my next caller. Thanks for calling the Department of Technology Assessment and have a great day!"

The screen went black, and the line went dead.

Shea slammed her hand down on the cutoff button. She could hear the plastic casing crack under the force, but she didn't care. Then, she wadded up the letter and threw it down on the floor in disgust. "How the hell can they do this?" she yelled, her face contorted with rage.

Meghan came in, hearing the pounding. "What's wrong?" she asked. "Was it something bad from the government?"

"Yeah, that's an understatement," said Shea. "What's wrong *is* the government. *That's* what's wrong. They've screwed us over for the last time, Meghan. Apparently, they really *have* rejected our patent. I don't understand it." She shook her head in shock.

"I'm sorry. I don't know what to say. It doesn't make any sense. You and Dr. Disone have worked so hard for this."

"Get Patrick on the phone. I've got to talk to him right away."

Minutes later, Meghan came back, "Your husband's on the line."

Shea pushed the *On* button, and Patrick's image appeared in three dimensions in front of her. "Patrick. Technology Assessment just sent us a letter. It says that ..."

"... that our patent was denied," said Patrick, mouthing the words before she could get them out.

"Uh, yeah. How did you know?"

"My people inside the department asked me a few months ago if I'd gotten a letter. I told them no, but they told me to watch for it. They didn't know exactly what it said, but they knew it had been issued. One person said they had questioned the patent approval months earlier. But there was too much fog – too much uncertainty to know anything for sure. So, I didn't want to worry you. I wasn't sure it was real. So, I waited. I guess it's official, then?"

"Patrick, what do we do now?" asked Shea, her voice trembling. "We've already started lining up our production and marketing. We're in it for millions right now. We can't cancel; a lot of those contracts have huge penalties if we pull out. We're sunk!"

"Don't panic," Patrick said, trying to soothe her worries. But she could tell he was too. He had promised her much during their years of marriage, and now, just when he thought he was about to deliver for her, the rug was pulled out from under them.

"What else can we do? If we can't sell the engine, we won't have the cash to make good on all of the commitments we've made," she said. After a long pause, she added, "We're going to have to file for bankruptcy." She could feel the emotions welling up inside her. She'd always tried to be strong, but this was about as much as she could handle.

"Bull sh*t!" Patrick said adamantly, the image of his face contorted with rage. "I'll *never* let the government force me into bankruptcy as long as blood is pulsing through my veins. If I'm ever going down, it's going to be because *I* was the one who failed – not because some pin-head in the government brought me down. And, as God is my witness, I'm not – we're not -- going to fail, Shea. I'm not going to let that happen. I don't care who's in the White House, and I don't care who's running things in Washington."

"Okay. So, what do we do?"

There was silence as Patrick gathered his thoughts. His face held a blank stare, but then came back alive. "I have to make a few calls. If we can't get this straightened out, we'll have to push this higher up. I don't know if there's anyone in D.C. anymore who listens to the common man like us, but it's worth a shot."

"You and I know people – but they're all the wrong people, Patrick. We're on the wrong side, remember?"

Now it was Patrick's turn to be quiet. Then, he said, "I don't care. Even if I get through to just one, that one might be able to make the difference. I have to try."

"Do you still believe that?" answered Shea, skeptically. "They've been gunning for our little company for years, Patrick. They're out for vengeance because we wouldn't play ball with them. We rejected their request to share our research with them, remember? That's 'cause we knew what that meant. It was like refusing their grant money with all those strings attached. That money would have been great, but the bureaucrats would have taken over our company in return."

"Not only that, but we know now that they only wanted to do that to kill our project. They hate fossil fuels and everything that has to do with them. That's been their aim for years."

"True, but let's just not make this thing any worse than it is. It's pretty ugly right now," said Shea.

"I'm afraid, my dearest Shea, that things are about to get a whole lot uglier," said Patrick.

"What do you mean?"

"Like I said, I have to make a few calls. I'll let you know what happens."

"Patrick …" she paused, "… don't do anything brash."

"You mean stupid."

"Well, that too," she said. "But then I know you'll do what you want to anyway, regardless of my admonitions. So, just be aware of what you're saying and to whom. As we're seeing, Washington is good at threats and vendettas and making good on both. It's a sport to them."

"Thanks for the confidence," Patrick said, sarcastically.

"Really, honey, you're not always …"

"I get it, Shea, okay?" Patrick was angry, and he felt badly about barking at her. Then, he calmed down and said more softly, "Okay, I'll try. And Shea …"

"Yeah?"

"Don't worry. I promise I won't do something stupid."

She kissed him and put her arms around him. He was life to her, as she was to him. "I love you," she said as she pressed her body into his.

"I love you too," he answered, drawing her closer and never wanting to let go. "More than you can ever know."

***

Patrick's next call was to an old friend, Congressman JC Sumner. He'd met him at a Freedom Party rally several years earlier. The Freedom Party was a new, third party that had been formed to try to draw like-minded political thinkers together. Many had come to the event just to see if there was anything to it – if there was enough support and momentum to make a new party viable. Most had been noncommittal, fearing that the time was not right or that it would only detract support from the current opposition party – the Constitution Party – weakening their chances overall, rather than improving them.

But many felt the Constitution Party unsalvageable – that it had become no better than the party in power – the People's Party. They believed the Constitution Party no longer represented its followers and had no chance to regain any clout in Washington. Had the Constitution Party politicians simply become complacent and comfortable in their cushy, well-paying, jobs, sitting pompously in their cavernous offices and content with idly watching the People's Party run the table on the rest of America.

At the rally, Sumner had confided in Patrick that watching his colleagues in the Constitution Party on Capitol Hill had disgusted him and that he was considering switching his affiliation to the new party. He had come to the conference to talk with party leaders to see if there was a fit with his own belief system. He had been impressed at that point, he'd told Patrick.

Yet, during the intervening years, Sumner had gotten cold feet, just as others had. Together with pressure from colleagues and an outright assault on the Freedom Party by all fronts, including the media, he had withdrawn his support.

Even so, the two men had developed a quick and lasting friendship. They were like-minded on many issues, agreeing on the sad state of America, the huge national debt, the deteriorating military, the skyrocketing interest rates and inflation, and the growing scarcity of jobs and resources. Each of these problems, left unaddressed for decades, had exploded into a national crisis. It seemed that those people attuned to what was going on in the country recognized it too; however, the other 95 percent did not. With the help of the media, such bad news never surfaced, and if it did at all, it was buried within other stories and watered-down to minimize the impact.

When discontent first began to arise, the reaction of the government was to label those who were unhappy with the state as anarchists. Such a label could destroy people's careers, their families, and their lives. Once an anarchist, they would be unable to get a job, be ineligible for government benefits, and become disqualified to hold a passport or travel visa. The penalties were stiff to facilitate compliance and obedience. Life was always easier if you just went along.

"Congressman, it's Patrick Disone. It's been a while. Thank you so much for taking my call. How have you and Maria been?" Maria was Sumner's wife of thirty years. She was a Hispanic beauty who had caught his eye when he was practicing law in Laramie. She had been his paralegal, and it hadn't taken long for them to grow fond of one another – eventually marrying once he left the firm to set-out for a career in politics.

"Just fine, Patrick. It's so good to see you again!" said Sumner, looking at the video image of his friend. "It's never a bother to get a call from you – you know that. How is Shea? She was working hard as ever last time we talked. I'm sure that hasn't changed."

"No, not at all. We're in the midst of a lot of changes right now, and that's why I'm phoning. You see, we are having some problems with the Department of Technology Assessment. If you recall, we were just beginning the development of our next-generation, high-efficiency combustible engine. For the last few years, we've been working to perfect our patent on that. You know what a nightmare it can be working with that agency."

"That I do, Patrick. It's not easy working with any of them, but some are worse than others. That's for sure."

Patrick smiled and nodded his agreement. Then, he continued. "Last October, nearly nine months ago, Shea and I received notice that our patent was approved. As you can imagine, we were thrilled. We immediately started to arrange financing and made commitments to begin production later this year. But today, we got another notice – it rescinded that approval."

"Wait, let me understand. You got approved last year, but the department took it back today? The Department of Technology Assessment?"

Patrick almost expected the Congressman not to react at all. He assumed that Sumner would have heard it all before and that Lenoir would be just one of many. To his surprise, Sumner truly acted shocked. Whether it was his honed political skills or genuine empathy, Patrick wasn't sure. However, during the short time he'd known the Congressman, Sumner had never once made him doubt his sincerity.

"Yeah. We called the department to see if it was a mistake, and they claimed it wasn't. Congressman, we're ruined if that's the case. We've guaranteed all of those contracts, and they came with some pretty stiff penalties. If we can't get the rescission letter overturned, we're out of business!"

"The DTA? That's Angel Ratner, right?" asked Sumner, haltingly.

"Yeah, she's the secretary, I think."

"I think she's just the deputy secretary, but that doesn't make any difference. She's a dragon – and I'm trying to be polite. Of anyone I can think of, she would be the one to eat her own children and not think twice."

"Shea says we should sue, but I don't see the courts taking the case, do you?"

"Not if you're dealing with her. You're wrestling with a thirty-foot Diamondback, my man – and that's a snake that will sink its fangs into you and watch you die. You're caught between hell and the devil herself, you know. Patrick, just don't piss her off."

"It's too late for that. She's gunning for us. I can tell. And if we lose, we're done – financially and professionally. Hell, we'll have to sell our home, belongings and everything else. Our life's work will have been for nothing. I just can't let that happen."

"You want me to make some inquiries?" asked Sumner.

Patrick stopped to catch his breath. He wanted more, but he understood how Washington worked. And although Sumner was a rebel, he too had his limitations. "Yeah, that would be a good start. I'd appreciate it, and so would Shea."

"Okay. I'll give it my best shot. Give Shea my best. I'll see what I can do."

Patrick turned off the phone, and Sumner's image evaporated. He knew it was a long shot regardless of whom he involved. Sumner was his best chance – their best chance. If he couldn't do anything, no one could. He would push the envelope as far as he could as the rebel of the Constitution Party. But they were dealing with a rattlesnake, as Sumner had described her. Even

Patrick had heard about her and the fact that no one who stood up to her survived for very long. She eventually had them destroyed. Even the delusional, yet pugilistic Joseph McCarthy wouldn't have stood a chance against her.

It was out of his hands now. All Shea and he could do now was wait. *****

CH 18 NO INFORMATION AVAILABLE

Weeks passed, and Congressman Sumner continued to be stonewalled by the DTA. His direct inquiries on the Lenoir Labs patent were met with derision and animosity. Responses from the recently promoted Assistant Deputy Secretary, Margola Vasilik, had been vague at best, recalcitrant at worst. Normally, such behavior toward a Congressman would be considered inappropriate and unacceptable, but times were different. Now it was just business as usual at the DAT, as it was at most departments.

Frustrated, Sumner finally ordered his chief of staff to march down to the department and confront the deputy secretary directly. However, his chief of staff only ended up sitting in the waiting room for over four hours – never getting a chance to get inside Ratner's office or even that of her assistant. So, Sumner petitioned the White House for answers, being careful not to speak negatively of the rattlesnake lady and her office. However, two more weeks passed without an answer or a reply of any sort.

"I'm sorry, Patrick. I don't know what else I can do," said Sumner, following up with a call to the Disones. "I'm blocked everywhere I turn. I've never seen anything quite like this – even for Washington."

Patrick was upset, but he didn't hold it against Sumner. He knew the Congressman had done everything he could. It was Washington. No, it was his anger that was growing more and more against the tyranny of the ruling elite in Washington. They were no longer representatives of the people – no longer doing the people's work. They were only doing their own.

"Congressman Sumner, thanks for trying. I wasn't expecting a miracle," Patrick said as positively as he could.

"I'm just sorry I didn't get any help for you," answered Sumner. "It used to be a lot easier to get things done for your constituents in this town. Now, it's impossible unless you're part of the People's Party or are owed favors by people higher up the chain. Even then, it's difficult to make them pay up."

Patrick said his goodbyes and hung up. Then, he called his attorney, Emery Lawson. "Emery, I want to file a lawsuit," Patrick declared boldly and assertively.

"Why?" said Emery jokingly. "Business for me is good these days. Everyone is suing everyone else. I think you're about the only one who hasn't sued somebody this past year. It's about time you joined in the fun."

"I wish this were going to be fun," said Patrick.

"Who do you want to sue, Patrick? You name them, and I'll sue them."

"The federal government, the Department of Technological Assessment and, specifically, Angel Ratner, the deputy secretary."

Patrick had always been blunt and to the point with his attorney. At a legal rate of twelve hundred dollars per hour, he felt he couldn't be otherwise. At the same time, he had known Emery for twenty years. In all of those years, he could only remember one other time when he'd called him about something that had really angered him – something that needed a legal response.

It had been years earlier, when Shea and Patrick had just filed incorporation papers for Lenoir Research Labs. Patrick had dreamed of having his own business since the age of seventeen, but many other things had gotten in the way. By his twenties, he had found the one woman with whom he wanted to spend the rest of his life.

Early on, after they had found success with early versions of an efficient combustion engine, they had faced severe pressure from the big automakers and the oil companies to shelve their plans. There had been a threat, although they never found out the source. But they understood it had come from one, if not all three – auto, oil, and ... Uncle Sam.

If they were able to produce a highly efficient combustion engine, it would cost both industries – the automakers in subsidy payments from the government and the oil companies in lost profits. The federal government would lose the most – credibility. Quickly, the state governments got involved. Worried about lost gas tax revenue, the states teamed up with big GovCo's to wage war against the upstart company to shut it down. The Massachusetts state legislators issued thinly veiled threats against any company trying to build a *certain* combustion engine. With the specificity of their definition, it was only intended to target Lenoir Labs. They wanted it gone, so they could keep their tax revenue flowing and maintain the *status quo*. More perniciously, they threatened any company that dealt with such a company, including banks.

The bank Lenoir Labs had used for years dropped them suddenly in the wake of these actions. It wasn't until Patrick found a bank sympathetic to their plight and willing to stand-up against the strong-armed tactics of the state, that they were able to carry on with their business.

148

But it was at that point that Patrick and Shea had contacted Emery Lawson. They had just received a threatening notice from a Massachusetts state senator telling them they were in violation of some obscure labor law that had been enacted before the Civil War. A cease and desist order from a state appeals court was attached. It stated in unequivocal terms that Lenoir violated many state laws and should halt all operations immediately. It took two years and hundreds of thousands in legal fees to Emery and his law practice, but they were able to win their case and stay open.

However, now things were different – the government, the courts, and what used to be called justice. They no longer resembled what they had been even a score of years earlier.

Lawson listened patiently as Patrick told him the series of events that had unfolded. It took longer than usual, as Patrick had the tendency to explain how to build the watch, rather than tell someone what time it was. However, when he finished, Lawson sighed.

"That bad?" asked Patrick, his fingers pressed together tightly and interlocking into an unconscious two- handed fist.

"I wish I could say otherwise, Patrick, but going up against the federal government and winning these days is harder than becoming CEO of GoogleSoft."

"But this will destroy us!"

"I know," Lawson answered. "I'll do what I can, Patrick, but I can't promise miracles. But if your Congressman wasn't able to get anywhere, I'm not sure what you expect me to be able to do. The DAT is about as iron-fisted as they come."

"Do what you can, then," said Patrick, dejectedly.

"May I ask what donations you made to the president's election campaign last time? Was it anything significant that we can support?"

"None!" exclaimed Patrick, trying to suppress his fury. "I'd never contribute a dime to that moron."

"Patrick, again, none of this helps. But, I'll see what I can do."

"Emery, I've heard that a lot lately, and I know what that means. You don't think you can do this do you?"

Lawson cleared his throat, uncomfortable with the implication.

"Years ago," said Patrick, "you didn't say that to us when we came to you with a problem with the government and the big union companies. You worked with us! You fought for us! And we won, didn't we! We won! ... Emery, we need you to go to battle for us on this one too. We really need your help. Will you at least try?"

"I'll see what I can do, Patrick. That's all I can promise. You see – those years ago --that was then. This is now. We have a president who isn't what they describe in the U.S. Constitution. The office isn't anything like that anymore. I don't recognize it these days. There isn't much of this country that I do recognize anymore, for God's sake! What else do I have to say?"

"Let me know, Emery. Just let me know." Patrick hung up, exasperated.

Patrick dreaded having to report what he was told back to Shea. It would upset her, and that was the last thing he wanted to do. Yet, he knew she would want to know. She was stronger than that for which he'd ever given her credit – still, he didn't like to see her in pain.

He knocked on the door to her office and cracked the door. She was busy looking at financial charts and other graphs on the performance of the company, trying to figure out how to make everything work.

"Shea, I've been on the phone with Sumner and Emery."

She looked away from her screens and, with a pensive look, waited for the rest of his briefing. "And?" she asked, simply.

"Uh, it seems that no one wants to take on the DAT."

"Even Emery?"

"Emery said he'd get back to me. He wasn't optimistic."

"What about the Congressman? What did he say?"

"He said he's tried and hasn't gotten anything back from the DAT or the White House. Nothing. He's at a dead end," said Patrick.

"Sh*t," Shea said under her breath and looking away. "So, where does that leave us?"

"I don't know. I'm out of ideas," said Patrick.

Shea sat for a moment. "I may have one. It's crazy, but at this point, what do we have to lose?"

"Go on."

"I know poly-sci was never your thing like it was for me, but would you consider helping me with an ad?"

"An ad?" he asked. "What kind of ad?"

"I'll talk to you about it tonight when you get home. It's something that was tried almost three hundred years ago. It may be the way to get some attention to our cause."

***

After attempting to contest the administration's power head-on, first with the Congressman and then his attorney, Patrick and Shea took another approach. *People understood two things,* Shea figured, *sound bites and commercial advertising. If only he could combine them,* she thought.

Their first paid ad hit the 3-D electronic billboards outside of Boston within a week. It was followed by Sat-TV and SI-net commercials that ran for only ten seconds. The ads merely read *Publius is Dead.* That was all. There was no explanation or narrative.

At first, the reaction was one of disinterest. So, Shea ran another one: *Do you remember Publius?* After several weeks, someone at the *Boston Globe* took up the promotion as a news story. *What did all this mean? Publius is Dead?* But getting answers was difficult. The buyer of the ads was a non-descript organization called Fathers of the Founder.

As awareness rose, advertisements in the paper and online grew in frequency, just asking the question Who is Publius? became commonplace around the workplace water cooler. Finally, an article appeared in the *Globe*, reportedly penned by one named Publius. In it, the author explained that the pseudonym Publius was used in honor of the Founders (a term used instead of Founding Fathers, which was considered misogynistic and banned), James Madison, Alexander Hamilton and John Jay who wrote the *Federalist Papers* at a time when the Constitution was being debated in America. Although not as eloquent as those of the eighty-five articles written by those authors in promoting the strengths of federalism within the draft Constitution, the new Publius article was short and to-the-point. Many wrote the paper asking who this Publius person was? They admired his bluntness and forthrightness as he confronted the twisted and corrupt practices of the Fourier Administration.

In the first article, Publius attacked the czar positions President Fourier setup to run his departments – positions outside the standard cabinet posts of department secretaries. Few department secretaries had any power and actually ran their bureaus. It was true that they had to be confirmed by a majority of the Senate, but they were there mostly for show.

Instead, most federal departments were run by the czars who were selected by Fourier and avoided being confirmed by the U.S. Congress. Under Article II, Section 2, the Constitution created principal officers of the Executive Branch, more commonly known as Cabinet posts. Many positions had been added since the original four were created in 1789. Now there were many more, and each required Congressional approval. However, President Fourier created seventeen ministerial posts called czars, allegedly only to advise these Cabinet positions. However, the czars ran the government, reporting directly to the president. He rarely, if ever, called Cabinet meetings any more, instead gathering his czars for briefings and direction.

In the second article, Publius criticized the use of executive orders by the president to avoid being challenged by Congress. In fact, there had been a secret document prepared by his Justice Department, arguing that neither Congress nor the Courts could not challenge his executive orders. Fourier's Attorney General, Dutch Welbourne, had been working on the details of the paper for months, but Patrick had learned about it from Sumner who'd gotten it from a source inside the White House. Publius chose to leak the story, citing a violation of the Constitution's separation of powers.

In the third and fourth articles, Publius blasted Congress's ineptitude and inability to pass a single bill of legislation. The Senate had long been written off as a worthless, do-nothing body, similar to what the House of Lords had become in England prior to its dissolution. On the other hand, the House had become so acrimonious with rebels like Sumner and others that it was being compared with the 37th Congress, which convened in 1860 to discuss the issue of slavery. The House was hot then, as it was now. The only difference was there were fewer fisticuffs on the floor now. Publius called them out for being obsequious to the Executive Branch – mere lemmings that were willing and able to follow it off the cliff and take the rest of America with them.

But it wasn't until the fifth article that Publius launched his attack on the Department of Technology Assessment and the managerial malfeasance of its minister, Angel Ratner. In the manifest, he cited the department for its capriciousness and prejudicial approach to granting or denying patent applications. He wrote, "It is the author's first-hand experience of receiving conflicting statements from the department – one moment approving a patent request and the next having it stripped away. The cost to the company was and continues to be enormous. Yet, there is no recourse against a government department; It is folly to think otherwise. It has total and absolute power, and it wields it with abandon."

Of course, references in the articles were more specific than Patrick's attorney, Lawson, would have advised. By the fifth article, the DAT had quickly tracked down who Publius was, and a warrant was made for an arrest. Within hours, the feds arrived at the Disones' home, bursting through the front door with a cement-pipe battering ram that shattered the fine detail of the mahogany doors with the first blow. Announcing that they were with the sheriff's office rather than the FBI, they stormed the library and yanked Patrick up off his chair to cuff him.

"What am I being charged with?" Patrick exclaimed, shocked at the violent intrusion.

"Sedition," said the federal agent. "You've been trying to undermine the power and authority of the federal government. As such, you will be charged as an anarchist and traitor to this country."

"What? What about my First Amendment rights -- freedom of speech and all of that?"

The agent laughed and strong-armed Patrick out of the house, pushing him into the back of an unmarked, black sedan. They whisked him downtown to the FBI's local processing center, scanning-in the new inmate's fingerprints and retina pattern as well as swabbing and recording his DNA profile for the rest of eternity. "Pickup your orange jumpsuit in the bin to your left and go down the hall. Your cell is Bravo sixteen. Can you remember that or should I write it down for you?" asked the obese, middle-aged agent, sitting on his ass behind the large, oak desk and a two-inch thick bulletproof glass that defended his position of authority.

"What about my call? Don't I at least get one call?"

"Is it in the Constitution?" the man said, not knowing and not caring.

"Yes, as a matter of fact," answered Patrick, "I believe it is, in some manner or form."

"Oh," the man said in reply. He rolled his eyes and looked back at his paperwork. Then, he mumbled to himself, "Then, I guess it's good we don't go by that *old* thing anymore."

It was the next day before they allowed Patrick to make that one call to his concerned wife and ask her to talk their lawyer. Shea had been frantic, contacting every hospital, police station and morgue within fifty miles of the city. None had any information on a Patrick Disone. She had not been home when they had arrested her husband, and 'disappearances' of ordinary citizens were becoming more and more frequent, especially those on the White House Enemies List, as it was known. She had tried describing her husband in great detail to each official too, in the mistaken belief that perhaps he had lost his identification, was unable to speak, or had realized trauma so he couldn't remember. However, no one took her histrionics seriously. There was even one sanitarium that asked for her information so that they might follow up with her later … as a potential patient.

Finally, she received the call.

"Shea, I'm okay," said Patrick, trying to be calm. "I'm here at the FBI center or whatever the hell they call this place. They haven't let me make any calls until now."

"Patrick! You're sure you're alright? I've been worried sick! I've called every hospital, clinic, and …"

"Shea, I'm fine. I just need for you to reach Emery Lawson. They've detained me for sedition. They say I'm a traitor because they allege I wrote those articles in the paper."

"I feel awful," she answered. "It was my idea and I wrote all of those. You shouldn't be there. It should be me."

"It shouldn't be either one of us," Patrick said. "It wasn't wrong, what you did. It was within our rights."

"How is writing articles traitorous? I thought that's what we're supposed to do as citizens?"

"I don't know. It's not the country we used to know, Shea. But right now, I need to talk to Emery."

"Okay. I'll get him for you. I'll get in the car and come down to post bond to get you out of there."

"I'm not sure you can. They told me you can't if I'm in for sedition. It's obviously serious. He said it's a capital offense."

"Patrick!"

"Don't worry, Shea. We'll get this sorted out. That's why you have to reach Emery. He'll know what to do."

"Patrick?" asked Shea.

"Yeah?"

"I'm so, so sorry. I'll come down there and tell them it was me. *I* was the one who wrote those articles," said Shea.

"No you won't," Patrick said. "You'll do no such thing."

"I have to. You didn't write them."

"In spirit, I was as much a part of it as you. And if you try, I'll just tell them you're just covering for me."

Shea huffed. "Okay. But, Patrick?"

"Yeah?"

"I love you."

Patrick smiled. This was a woman he had loved from the first day he'd met her, and it had only gotten stronger with time. They understood each other; they cared for each other; they worried about each other; and they would be with each other in one way or another through it all, no matter what. He just had no idea just *what* that might be.

"I love you too, Shea. More than you could ever know."

***

Emery was efficient and amazing. Undaunted by the sedition charge, he pushed hard against the allegations and invoked the help of several federal judges he knew who were still independent and willing to defend the Constitution that they took an oath to defend to force the bureau to recant their accusations. Within twenty-four hours, Shea had Patrick out on bail. But, they would soon learn that this was only going to end up being a minor skirmish, compared with the greater battles ahead. Their war had only just begun.

*****

CH 19 PUBLIUS RETURNS

At first, the Justice Department was eager to get the news out about Patrick's arrest, hoping it would silence others who might try the same ploy. The attorney general covertly leaked the information as an "unidentified source" to reporters he knew would spread the word. Initially, it was successful. The coverage was slanted, just as he'd hoped – painting the Disones as anarchists and a threat to society and the country at large.

But the aura of éclat was short-lived. Publius had struck a chord with people – one with which they agreed. His (or her) tone had been challenging of the government while empathetic to the people they ruled. It had been the right balance at the right time.

The SI-net was awash in backlash. Even sites that normally were supportive of Fourier were issuing scathing rebukes based on their readership. On-line virtual discussion groups showed images of angry subscriber's avatars jumping out of their digital chairs and shouting down speakers trying to defend the police-like action.

Within days, Welbourne wished he had muzzled the news instead and issued new, more-formal instructions *advising* all mainstream media outlets not to mention it for fear of creating civil unrest. Its comminations covered most media outlets, but not all. It was impossible to address all of the blogs and other social media venues that had proliferated on the SI-net, many of which used masking technology to make government blocking difficult. These sites continued to cover the story and the uproar.

Publius Uncovered! Government Cracks Down!

At Last, Publius ID Known! Police Raid – Torture Him!

The news included detailed accounts of the sedition and treason charges that the Justice Department was going to bring against Patrick and the Brown-shirt style tactic to arrest him. Of course, there were exaggerations and outright fabrications too. Miscalculating, the Justice Department thought only the few people who really paid attention to what was going on in the world or, at least in the country, would be upset over the violation of his constitutional rights. Instead, far more were.

Publius had done nothing but express his opinions as was protected by the First Amendment. Ad hoc news programs on the web presented the facts – that he had published his thoughts as protected by the Bill of Rights to the

Constitution; that the government had arrested him and thrown him in prison; and that they intended to persecute him without due process of law. Although there were no reported protests, there was a level of vehemence in the comments and a disturbing degree of vitriol that was unsettling and unnerving to the White House. Unable to give rifle shots to kill those sites creating the problems, Fourier clandestinely ordered the entire SI-net shut down.

It was the cry heard around the country, and it was shrill.

"Why is my net down?" everyone was asking, as well as, "What's going on?" and "Is there some conspiracy going on that caused this?" Commerce and social activities within the country shut down, and the White House was on the defensive.

Because of the severity of the matter, Ken Beister turned over the emergency video press conference to the Chief of Staff, Trevor Allen. "I have a brief statement before taking two questions," said Allen. "There was a disruption to the SI-net this morning caused by Chinese hackers trying to infiltrate our defenses and security. President Fourier was on the line immediately with the Chinese premier, who told him he would investigate immediately. The problem was fixed within hours, and the Chinese premier said the offenders would be prosecuted." It was a lie, but since everyone came out smelling like a rose, neither the Chinese nor the Administration had any objections.

The first question was a softball from a hand-picked journalist of an Administration friendly news organization. "So, to clarify," said the young woman reporter, "President Fourier was able to bring back the SI-net by taking a hardline with the Chinese premier. Is that right?"

"Yes, that's right. President Fourier's quick response to the problem led to the restoration of the net and saving the country billions in trade and losses," said Allen.

Next, he pointed to another pre-arranged journalist on the other side of the room, but instead, another stood up right behind her, taking the spotlight and the question. "But as I understand it, the SI-net has many, separate servers that run independently all over the world. If there was an attack, the entire net would have gone down, not just within the United States. How was it that just the U.S. service was disrupted?"

The conference was being broadcast live on all channels, and interrupting the program due to technical problems in the wake of the SI-net issue would have been even more disastrous. Allen was stuck, and he wasn't use to that. So, he started making things up.

"Perhaps, usually, but in this case the Chinese attack was only on the U.S. nodes."

"From people working at one of the U.S. sites, they tell me that the hackers' code was something they know was developed by the NSA a few years ago. Why would the Chinese use the same code?" asked the reporter.

"They stole the code from the NSA. That's all we know at this point."

"But if they stole the code, why didn't the Administration ensure that the U.S. nodes were protected from that code – being that, as you suggest, the White House knew about the theft?"

Allen was digging himself deeper, and he knew it. He smiled, "I think that's all I have time to address today. As we have more information on this issue, we will be sure to make it available to everyone. Thank you." And with that, he abruptly left the room.

"What the hell is going on?" shouted Fourier, looking out across the South Lawn of the White House toward the National Mall where a few protestors were starting to gather. "Why can't you get this thing under control?" The president was visibly disturbed by the press conference disaster and Allen's abysmal performance. The hint of any massing of people on the mall, those challenging his actions, could pose a clear and present danger to him and his authority.

"Mr. President, I truly am sorry, but we are sending in more manpower to quell the crowds," said his head Chief of Staff. Next to him stood General Shontal Washington, head of the Joint Chiefs of Staff. Fourier had summoned her in the event more extreme measures would be required.

"It's been twenty-four hours now, and you haven't made this go away!" said Fourier. "All you've managed to do is screw things up worse than they were!"

"Our intelligence reports say we could have between three and four hundred thousand out there by tomorrow," said General Washington.

"So, what *have* you done, Allen?" asked the president.

"Sir, we did have some problems; that's true. But we managed to kill the story coming out of major news outlets. That's where most people get their information. If those outlets do report on it, we'll pull their communications license. That was my threat," said Allen.

"It doesn't matter!" shouted Fourier. "Others are still reporting it. And after that fiasco you call a press conference, I'm sure they'll be more!"

"Mr. President," said General Washington, holding her small, thin frame rigid and formal, "we are contacting the Chief of the National Guard Bureau to bring in their units from Maryland and Virginia. They should be arriving shortly. We will be prepared for any unrest."

"Thank you, general," said Fourier. Then he turned back to Allen, his hands shaking with anger. "I want this cleaned up within the next hour. Do you understand me?" he shouted, stabbing his finger into Allen's chest. "I don't care what you have to do! Just get it done!"

"Yes, sir," said Allen, turning and walking with the general out of the Oval Office.

Moments later, Abigail, Fourier's wife barged into his office. "Jack! Jack! What's going on out on the mall?"

"What's wrong, dear?" Fourier asked, trying to emote some empathy.

Abigail came in and seated herself on one of two the moss-colored, Chippendale-style chairs placed alongside the two sofas that bordered the presidential seal in the center of the room. "This worries me. You shouldn't have to put up with protests like this. You're the president, for God's sake! They're supposed to do what you want them to, right?"

Fourier's face flashed with anger. "Abigail, I told you never to speak of *God* in this office! Do you understand? There is no room for such nonsense. I have a country to run and have a lot of pressure on me right now. I can't have my wife running off her mouth about what God has to say about things. God doesn't exist – never has, never will! It's just a matter of convincing the other poor bastards who go to church every Sunday. They should be giving their tithes to *me* instead of the damn church!"

"I thought you changed that last year?" she asked, tilting her head.

"I did. We now can tax the hell out of the churches. It's really boosted revenues for the country. Finally, we're getting our piece from those Right-wing, whack-jobs – those ignorant Bible thumpers. Hell, they'd be out there dancin' with their snakes, if we let them. But what we really need is their money. So, when you have trouble getting more money one way, you just have to try another. It's called creative taxation," he said, rather proudly.

"So, what are you going to do about the *low-lifes* out there on the Mall who are gathering to cause us trouble?" asked Abigail.

Fourier shook his head. "If Allen can't get it done, then I'm done with him. He said it would be handled within the hour. We'll just have to wait."

General Washington contacted the Secretary of Defense and within minutes a squadron of F54 fighter jets from Andrews Air Force Base flew in, only a hundred feet off the ground down the center of the Mall, having to bank sharply to fly around the Washington Monument. The crowds stood in fear as they watched their own military threaten them at near Mach speeds. After a few faux strafing runs, they dropped concussion bombs, which made the protestors scatter in all directions. It was enough time for the tanks and armored personnel carriers, helicoptered in from nearby Fort Belvoir, to arrive. It was reminiscent of the Soviet invasion of Hungary to suppress its revolt in 1956, as the tanks rolled down Constitution and Independence Avenues.

It was over quickly. The protest was crushed, but the revolution had only just begun.

*****

CH 20 THE SILVER DATA STICK

Sumner was groggy as he answered the phone at 2:35 in the morning. He was accustomed to getting late-night calls from lobbyists who were desperate for one more vote on their behalf. However, it had been years since that had been necessary. It seemed like forever that the president's People's Party had dominated national and even local elections. Close votes were rare, and most of the time those in the minority party, the Constitution Party, would not even show up on the floor of Congress to cast their vote. Outnumbered five to one, they knew it was pointless.

"Hello?" Sumner asked, gazing blurry-eyed at the white diodes blinking on his phone. The imaging portion was turned off for the sake of security, but voice calls were permitted. Still, Randy Marston, the Congressman's aide-de-camp, usually screened evening calls, or if very late, it was the Congressional answering service. However, calls this early in the morning, sometimes got through unfiltered – much to Sumner's annoyance.

"Congressman? This is Alan Gerrard, we talked not long ago about …"

"Listen, it's not even morning yet. Can't it wait until tomorrow?" Sumner said, stating it as more of a point of fact than a question.

"No, Congressman. It's about that oil refinery just outside of Baton Rouge that I mentioned when we were at your D.C. fund raiser. I told you what the Environmental Protection Agency was trying to do – their chicanery to find something bad they could use against the refinery – some safety violation or something big enough to shut them down."

"Uh, yeah. I guess so, but can't it wait until …"

"They've thrown all sorts of things against the plant to stop it, but they haven't been able to keep the oil from flowing – until tonight."

Sumner sat up and rubbed his eyes. "Go on," he urged, now more interested in the call.

"Over three hundred are confirmed dead at the refinery alone, and many more are presumed dead in the surrounding towns. Two thousand are injured and flooding hospitals. We haven't seen anything like it in this country – ever!"

"What? What happened?" asked Sumner, now wide awake and shaking.

"My life is in danger talking to you. I've almost been on the line too long now as it is. You'll need to meet me at the corner of 17th and M Streets. Be there in thirty minutes." The line went dead.

Sumner glanced over at his slumbering bride. Maria was a sound sleeper and wouldn't wake unless a fifty-car, diesel freight train roared through their bedroom. Rather than wake her, he left her a note and put it on her night's stand before quietly throwing on some clothes and hurrying downstairs to the garage. Since D.C. shut its Metro down after midnight and his car was in the shop, he took his wife's, hoping it had gas in it.

Twenty minutes later he pulled up along the curb at the designated intersection. By that time, the partiers had largely gone home to sleep off their revelry, and the sidewalks were quiet, except for the more numerous homeless persons moving about amongst the dumpsters and shadows of the commercial office buildings.

The clock continued to tick -- 3:05 a.m. turned into 3:15, which dragged on to 3:30. He was willing to wait another five minutes, when finally, Sumner saw an odd, shrouded figure emerge slowly from the closed Red Line Metro Station. The ember of a banned cigarette burned brightly before a puff of gray smoke wafted upward into the night's darkness in violation of municipal law. The man flicked the cigarette to one side and walked rapidly and deliberately toward his tryst mate.

"Congressman," whispered the man, extending his hand, "so glad you decided to come." The streetlight overhead was burned out, and the one next closest to the car was faint and sputtering. The sporadic reflection of the light off the man's face made it difficult to see it clearly. He wore a dark jacket and pants, probably gray, but Sumner wasn't sure. "Let's go someplace where the street cams aren't zooming in on us as we speak," the man said, pointing down the street to some assumed, but unseen and unwanted chaperone watching their every move.

They walked a short distance before turning down an alley lit by a single overhead bulb that also blinked on and off intermittently as if controlled by the same invisible, spasmodic hand on a light switch. Sumner was uneasy and now wished he'd brought his .45 cal. Colt pistol. Even though all guns were still constitutionally permitted, D.C. had made ownership virtually impossible by imposing a district tax of 18,500 dollars to purchase of a gun license. Combined with a six-month training class and a three-year wait for the background check, gun ownership had largely become non-existent – except for the criminals.

"I checked the news channels before I left the house. There's no word of any disaster anywhere. Are you sure about this?" asked Sumner.

The stranger grabbed Sumner by the arm and pushed him back into a dark recess where no light could find them. Fear shot through every pore in Sumner's body. "What are you doing?" asked Sumner with an air of panic.

"Keep your voice down!" whispered the man in a controlled, but angst-ridden voice. The stranger held up his PCD, which projected a holographic image just above its large, pixilated colored screen. The words from an AP report floated in the air front of them:

Disturbance Near Oil Refinery in Louisiana.

Sumner began reading about the shock wave felt throughout Baton Rouge and New Orleans, only sixty miles away.

> *... Residents called local fire and police complaining about a tremor that shook the capital early this morning. First indications were that it was not caused by any seismic activity, as no earthquakes were recorded in North America by the U.S. Geological Survey Group.*

Then the screen went blank. Seconds later the moniker **404** appeared, indicating the website was no longer available.

"I knew they'd pull it. I wanted you to see it before they deleted it," said the man.

It was dark, but the man kept his coat collar pulled up tightly around his face to shield it from the street cameras that were continually scanning the streets and even many alleyways, monitoring activity. There were over ten thousand cameras within the district's borders – an area a little over eight square miles in size.

"Tell me what happened," inquired Sumner. "What do you know?"

"As I told you before, the EPA sent their goons in to sabotage the operation. Most were twenty-somethings that didn't know a coker from a cracker in a plant. All they cared about was creating some chaos so the EPA could declare the plant unsafe and force it to be shut down. We think the thugs only intended to cause the plant to release pollutants into the air - as much as possible – to violate the department's edicts. Better yet, they may have hoped for some massive, uncontrolled oil spill. But obviously, something went terribly wrong. Most people at the plant were killed, so I don't have much good information. However, I did get these computer logs emailed to me that show User Names and instructions sent from computers that run the alky and scrubber units. I think this is what you need."

The man handed Sumner a small, silver data stick.

Sumner took it and looked at it curiously. "I'll take a look. But if it's as bad as you say, they won't be able to cover it up," said Sumner.

"They will. The White House lights were on when I walked past there tonight. They're working overtime on something."

At that moment, they heard a car door open and close at the end of the alley and the sound of footsteps racing toward them.

"We have to go," said the man urgently, his dark brown eyes opened wide and showing alarm.

The first shadowy image rounded the corner of the building, stumbling over an old, rusty downspout that had broken off and lay in the middle of the ally. The second figure nearly fell over the first, rolling out farther into the narrow opening to avoid the collision.

Realizing they could be trapped, the mystery man pushed against a peeling green door next to them, but it was locked. He tried to force the handle, but it didn't budge. "Push on it again!" shouted Sumner, fear closing in on him.

Suppressed muzzle fire sprayed bullets everywhere, bouncing off the brick walls, waste containers, and fire escapes. Two hit the Congressman and a third hit the man in the dark jacket.

"Sh*t!" cried Sumner, "I'm hit!"

"Come on," growled the man, pushing two steel points into the lock and raking them back and forth.

The lock popped, and the door flung inward, crashing against the wall to the right side. Grabbing Sumner by his coat lapels, he pulled him through the opening before slamming the green door and throwing the deadbolt lock. "Get down!" yelled the man, pushing the Congressman's head down to the floor and bruising his nose.

They heard the sound of footsteps run up to the door outside. Then, there was a horrific sound of machine-gun fire as bullets shredded the doorway, sending shards of green splinters over their heads. Next came the banging of a rifle butt against the door's lock, trying to break through.

"We have to get out of here," said the man, pulling on Sumner to get up.

Sumner clutched his abdomen with his right hand. Blood poured freely through his white cotton shirt, soaking it down to his black, alligator belt. Dazed, he pushed himself up and followed his informant friend down a hall lined with black-framed, motivational posters and into a small office. It looked like a scene out of a 1950s mobster movie, with a metal desk and filing cabinets as the most prominent pieces of furniture in the room. To the side stood a series of wood-laminated bookshelves stacked with business papers, mostly haphazard and chaotically arranged on the ledges.

Sumner collapsed into the metal chair, covered with green vinyl and foam, while the man opened his PCD and dialed 911.

"Yes, I'd like to report a strange noise coming from the alley next to my business. I'm working late tonight, and it sounds like a couple of drunks are in a fight outside ... Yes, I'm at 2411 M Street. Yes, thank you." He hung up the line.

Down the hall, they could hear the assailants continuing to breakdown the door, taking it apart plank by plank. But it wasn't long before there was another sound – that of sirens getting louder. That's when the banging stopped.

"The cops will find us in here," said Sumner, wincing in pain.

"No, I gave them the address of the building across the street. It was enough to scare away the guys shooting at us," answered the man, looking over at the wounded Congressman. "How are you doing? You look pretty bad. I'd better call an ambulance."

"I'm okay. I'll be fine," said Sumner, growing feint.

"You're losing a lot of blood," said the man, becoming increasingly alarmed. "I'd better call an ambulance. But just remember, you have to guard that data stick. It's got all of the ..."

Sumner's head was spinning. He could feel the data stick slipping from his clutched fingers. And, as the man continue to talk, his eyesight went gray and then faded to darkness. Then, there was nothing.

*****

165

CH 21 THE TAX MAN COMETH

As time went on, Angel Ratner became more and more engrossed in the Disone Affair, as it was becoming known. To her it meant career success or failure. It had all started within her department and the focus was on her. It was attention she did not want.

She knew her higher-ups felt this was fast becoming a litmus test -- one at a critical time in the Administration's tenure, if not the nation's history. She too viewed it as a Tiananmen Square event, as the Chinese had faced in 1989. In that year there had been an uprising in China – the result of protests after the death of Hu Yaobang, a Communist Party reformer who wanted to change the communist system. Millions gathered in Tiananmen Square in Beijing asking for freedoms previously unheard of in China, but freedoms enjoyed by Americans and guaranteed by their U.S. Constitution. However, Deng Xiaoping, the premier of the country, had other ideas. In a brutal show of force, he sent over three hundred thousand troops into the center of the city to quash the demonstrations. Hundreds were killed; a few thousand were injured. He succeeded in crushing the protests and arresting the "anarchists." Most were never heard from again. The government had prevailed, and the young flame of freedom had been quickly extinguished. It was the perfect outcome as far as Ratner was concerned, and one she wished she could emulate to rid herself of the albatross that was suspended around her own neck.

Like Deng, she would win – regardless of the cost and the sacrifice. It was all worth it to further the cause, which was, of course, herself and her own career. This was something that had resonated with her ever since she'd been a sophomore in college when an English literature professor had told the class, "It is the ends that are important. Whatever is necessary should be done to achieve your goal, if worthy either for you or for those of intellect who know what's best for all others." He had said that "one just had to remake or mold one's reasoning to make it appeal to those less educated or blind. Ideally, one's ideas should sound grand and altruistic. If framed properly, one can make a position so attractive that people will follow it, and its proponent, anywhere. When one understands that the goal is just and right, there is *nothing* that can be done that is illegal, immoral or unjust if its sole purpose is to achieve that end," said the professor. "Simply put by Machiavelli in 1512: The ends justify the means."

So to Ratner, all games were simple. They were *all* zero sum. One person won and one person lost. That was it. There was no room for compromise – ever. She had the answers, and for others not to see that – well, they were incompetent fools. For her there could be only one outcome – her outcome -- and she was not about to lose – ever.

"Bailey, how are you?" asked Ratner, rocking back in her pin-cushioned, red leather chair. "Listen, remember when we talked last week about the Disones? Well, I need you to make sure that they are making good on the taxes they owe you over there at the IRS. I have some information that may suggest that an audit of their financial records and tax returns is in order. Would you be able to look into that for me?"

The Secretary of Taxation, Bailey Griffin, had been in the Illinois state house when Fourier and his lieutenant governor, Preston Brooks, had ruled the state. At then Governor Fourier's request, Griffin had attended the Governor's Conference in Boston when it had been held there over twenty years earlier. It was in Boston where Griffin got to know Fourier, and they became good friends – a friendship that lasted into the governor's presidential campaign and culminated in his winning the top spot. Griffin had worked tirelessly to get his mentor elected, and in return he was rewarded with a plum job running the IRS, soon after renamed the Department of Taxation Compliance. He was nominated to the new Cabinet-level post of secretary even though he had neither formal education in accounting or taxation, nor any related experience. He was merely a political hack sent to do the president's bidding and prey on anyone the president listed on his Enemies List.

"Angel. You understand that it is my responsibility as secretary to make sure that each citizen pays their fair share of taxes to this country," he answered, laughing mockingly. "But, sure, I'll look into it for you." But his language was also intended as 'cover-your-ass talk,' just in case the call was being monitored. They had been warned to use b-crat speak to ensure that if any tapes surfaced of their conversations, that they would not be directly incriminating. It was important to keep the wall as high as they could make it between the tax department and all other departments, including and most importantly, the White House.

Two words were the watchwords of the Fourier Administration – *Plausible Deniability*. Fourier always wanted to be able to say he knew nothing about whatever problem surfaced. It was what he joked was his *Teflon maneuver* – making sure nothing stuck to him. And that went for just about everything that went wrong. Regardless of what happened, nothing was to be traceable back to the White House –nothing.

"I do understand, Bailey. That's why I called you. I knew you would make sure this was handled correctly. Thanks," answered Ratner.

"Of course," Griffin answered, the warmth in his voice suggesting there was more than just a business conversation taking place. "For you, Angel, it's never a problem. You know that."

Within two days, a certified electronic message came to the Disones' home computer. It was addressed to:

> *Dr. and Mrs. Patrick Disone*
> *500 Patrick Boulevard*
> *Needham, MA 02494*

Patrick never saw the message, but Shea found it in the certified urgent file as she was reviewing her messages that day. Meghan was off, and she began going through the mail to get a head start on the day's workload.

Shea tapped on the envelope, and it jumped off the screen, opening itself in mid-air and reading itself in a harsh, gruff tone through the audio outputs on her computer. The sound was so loud and shrill, as tax letters often were, that she had to cover her ears to keep them from ringing.

> *Dear Taxpayer,* said the voice, loudly.
>
> *Based on the review of your 2043 1040 tax return, we have determined that a more thorough assessment of your tax submission is in order. Therefore, our Tax Compliance Agent (TCA) cited below will be contacting you within the next thirty (30) days to schedule a meeting to discuss certain problems in your submission. You may have your accountant or legal counsel present at the time: however, this is merely a preliminary formality to clarify some of the items you have presented in your return.*
>
> *It is important that you gather your documentary evidence supporting the deductions you claimed on the return and have them available for the TCA when he or she arrives. Currently, we have openings for such a meeting with (fill in name) Ms. Spencer between the dates of (fill in dates) October 2 at (fill in times) 3:30 p.m. You are expected to attend. There will be no exceptions allowed. Please contact our office at 555-989-3922 if you have any*

questions. This is not an optional meeting. You are required to be present at this meeting.

Please have a nice day!

Very sincerely,
Your humble servant

B.T. Griffin III

Bailey T. Griffin, III
Secretary

Of course, it was stamped with his signature to be as impersonal as possible. Likewise, the errors in the letter – leaving in the prompts for names, dates and times – was also not uncommon.

Shea had gotten letters from the IRS as everyone eventually did, but not like this one. Usually, she would send them off to her accountant to be handled. However, for this one, she called him directly.

"Andy, it's Shea. How are you?" she asked. They spent a moment exchanging pleasantries before she got down to the matter at hand. "So, what do you think about this letter after what we're going through with the Department of Technology Assessment? It's a little too coincidental. Don't you think?"

"Oh," was his answer, revealing an element of surprise. "Shea, you'll need to send that to me so I can read it and study what it's implying. Let me do that before we move forward, okay? There have been a lot of these types of letters going out lately. It's troubling, actually. But … again, let me take a look."

It was later that day when the accountant sent her a rather cold, detached form-letter message, informing her that neither he nor his firm was going to be able to represent them at the hearing. In part, it read:

Dr. and Ms. Disone,

I regret to inform you that we will be unable to represent you and your husband at the department meeting cited in your letter. Due to special circumstances and the uniqueness of your case, we feel it is best if we recuse ourselves at this time. We do, however, wish you the best of luck.

Andersen Evans

Buckley, Evans & Baker, CPA's

Even Emery, their attorney, was unable or unwilling to help, citing a conflict of interest of some sort. It made no sense to either Shea or Patrick, but by the time October arrived, they had no choice but to show up by themselves to see what awaited them.

***

On October 2, Patrick and Shea arrived at the hearing at 3:30 at IRS headquarters in Washington, D.C. carrying several 5,000-terabyte storage devices that contained the thousands of documents demanded by the taxing authority. Alone, the two went into the small, cramped interview room and waited. The building was relatively new, with a multi-billion dollar, high-tech level of electronic sophistication – from the 4-D, holographic projectors in every room, to the auditorium-sized 360-degree video conferencing capability. Considered more minacious than the DTA, few messed with the IRS, and if one did make that mistake, it could be a lifetime, or at least several generations, before the claws of the agency would release its throat-hold on those accused of being scofflaws.

The Disones had made such a mistake.

Two and a half hours later at six o'clock, the door to the interview room opened and a young woman walked in. She was carrying neither a briefcase nor a stack of papers. She was short and stocky, with straight-black hair and bright, pink-framed, plastic glasses. Pursing her lips, she began to speak in a soft-spoken voice, almost apologetic in tone and tenor. At the same time, it seemed like a speech she had made hundreds of times before. There was little expression in her face and none in her monotone voice.

"Mr. and Mrs. Disone? I'm Patrice Stewart," she said, not caring that she had mistakenly addressed Patrick as Mr. rather than Dr. "I am afraid that your TCA has been detained and will not be able to meet with you today. You will have to come back tomorrow at the same time to meet with him," she said. There was no attempt at an apology, and they were given no other options. Then, without waiting for a reply or reaction, she simply walked out of the room.

"What?" said Shea, angered by the delay and the rescheduling. Her face grew red, but Patrick put his hand on her arm to calm her.

"I see," Patrick said, interjecting calmly. "So, when will the meeting take place, then?"

"We don't know," the woman said coldly.

"You don't know?" asked Shea. "So, we flew all the way from Boston for this mandatory meeting at 3:30 and now you don't know when it might be?"

"We don't know," repeated the woman. "You'll just have to come back tomorrow."

"Tomorrow, then? At, what, 3:30?" asked Patrick, keeping his reserve. "Is that what you're saying? Is there a reason the agent can't see us today?"

"I'm sorry. I don't have that information. All I know is that he's not available. You'll have to return tomorrow." And without another word, she turned on her heels and walked out the door.

Shea looked at Patrick, but he shook his head, chiding her. "Don't Shea. You'll only make things worse."

She knew he was right, but she really wanted to go-off on someone at that moment. Instead, she took a deep breath and looked up at the small black disc of a camera in the corner of the room that was recording every word and image. "Okay. We'll just come back tomorrow, then. I'm *sure* we'll get this straightened out and we can all go home." Now she was hamming it up for a viewership she knew she would never see.

However, the next day the same young woman told them the same thing, and then the same the following day. Finally, on the fourth day, an older man walked slowly into the interview room about an hour and a half late and set his brown, scuffed briefcase down on the table. He offered no apologies for being late or for postponing the meeting for four days. The man was tall and lanky. His ill-fitting, navy suit was wrinkled from the straight, un-cuffed pant bottoms to the tips of the suit jacket. Shea wondered how long it had been since he'd had it dry-cleaned, and how many times he'd worn his $10 white shirt before he would wash it again.

The man opened his thin satchel and pulled out several, thin manila-colored folders, placing them on the table beside him. It was an almost archeological scene to Shea and Patrick, who had forever dealt with data sticks and e-transmissions of images and information. Manila folders were as old as buggy whips to them, and to think the government still used such things was … well … mind-boggling.

"I'm Agent Toiken," the man said, not even looking up at them. "I'll be looking at your documents today." He then opened a folder and flipped a few pages inside. "I see that this review is supposed to be for 2044 through 2046; is that correct?"

"Uh, no. The letter said it was for 2043," said Patrick, offering his simple correction.

"No. My audit order is for 2044, 2045 and 2046, and that's what I'll be looking at. So, I will be needing every invoice, receipt, purchase order, shipping bill of lading, canceled check, bank statement, financial statement, sales order, sales quote, and any other document that will support your business tax filings. I presume you brought everything?"

The auditor knew full well the review letter had said 2043 and that this was a setup as an ambush. If the citizens were unable to provide the information requested, in the time requested, they would get put on the Enemies List -- and that was the only point. He'd been ordered to do this before – it was not the first time, and he had always carried out his mission with skill and perseverance. He had never failed.

The amount of information he had requested was mammoth for one year, let alone three. Even on portable storage drives, it would take time to compile and download. To ensure the Disones would not be able to comply, he was told to change the audit period on them, so even if they had brought the required information, they would have the wrong year.

This time Patrick's face grew stern while Shea's demeanor was now beyond anger. To relieve the pressure mounting inside, she stood up and paced behind her chair.

Now it was Patrick's turn to explode. He too started to rise from the table.

"I'm sorry, but you'll both have to be seated for this meeting," said the pencil-necked man.

At that moment, Shea looked as if she would strangle that auditor's skinny little neck when Patrick again gave her the look for restraint.

She sat back down in her chair, and more calmly she said, "I … I don't understand. It's highly unusual to request all of those documents when you haven't even begun your audit. This was supposed to be a preliminary interview, and it was clear in this electronic message that the year to be audited was 2043." She held up her personal electronic assistant, showing a copy of the message.

The agent didn't bother looking at it. "You obviously altered the document. That was not the one sent. I have the original right here." He showed her his device, which revealed the same document, except the dates were 2044, 2045 and 2046.

"That's not right," said Shea. "That's not what we received."

"My records show that you were sent this copy many weeks ago."

"No, we weren't," said Patrick, defensively.

This time the agent did look up, but he was not showing an expression of empathy or understanding. In fact, it was one of contempt. "I could have you both arrested right here and now," he threatened.

Shea reacted with shock. "What?"

"Yes, I could have you thrown in prison for falsifying a government document. That's a felony you know."

"But we didn't change anything! This is what we got from your department!" shouted Shea, the anger returning.

"Are you calling me a liar?" asked the man, holding all the cards in the game.

Shea bit the inside of her cheek to prevent herself from saying something more she would have regretted.

"I thought not," said the agent. Then he closed the file and folded his hands in front of him on the table. "Why is it that people like *you* think you can skate by in life? Do you really think that the IRS would go to all this trouble not to turn over every rock in your tax history? No, Mr. and Ms. Disone, not only are we going to look at everything for 2044 through 2046, I'm going to order expanding the scope of the audit to include the previous five years – that is, from 2039 through 2043" His tone was imperious and uncompromising.

"You can't do that!" said Shea, letting her emotions flow more freely. "You can't just pick a whole bunch of other years without cause. Plus, you can't go back more than three years! It's the law,"

The agent smiled insincerely. "You have shown obstruction to my efforts here today. Your unwillingness to comply gives me no other choice but to expand our audit," he responded.

"Obstruction?" asked Patrick. "We haven't done anything!"

"Your resistance and uncooperative nature in these proceedings is clear. You've raised your voice as well, showing disrespect for my position and what I, as a servant of the public, have been charged with doing."

"What have we done that's uncooperative?" Shea asked, listening to the ridiculous accusations. "We have not refused to comply at all!"

"It's pretty obvious. You were demanding that we reduce the size of our audit scope, which means you must be trying to hide something. It's a clear case. And, if you give me any more grief, I may have to have the Department of Justice step in and detain you until we get the information it appears you are unwilling to produce."

"We're not unwilling!" said Patrick excitedly. "You changed the dates of the review without notifying us. You're just being a horse's ass!" It was a rare explosion out of Patrick, but he could hold it in no longer.

The agent got on his PCD. "Guard, please come in right away. I have two belligerents in review room 14B who are threatening me. We need to have them locked up until we can get the situation under control."

Patrick could only look over at Shea in utter amazement. He didn't dare say another thing for fear the charges would be upped to something like attempted murder or worse.

Moments later, both Patrick and Shea were cuffed and hauled away, put into separate gray, cinderblock prison cells in different sections of the building. Running out of cell space for criminals, the federal government had constructed detention rooms specifically for the IRS to house those who violated tax laws. It was the second time in as many months for Patrick, and it didn't take a third time for him to understand that he had become a marked man. Now, Shea had joined him on post office walls where the *Enemies List* was usually mounted, right next to the *Top Ten Most Wanted* criminal mug shots.

*****

CH 22 EDICTS FROM 1600 PENN AVE

Change was coming fast and furious, and it was all Congress could do to record the blizzard of Executive Orders being issued by the white mansion at 1600 Pennsylvania Avenue. The guise of Congress passing laws and sending them to the White House for signature was becoming an extinct practice. Congress and the Supreme Court were quickly being pushed to the sidelines and being made increasingly irrelevant. Like many Articles in the Constitution, the first three – those pertaining to separate but equal branches of government -- were interpreted differently by the president than had any other since George Washington. To Fourier, the Constitution intended three equal branches, but that the Executive Branch should, by necessity, be the *first* among equals.

Besides the health- and food-related orders, Fourier unleashed a barrage of others. Most devastating to the economy was his new 20 percent VAT, or value added tax, which taxed goods at every stage of production through to their sale to consumers. It had been commonplace in Europe for nearly a century, and was spreading quickly to other economies desperate to tap more revenue out of their patrons. In addition, the president implemented a tax on high-end items, a luxury tax of 50 percent. As a result, a typical car that cost 35,000 dollars to build and was previously priced at 76,900 to customers, now had a price tag of 174,600. All cars were now considered luxuries, as the average person was not able to buy a new car. As a result of the tax, car sales dropped to almost nothing, and car manufacturers began going out of business – first Ford Motor, then Chrysler. General Motors, which was still under government control and protection after its second bail-out several years earlier, was still operating even though they were hemorrhaging money every year, with losses in the billions.

Yet, that wasn't the end of the VAT drama. The Department of the Treasury moved quickly to re-interpret the president's order and implement the *coup de grâce* of all taxes – a progressive VAT. It was based on the idea that progressive taxes were the best way to redistribute wealth – taking it from those who had it and giving it to those who didn't. Progressive VAT charged people a national sales tax based on their wealth. Everyone was required to submit a personal financial statement to the IRS with their tax forms, telling what they were worth. The IRS issued federal Identification cards designated a code for each person or family. Each was placed into to one of ten different wealth categories. The wealthiest, in the top category Group One, had to pay the highest sales tax – 75 percent of the value of the item purchased. This rate was in addition to state and local sales taxes that had to be paid on purchases. Therefore, if the item purchased were 1,000 dollars, the total, including the Group One VAT, was 1,750 or perhaps 1,850, including the state and local encumbrances. If a person did not present a card, they were automatically charged the highest rate. Those in the Groups Four through Seven paid almost no tax, and those at the bottom, in Groups Eight through Ten, actually got discounts on their purchases. As a result, someone in Group Ten could buy an item priced at 1,000 dollars and pay no more than 250. It was a quintessential Marxian program, and it was the crown jewel of the Fourier Administration's accomplishments during its first term.

Many producers packed up their bags and left the country, and in the end, the tax was a disaster. It brought in very little tax revenue, as those who had the means to purchase things, didn't. Within months, manufacturers shut down and distributors stopped stocking products, as inventories grew without being sold – sitting on shelves collecting dust. Eventually, as these things were sold, there were no producers left to offer any replacements. Thus, the shelves went from being jammed with unsold goods to an emptiness that presented only the picturesque shelving paper that had been used to wrap them – little more. In malls across the country where stores had once carried everything from diapers to tires, most shops were closed. And where stores were open, the only things available for purchase were a few expired packs of batteries and some old magazines.

But there was a far bigger target of the Administration than diapers and toilet paper. They believed it was time to dismantle the fossil fuel industry once and for all. President Fourier had fought the oil companies for years, trying different ways to have Congress pass laws making it difficult for them to do business. However, at every turn, these businessmen found ways around these laws and regulations. Supported by the vast majority of Americans, the refineries kept pumping out diesel and gasoline for automobiles. Electric cars were unreliable and still prone to fires. Autos using liquid natural gas were heavily subsidized by the government. However, as they were produced largely by GovCo's, they were of poor quality and subject to frequent recalls.

The sustained popularity of fossil fuel automobiles and the lack of an appealing, profitable alternative galled the president. He finally the EPA to find ways to put Big Oil out of business. Together, they came up with several strategies. First, they imposed regulations on gas stations so strict that it forced most to close. Second, they increased the federal tax on all gasoline, increasing the dollar price of gas from 5.50 per gallon to over 15.50 in many areas. Next, they added a national mileage tax to toll drivers based on the miles they drove. However, this only applied to fossil fuel automobiles. And lastly, they issued new emission standards so low that no fossil fuel engine then manufactured could meet them – until the SECE engine, that is. It hadn't taken long for news of the SECE's ultra-low-emissions to travel across town from the DTA to the White House, and within a month, new orders were issued specifically banning that engine from use within the United States. All the Administration would say was that certain 'irregularities' in the test data made the use of the SECE engine a *danger* to the public. When Patrick had pressed the DTA on the nature of the irregularities they found, they were told the data was 'classified.'

Coincidentally, at the same time, Congress voted to grant three billion dollars to a relatively new electric car company in the U.S. called *Ampitup*. It was owned by friends of the president's, as well as donors to the campaigns of the House Speaker and Majority Leader of the Senate – all from the People's Party. The spokeswoman for the company was careful with her answers to journalists' questions on the subject, saying that it was just fortunate that the company had received such monies at this time. However, rumors abounded that the company would still have to file bankruptcy within the next nine months. Conveniently, the grant bill also offered the shareholders immunity from the default if such an event took place. And it did. All the money was lost.

Hearings were held with big business executives moaning to Congress about the terrible impact the directives – particularly the VAT taxes -- were having on their businesses. They were dying, yet no heed was made by the Administration. It wasn't until big labor union jobs were threatened and thousands of voting members risked losing their jobs that the president acted – issuing another Executive Order fix the mess he'd already created. This one barred companies from lowering the pay of their workers or cutting jobs, citing that shareholder dividends should be cut instead. However, that action only the hole deeper – accelerating the number of companies unable to keep the same level of staff and pay, while sales dropped. There was nothing to pay for the expenses of the business, and most filed bankruptcy. As of then, there were no laws on the books that forbade that.

In years gone by, a dip in America's economy would have sent reverberations around the globe. But this was no longer true. The world had become independent of the U.S., and the drop in productivity was merely a

178

inconvenience for most foreign banks and economies. According to the newly created Department of Facts and Statistics, a centralized propaganda arm of the Executive Branch, the gross domestic production (GDP) number stood at 5.4 percent; unemployment (U6 number) at 2.3 percent; and inflation (CPI) at 3.4 percent. All were lies. The real numbers, as presented by the independent Foundation for the Accuracy of Economic Statistics or FAES, showed the GDP at a *minus* 4.1 percent; unemployment U6 at 21.8 percent; and inflation (GDPD) hovering close to 15.9 percent.

Since the other orders had failed miserably, the White House sought to issue more to fix the problem.

NEW EXECUTIVE ORDER TARGETS PROFITS

(UPA wire) Washington, D.C.: The White House issues Executive Order EO 16351, the fifty-third of President Fourier's Administration, which targets businesses that make more than $1 million in profits and labels them as un-patriotic. Our president issued the new tax orders unilaterally without Congressional approval. These orders impose a 100% tax on all profits in excess of the $1 million threshold. Although phased-in over three years, the order will instate the tax rate on profits below that level after the three years, taxing 100% of profits over $750,000 and then $500,000 during the following three years.

House Minority Leader, Milford Rose, expressed outrage, as he claimed only the House of Representatives is empowered by the Constitution to propose tax bills.

White House Chief of Staff, Trevor Allen, defended the president's order, stating that "The wealthy of this country have gotten away without paying their fair share for too long. We, the rest of America, built this country. We made it possible for them to succeed and become wealthy. They owe that to the poor of this great nation."

When asked why special exceptions were made for certain large corporations and union leaders, Allen said, "Because they didn't succeed on the backs of the middle class. The unions are the middle class, and certain companies and their executives exempted from the new 100% tax rate have demonstrated a special commitment to America. They have provided their goods and services to this country through thick and thin – through good times and bad. It is the least we can do to offer them an exemption. They have already paid their fair share."

The wire went on to extol the virtues of other EO's that had been issued during the previous months, ignoring the utter failure of all of them. It concluded its polemic by stating:

> *According to the Administration, these measures will successfully redistribute the wealth that would otherwise go to the already wealthy Americans and force companies to pay their workers more. It is the middle class that needs the money. Therefore, the money will go to either the middle class work force or to the government, which will ensure that it is funneled back to those in our society who need it most.*

Thus, while the American economy kept falling, other nations were more than willing and able to fill the void. The New People's Dynasty of China, the Federation of Russia, and the Southern Union of Islamic States, together with Iran, all nuclear superpowers, began vying for the top spot. Europe was no longer a modern, industrialized region. Long fractured back into its component parts, the once-promising European Union had crashed from its own debt burdens. The Middle East War had resulted in the rise of two nouveau-Persian empires – the Sunni Union, dominated by Saudi Arabia, and the more radical Shiite Islamic Republic of Iran, which also included Lebanon, Syria, and Iraq. Still hanging on by a thread was Israel -- alone, isolated and surrounded by nuclear enemies on all fronts. And while the UN and the world watched and did nothing to intercede during the Middle East War, China struck quickly, subsuming Japan, Taiwan, Korea, Vietnam, Laos, Cambodia, the Philippines, Indonesia and Malaysia under its rule. These countries, that had once constituted independent cultures within Southeast Asia, were all annexed by China. As for the rest of the world, it continued to watch and do nothing.

*****

CH 23 THE DEBATE

During the months following the initial meeting, Agent Toiken stepped up the harassment. And as a result, the Disones had to spend every minute of every day working with their staff and accountants to meet the document demands of the IRS. The list was long, and it intentionally got longer. Hours were spent searching through years of files and meticulously explaining every invoice paid and every deduction taken on all of their tax filings going back to 2039. Soon, the company ground to a halt, and that was exactly what Toiken and his bosses, Griffin and Ratner, had intended.

"And why was *this* purchase made?" said Toiken, pushing an invoice for three cases of coffee across the table toward Shea.

Shea rolled her eyes. After five hours of this type of questioning, she had taken enough abuse. She had hired another outside accounting firm to help with the struggle, but at eight hundred dollars per hour, it was draining them. So, Patrick and she took turns sitting through the inquisitions, suffering through them hour by hour.

"Really? Coffee?" she asked, her distain showing through.

"Three cases seems extreme for a company like this," said Toiken, harshly.

"We have over one hundred fifty employees!"

"Certainly it's a luxury you indulge your employees with, I guess," asked the agent. "But then again, you're a rich company, so you can do that."

"A lot of people drink coffee," Shea answered. "You do! You have coffee machines all over the place here."

"You just don't know how to run a business," Toiken said sarcastically.

"Then why do *you* have coffee?" she asked

"We aren't a business, ma'am. We're the government," he answered, coldly.

Shea could tell he was enjoying this. In many ways, he was a sadist, and his occupation fit his need to inflict pain on others. She figured he must have been powerless in his life outside of work; so, he took advantage of his position within the IRS to make life miserable for others.

It was then that Shea snapped. "I suppose you're right," Shea said. "But maybe you can tell me this? Where do you get the money for *your* coffee?"

"What do you mean? It's in our budget."

"Where you do get it for your budget?"

He looked at her blankly.

"You get it from me!" she blurted out. "That's where! *I* paid for your coffee!"

"No you didn't," he retorted, "'cause you don't pay your fair share!" Now it was the agent who raised his voice. "You rich bitches – you think you own us, don't you!"

"All I own is my business," she said. "And a lot of people earn a paycheck because of my husband and me. And they pay taxes on that too – for your coffee! So, what have you done lately to create a livelihood for other people?"

"Ma'am, you are in business to pay taxes – pure and simple. That is the only moral reason the government allows you to be in business at all. Profit is *evil*. It is self-centered and egotistical. You people in business are only looking out for yourselves. You don't give a damn about anyone else! You don't care about your community, your state or your country. Why do you think everyone believes that you capitalists are a bunch of greedy bastards? Hell, even our president says so."

"Why would anyone risk everything they have to start a business, then? Just to pay taxes for your benefit?"

"To help the rest of society. That's why!" said Toiken. His sense of importance was growing by the minute.

"And if I succeed, and all I get from it is paying for everyone else, you're saying I should get nothing out of it?"

"The satisfaction of knowing that you're helping your fellow man. You have to think of other people; not yourself!"

"I do that by giving fifteen percent of my earnings to the charities of my choosing; not by paying it in taxes to the government," she said, countering his argument. "I want to decide who gets my money and for what cause – not the government."

"But the government can make much better decisions about how to use that money than you can. You only see a miniscule picture of things – the proverbial leaves on the trees. Like your mind, you only see small things. On the other hand, *we* see the forest. We are able to see the grand scheme and what is needed for all of society to prosper."

"Really?" said Shea, skeptically. "Is that why all the credit agencies have downgraded U.S. debt to junk status? The government has wasted so much money for so long that few countries in the world will even accept it. We continue to spend billions a year on what you call charity -- to people capable of working, but who are too lazy to find a job or try to keep one after they get it. Other untold billions are scammed by people playing the system to make money. So, in the end, we've got sixty-five percent of the population sitting on their asses at home watching their 4-D movies and getting drugged up in their TV rooms, while the rest of us work *our* asses off to support them. After eighty years, and you still haven't won Johnson's War on Poverty?"

"We can't win because *you* people are stealing all the money out of the system! If you'd pay a decent wage, maybe there would be jobs and people would work!"

"First of all, I pay very good wages. That's why people stay with me. But, let's assume I pay people more, then the cost of my products goes up. If the costs go up, my prices go up. If my prices go up, fewer people can buy them. If fewer people buy them, I produce less. If I produce less, I lay off people. So, thank you very much, you've just made unemployment in this country worse!"

Toiken continued his assault. "Don't raise your prices then. Eat the cost."

"We don't make much money as it is. If I don't raise my price to cover the higher cost, I'll either go bankrupt or won't make enough to reinvest in the business. We take very little out of the company. What we make generally goes back into the company to expand and build the business, and yes, employ more people. But let's say I even do all that, and I'm just breaking even. What will happen to my business?" she asked him.

"Nothing. You'd just make a lot less. You wouldn't be able to buy that new Rolls Royce, maybe," he said acerbically.

"Wrong!" Shea said sternly. "My competitors would reinvest their profits in research and development and come up with better engines. They would pass us by, and we wouldn't be able to sell anything anymore."

"They'd be in the same boat you are. They'd breakeven too. We'd make sure all of you just broke even."

"No, they'd be competitors in other countries who wouldn't be fettered with the massive regulation and taxes I am. They'd have money to reinvest."

"So, you'd probably send your jobs overseas and pay those people pennies to do crappy jobs while they live in poverty and squalor? That's what you'd do, like everyone else. Is that moral?"

"Yes, because it's more than just pennies to them. Those *crappy* jobs you're referring to are a godsend to those families who would otherwise be begging in the dirty streets of their capitals or dying of starvation. It allows them to put a roof over their family's heads and buy food from the local market. Their cost of living is much lower and, of course, so too is the standard of living. But those wages pull those people out of poverty – *real* poverty. That's something most here in this country can't understand. To them, poverty is having their favorite TV show pulled from their SAT TV channel, or having to actually cook a few meals instead of getting fast food. Sure there are those in need here, but they can be served by the churches and charities, if the government would let them."

"So, you're saying that stealing jobs from people here in this country is a good thing?" asked Toiken, not budging from his position.

"If your government won't create an environment here that makes people want to setup a business and employ people, then yes; I'll take my business and employ workers overseas."

"That's why we need tariffs on overseas products, missy! That would stop you from screwing over the American worker. A thirty percent tariff on everything would stop that! It would save jobs here and strengthen our unions."

Shea smiled. "Okay, you're just going to levy a thirty percent tax on *everyone*, then. So what does that do to the price of, say, a PCD? Most are manufactured overseas, right?"

"Yes. But that's the problem. They should be made here in the USA!"

"So, let's say a worker in Burma is paid fifteen dollars in labor to make a PCD. With materials and shipping, the manufacturer's cost to sell it in America is one hundred. With your tariff, that's one hundred thirty in costs. By the time it gets to the retail store, its price to the customer is two-thirty."

"That's right," said Toiken. "One of your greedy capitalist friends sells it and pockets the one hundred dollars. That's wrong!"

"Really? No, that's not what happens. The PCD that's shipped from China has to be received at a dock, transported to a central warehouse where its stored until it's needed. That costs money. From there it's re-shipped to a retail store that needs that item to sell, which requires gas, truck maintenance, tolls, driver wages, etc. Government paperwork and forms must be filled out by truckers and transport agents and submitted all along the way – taking time and money. The PCD is then unloaded from a pallet, unwrapped and placed on the shelf for sale at the store. The store has to borrow money from the bank to pay for that PCD until it gets it back when it sells it to a customer. That's interest cost. The longer it sits, the higher the cost. If it doesn't sell, the company has to discount it until it does. But then, the store has to pay its employees at the store, plus the rent on the building, plus the utilities, plus bags and supplies, plus, plus, plus. That's not to mention the computer systems and bookkeeping costs to keep all of the business transactions straight for outside auditors and tax men like you. The cost for that PCD just went from one-thirty to one-ninety. The store also has losses from theft and returned product they can't send back to China. They also have costs for insurance to pay for risks from fires, fraud – hell, even customers who fall in the store and try to sue the store out of existence. But I've forgotten all the taxes and fees the business pays to be in business – social security taxes, unemployment taxes, medical taxes, communication taxes, sales and VAT taxes, gas taxes, heating oil taxes, conservation and reclamation taxes, personal property taxes, use taxes, business registration fees, franchise taxes, audits from federal, state and local agents, and any arbitrary fines and penalties you guys throw in – and that's *before* we get to income taxes! In the end, its cost for that PCD is goes up to two-twenty. So, when a business sells it for two hundred thirty, it will end up making all of ten bucks on that PCD, less than five percent, if they're lucky. And if another company comes out with a better PCD, the store won't be able to sell what they have on hand at all. They'll have to discount it to, say, two hundred, losing twenty bucks ... Oh, but I forgot. Business is easy – it's just about sitting back and making money, isn't it?"

"You're exaggerating," replied the agent.

"Not at all. The retail store has to pay rent, salaries, communication and computer costs. They have to buy shelving and equipment for the products they sell. They have to advertise and market their store and its products. It's all expensive, and it's a risky proposition."

"No! They would have made one hundred dollars on that PCD," Toiken said again, refusing to listen. "If they lose money, it's their own fault. They're incompetent."

"That's why capitalism is efficient. With certain restraints, capitalism is the best system mankind has ever created. But, it is hard work! You're right – some people aren't good at it, and they will fail. But, those who succeed will compete for consumer dollars and keep the prices low for everyone. The problem is that government makes it even harder each day to be successful. The socialized medicine tax first imposed on citizens thirty years ago was shifted entirely to businesses and is killing the economy. And what did we get for it? Waiting times for cataract surgery are over a year long, when they used to be weeks. And mortality rates are up! Development of new medicines and medical devices has all but dried up. People are going to Canada and Australia for treatment. And it cost Americans one hundred fifty thousand dollars per person to fund that abomination. Add that to all the other stupid burdens on business and in the end, they're lucky if they make that ten dollars on that PCD. Today, it's closer to five or even one, if they can make that. Working fifty to sixty hours per week to make one dollar? Why, when they could sit at home and collect more from the government handouts."

"You can just raise the price to cover the costs," said Toiken, getting confused in the conversation.

"But you told me earlier that I couldn't do that," said Shea, "that I couldn't or shouldn't raise my prices."

"I ... I did not," Toiken said clumsily.

"You did. But, I'm used to liberals changing their positions as it best suits them. I'll look past that and let you argue for increased prices. So, if we do that, do you realize what you've just done? We're right back where we started from, aren't we? People now can't afford what we're selling. And, according to you, we again have to raise people's wages so they can afford the higher-priced things. How many times do we have to go through this charade before it's obvious to you that it doesn't work? We just end up in an endless spiral upward. Eventually, we have nothing on the shelves and money that can't buy anything. That's just what people in Communist Russia found in the twentieth century, and they do again now. They get poorer and poorer but don't understand why."

"But the companies should suck it up! Like I keep saying, they shouldn't make *any* profit at all. That show go to the workers who make it all happen!" said Toiken, back to his old mantra. "Jobs should stay here – not go overseas!"

"Oh, then how does that work?" Shea asked, challenging him for some modicum of rational thought.

"Well, for one, you'd create a lot more manufacturing jobs in the country if you paid more. People would want to work and would have more money to spend. That would stimulate the economy. A tariff would protect their jobs as would giving our unions more say. Higher worker paychecks would fund the purchase of those more expensive PCD sets."

"Okay, just by paying more, we'd create more jobs. Is that your theory? Why?"

"Because people will want jobs if they pay more, of course," said the agent, acting as if it were common sense.

"But there are only jobs if a company has a need – *not* if people are lined up outside applying for million-dollar jobs that aren't being offered."

"It would all work out in the end," said Toiken, dismissively.

"And if we did magically raise wages and were able to sell some within this country, what about selling our products overseas? Do you think anyone outside this country is going to pay three hundred and twenty dollars for a two hundred dollar PCD? China would still be producing them at a hundred bucks."

"Like I said, you'd still have a market inside this country."

"But you understand that if we raise tariffs on imports here, that other countries will do the same with all of our products. So, U.S. industries that rely on exports to other countries will get crushed. Their workers will be in bread lines … oh, no, I forgot … they'll just collect unemployment for the rest of their lives."

Toiken was silent for a moment. Then, he said again, having nothing else to argue, "You greedy capitalists just don't get it. There are stories every day about some new billionaire buying a new yacht or even a new island someplace."

"Of course you don't believe me because you don't want to. You don't want to understand the reality of what is happening today. You only hear what the Left-wing media wants you to hear. They take that one unusual case and make it seem like it's happening to everyone – whether it's a greedy billionaire or some family down on their luck after trying to find work or support their eight children. Their story always fits the media's narrative, their template. If it doesn't, they don't air it.

"Have you heard anything about the 185,000 businesses that went bankrupt last year because they couldn't make it? You didn't, did you? Sure, there were over 633,000 new businesses created last year?" said Shea, continuing her lecture. "But the odds are high that most will be out of business within five years. If there is a billionaire minted from one of those new companies, it would be one every seven years. That means all of those billionaires you say we create, those who run rampant from uncontrolled capitalism in our country, they amount to one out of every 4.2 million companies that are formed. But that number, which comes from your own Department of Statistics, doesn't fit your model of the way things should be; so, you don't hear about it, do you? Of course not." Then, she paused. "Your chances of becoming a pro athlete and making hundreds of millions are far greater than becoming that wealthy from a business.

"Have you *ever* had an economics class, Mr. Toiken?"

"I don't need an economics class to understand how capitalism is ruining the country," he answered.

"Perhaps you do, or you'd understand better what I've been saying."

"Oh, I understand you well enough, Ms. Disone, and you haven't said a thing that will convince me."

"I don't expect to," she said. "You're too brainwashed to believe what you believe."

"So are you."

"Perhaps you're right, Mr. Toiken. But at least I can think through things logically and understand the cause and effect of things, where, I'm afraid, you can't."

"I absolutely can!" he shouted. "It's all about you winning and everyone else losing. That's the way you like it, isn't it?"

"But you want me to put everything at risk so I can pay the livelihoods of others. I see. So, what do I get if I win?" said Shea, standing up next to the table.

"Excuse me?" asked Toiken, not understanding what she was saying.

188

"What's my incentive," she said. "I'm an entrepreneur. I create, develop, and run a company. I pour my blood, sweat and tears into that company using all my savings and spending all of the most productive years of my life to do it. You've told me it's my responsibility to pay taxes if I win, so what do I get for all my efforts?"

"Like I said – you have a responsibility to your fellow man."

"And what are you doing to better mankind?" she asked, staring at him. "Is auditing people and making them hand over everything they've ever worked for bettering mankind?"

"Yes. We use their money to do ..."

"What *you* think is right?" Shea said, finishing his sentence.

"Yes, of course. What we *know* is right!"

"What if I don't agree with what you think is right?" she asked.

"Then you're wrong," he answered. "You people are usually wrong about that stuff. You're all about yourselves, like I said."

"But, if I'm Jewish and you're Catholic, and I want to donate to the synagogue. You may disagree and say I should be donating to the Pope instead."

"That's a religious matter."

"It still wouldn't stop you from disagreeing. And if my family has a history of dying from Parkinson's disease, and I donate to that. You're family has a cancer history, and you donate to that. Which is right?"

"They're both right. They benefit mankind."

"But, if ninety-nine percent of the people donate to Parkinson's causes and only one percent to cancer research, you wouldn't think that is fair, would you? You'd be upset that more money wasn't going to cancer labs, and most likely, you would tax me and all the other people who contributed to Parkinson's research so that you'd have the money to spend on cancer research, right?"

"Well, probably, but..."

"You'd tax me until there was nothing left to tax. Then where would you get money for what you think is important? What about those things that other people in the Administration feel are important? Where are you going to get the money for those? You'd want as much of my money as you could get to spend on causes all of you believe are important. But, you know. I am the one who earned that money; not you. And I'm the one who should be able to give it to the causes that *I* think are important; not the ones you think are."

"You don't know enough to know what's important."

"And you do?"

"Yes, I've gone to college. Got my undergraduate degree in accounting and got a job here at the IRS."

"Graduated at the top of your class, I guess?" asked Shea.

"Uh, well, I did very well. I don't need to defend myself to you!"

"But you want me to defend myself to you!" she retorted. "And what do you know about me? I guess, since I don't agree, I'm pretty stupid by comparison. There's no way I should know anything about anything, as I'm not a Progressive like you."

"Did you even *go* to college?" he asked.

"Yeah, just a little university called Boston College, graduated summa cum laude with a double major in economics and political science. I also graduated with honors from Harvard law school, but not that any of that would register with you. After all, I *am* a cave-dwelling conservative."

Toiken laughed, "You said it. I didn't."

"It's what you believe, though."

"Maybe. But the one thing I do know is that you rich people don't pay enough. You don't pay your fair share. If we had more money to spend on programs for the poor, they'd have a chance."

"That hasn't worked -- ever. You've been brainwashed by your own government – or you were born with the liberal mental defect. Some tell me liberalism is a mental disorder, something written by a well-known author named Savage sometime around 2005, I believe. I'm starting to think he was right. You use the same argument the government uses – if we just spend more on programs, we'll get the poor out of poverty and create more jobs for them. We've spent trillions on social programs, and we still have sixty-five percent of people not working," said Shea.

"We just haven't spent enough," said Toiken.

Shea smiled. "Ah, now you've reached the end of your argument. It's always the point you Lefties go to when you run out of reasonable thought. There is no way to prove a negative is there? We can stand here forever and excuse a failure by saying there was never enough money, or time, or effort, or some other resource available. That's when your argument fails."

The argument was over, and both of them knew it – but for different reasons. Shea, because she presented her argument based on logical thought; Toiken, because he held the power. Indeed, the argument was over. But in the end, power trumps logic, and Shea was the loser. She had won the battle but lost the war, and she knew it. She had gone too far, and she realized that Patrick, she and Lenoir Labs would pay the price.

Toiken closed his computer "I can see I'm getting nowhere with you. You'll just have to be indicted for tax evasion."

"What! How do you get that? We've given you every invoice, purchase order, ledger and receipt we've produced during the past eight years. We've answered every question and come to every meeting. Patrick and I have cooperated fully, and you have yet to find a single problem with any tax return. You can't do this!"

"I can, and I will. Good day, Ms. Disone." And with that Toiken left the room, letting the beige door slam behind him.

Shea sat in stunned silence. She had told Patrick she wouldn't fly off the handle like that, but Toiken had pushed her too far. Patrick and she would pay the price, and she feared that it would be more than they could ever afford.

*****

CH 24 SHARED BURDEN

The next thing of which Sumner was aware was awakening, hooked up to monitors in some hospital critical care unit. He didn't recall how he'd gotten there or by whom. However, he felt as if he'd been hit by a D.C. Metro train and then backed over again. A breathing tube was stuck up his nose, and intravenous fluids were running full stream into a vein in his arm. They'd given him an injection of thousands of nanobots that were flowing through his system and reporting back any anomalies they found so the doctors could find out the extent of his trauma and treat him.

"We thought we'd lost you," said a voice from across the room. "I guess I'm lucky I happened to be here when you finally woke up."

Sumner's eyes focused on the visitor and finally put the face with the voice. "Hi, Patrick," said Sumner, unable to generate even a smile. "It's good to hear at least one of my constituents hasn't given up on me."

Patrick chuckled. "Yeah, I may even vote for you again. If you make it through this, that is."

"If I don't, I'll still be sure to vote for myself at the next election," said Sumner in reply. They laughed.

At that moment Maria came into the room. "JC! You're awake!" She ran over to his hospital bed and grabbed the hand that didn't have the intravenous tube inserted into it. She caressed it against her cheek and began crying. Tears streamed down her face as she clutched his fingers in hers.

Maria was petite, standing only about five feet tall. Slight of frame, she had long, thin arms and tiny fingers, making her almost doll-like. Her dark, brown hair flowed in waves down to the middle of her back and over her fragile-looking shoulders. Maria's face was beautiful, with high cheekbones, thick, lush lips, and perfectly white teeth. Her long eyelashes were men-magnets and highlighted her big, brown eyes. And in both ears, she had multiple piercings, the traditional earlobe and two with small, gold rings at their apex.

Sumner tried harder to smile, and then he said softly, "Maria, it's nothing. You know I wouldn't leave you without saying goodbye. It wasn't my time, but I'll let you know when it is."

She grinned, but the tears kept coming. She wiped them from her eyes with her finger, yet that did little to stem the flow. The loving twinkle in her eyes said it all. They'd been married for a long time and had raised two children, both off to college, and a five-year-old golden doodle, named Enzo, that was just as much part of the family as everyone else.

"You do that, mister," she said right back to him. "You let me know when I'm supposed to plan the funeral. I don't like surprises."

Patrick backed up and moved toward the door to give them time together.

"Where are you going?" Sumner asked, spotting Patrick before he could get out the door.

Sheepishly, Patrick answered, "I just thought you two would want some time …"

"We've been married twenty-two years Patrick. And, we'll be married another twenty-two, so stay – please," answered Sumner.

Maria turned, suddenly realizing that she was not alone with her husband. "Oh, I'm sorry. I didn't notice someone else was in the room."

"This is Patrick Disone," said her husband. "He's a friend and one of my – of our – constituents. I've talked with him on several occasions about different things that are important to me … to us. He and I seem to see eye-to-eye on most things, and he's got a lot of good ideas about how to …"

"Okay, dear. Take it easy! You need to pace yourself. You've been unconscious for three days. The world hasn't changed that much in that time. Don't drain all of your energy at once!" she said, castigating him.

Patrick came over and extended his hand to the congressman's wife. "Pleased to meet you," he said with a grin. "The congressman has said a lot of good things about you."

"I hope so," she answered, playfully. "That's why we've been married for twenty-two years."

Then, still confused about his condition, Sumner asked, "How the hell did I get here?"

"Some man brought you into Emergency," said Maria. "He was told to wait for the police, but when they went to find him, he'd vanished."

"He didn't leave a name?" asked Sumner.

"No. But, the police have a BOLA out for him. They want to talk to you too, of course. Where did you go Tuesday night?" she asked. "When I woke up, you were gone. I had no idea where you were. I was worried sick! And I guess I had every right to be. You should have said something. What happened?"

"It's a long story," Sumner began. "But I'll just say that a man called me on my private line. He said he had to tell me some things, so I went to meet him downtown."

"At 3 a.m.? What in God's name would get you out at that hour in the morning? You must have known the man to do something like that," Maria said, suspiciously.

"I didn't want to wake you. I left you a note, though."

"Yeah, some note," she said, her irritation showing. "All it said was: *I've gone out for a bit. Will be back home before you probably read this.* Boy, was that ever wrong!"

"Maria, there is something I urgently need to talk to Patrick about. Do you mind giving us a minute?" asked JC.

Maria was taken aback for a moment. "What? Really, JC? Why can't you talk to him in front of me?" There was hurtful indignity in her voice.

Sumner could tell she was upset by it. "I don't want to hurt you any more than I already have, and if you learn what I'm about to tell Patrick here, then I'd be putting you in danger. I'm only trying to protect you, Maria. But, I can see that it would make it worse for you if I didn't tell you than if I did." Then he added, "What I have to tell Patrick is why I was shot tonight. There are people after something I have, and apparently, they're willing to kill to get it. I don't want you to know any more than that, Maria. If you do, your life will be in danger too. Do you understand?"

She looked at him – the hurt draining from her face. She had lived with him long enough to know how protective he was; yet, today, she could tell he was struggling with that. "Okay, JC." she said, her temper abating. "I guess I have to trust you on this. You've never lied to me before."

"I just don't want to put our family in any more peril than it already is," he said. He looked at her, hoping that she would understand him.

Maria's brown eyes softened. "I understand, but I still don't like it. I want to be there for you," she said, pressing her hand into his.

"You are. You're always here for me," he answered.

Maria finally let go of Sumner's hand and grudgingly left the room. She glanced over at him in his hospital bed once more with loving eyes before she vanished through the opening.

Patrick came over, closer to the bedside. His body was rigidly tense, and his mind racing. *What could be of such importance that the Congressman's family could be in danger?* he thought. "What is it, JC? What's going on?"

Sumner asked Patrick to bring him the hospital bag that contained all of his personal belongings. After taking the bag, Sumner pulled out everything inside, placing them beside him on the bed. Before him lay his black, deerskin wallet, an Audi car ignition chip, a electronic card clip, and a pocket-sized, paper version of the U.S. Constitution. Lastly, he took out a small, silver data stick.

"You need to take this and see what's on it," said Sumner, handing Patrick the stick, no bigger than the end of his thumb. "There was an accident at an oil refinery just outside of Baton Rouge the other night. This stick holds information on what happened. Did you hear anything about it?"

"Yeah, but the news was confusing," Patrick answered. "At first, they said there had been a major explosion at an oil refinery and that there were possible deaths; however, pretty soon after that, they said it wasn't that serious and there were only minor injuries. The story just topped after that. There hasn't been anything more."

"I'm sure the Administration pressured the media not to pursue the story. The locals must have started running it, I'm sure, but they were forced to abandon it quickly. The reality of it is that several hundred died in the explosion, and several hundred more were injured," said Sumner.

"What! That can't be. We would have heard about that! It would have leaked out."

"It will eventually. But that's not the worst of it. You'll find on this data stick computer logs that may show unauthorized access to the computer programs that ran the plant and the processing stations. The logs supposedly indicate that this was no accident. It was caused by saboteurs directly linked back to the current Administration."

"You mean, the White House was involved?" said Patrick, trying to clarify.

At that time, the nurse came into the room carrying a tray of medicine. "Time for your afternoon meds," she said cheerfully. She was young and spunky.

Just starting her shift, she still had nine hours ahead of her, but she tried to be positive all the time for the sake of her patients. Sumner liked that about her.

Patrick looked searchingly at Sumner, waiting for him to finish his sentence, but the congressman shook his head. "You'll find what you need, I think. Just make sure you make a copy and keep it in a safe place."

"I understand. I'll make sure of it."

Patrick left the hospital room wondering just how incriminating the data on the stick was. How high up did the connection go? Sumner said it was the Administration, but who in the Administration? Did it include the president's inner circle? Was it the president? No doubt, it was high enough to try to kill a congressman to get it. But, then his mind went to Shea. Getting involved might also endanger her. *It was grossly unfair*, he thought, *for the congressman to pick him for such a job.* However, perhaps he had just been in the wrong place at the wrong time or the right place at the right time, depending on how he looked at it. As he left the hospital floor, he noticed two policemen now stationed beside Sumner's hospital room door. *Indeed,* he thought, *this is anything but normal.*

Patrick walked to his car and said simply, "Open." The car door popped open upon command, and Patrick climbed in. "Home," he said, his voice tired and drained. The azure blue BMW understood and followed the directions voiced by its master and pulled out of the space. Automatically pushing down on the accelerator, the car sped up, rising to thirty-five getting out of the parking lot, and then forty-five once on the main road. Normally, the speed would have leveled off, attenuated to the signals given off by the roadside speed markers; however, instead, the car continued accelerating ... *fifty, fifty-five.* Patrick tapped on the pedal a couple times to override the car's computer, thinking it was stuck, but it did nothing to slow the car's speed. *Sixty, sixty-five, seventy* ... still the car kept going faster ...*seventy-five, eighty.* Panic started to grip his brain, as his efforts were proving futile. *Stop!* he thought. *Stop!*

Sweat started beading-up on his forehead, and his palms were cold and clammy. His heart, pounding through his chest, began to interrupt his ability to think. He again stomped on the brake, trying to halt the car from its out-of-control trajectory, but his foot went right to the floorboard.

"What the hell!" he exclaimed, his eyes as big as saucers.

He came up on another car fast, almost slamming into the back of it. But the car's computer kicked back in, and it swerved sharply, missing the back end by inches. Other cars next to him screeched their tires, careening away from an impending accident. But Patrick's car didn't stop; it continued at a furious pace, weaving in and out of traffic to avoid a collision. He suddenly heard the engine race – the RPM's jumped from five thousand to nearly eight thousand at the red line – sending sounds out screaming from under the hood.

Patrick's heart began beating as fast as the car engine. Streetlights, holographic billboards, and buildings with streaming video ads flew by at high speed – all becoming more a blur. His hands trembled at the wheel, as he tried futilely to gain control over the renegade auto. In a last-ditch effort, he pushed the car's bright-red emergency disconnect switch to kill the engine and disengage it from the drive train. The car reacted violently, vibrating as if it would fly apart. It began careening sideways, heading toward the sidewalk and a light pole.

"Oh sh*t!" Patrick shouted to himself, bracing for impact. He held his breath, anticipating the crunching of metal, as the car would wrap itself around the pole and him with it. All would all be over in seconds.

But the car hit the high curb in front of the pole, ripping off the front axle and causing Patrick's cocoon-like safety bubble inside the car to blow-up around him. He could hear the tie rods and bearings separate from the wheels under him, and the car skidded on its underbelly for several yards before stopping. Dazed, but largely unhurt, Patrick moved to deflate the safety bubble around him. He felt a severe pain in his left side, possibly from a cracked rib, and other bruises that made any kind of movement agonizing.

Patrick pushed the emergency 911 button on the dash but then saw that the computer screen was broken. He got out and staggered up and onto the sidewalk, but just as quickly, he sat down. The images around him began to blur as the blood drained from his head and he felt feint. He put his head down between his knees and felt his mind begin to clear.

But with all of the commotion and drama, no other cars stopped to help him. All of their drivers had set them on automatic pilot to get home, and they were not about to let their nap or reading time get interrupted by someone else's misfortune. It was just the way it was.

Several minutes passed before an ambulance arrived and the paramedics got to him. They first asked him for his papers -- specifically, his government-issued identification card. It didn't matter whether he was legal or illegal in the country, as the distinction had long-passed being meaningful. One could go to any government bureau and ask for an official identification card or even a voting card without any verification or background check.

An autopsy on his car later revealed that the computer program had been altered to send a signal to the electric engine to give full throttle and disengage the brakes above thirty miles per hour. It was simple enough, just some software modification that could easily have been uploaded while he was in the hospital. Still, the police reviewed the totaled car and declared that they would follow up on what evidence they came up with. Patrick wasn't overly confident that they would find anything.

***

When he got home, Shea was gone. She'd had plans to go out with two of her girlfriends to dinner that night. Patrick would explain the wrecked car to her, but he didn't want to alarm her with what had happened in the hospital or the sabotage of the vehicle's computer system. *She had enough worries right now,* he thought.

Sitting in his study, Patrick fidgeted nervously with the silver data stick, his fingers passing it back and forth between hands. Then, he stopped, examining it as if clutching the Hope Diamond with its priceless beauty but equally-notorious curse. Finally, he uncapped the top and turned it on. Within seconds, a holographic image projected out of the top, and a video began to run, showing a man, probably in his late sixties, sitting nervously in a hard-backed, wooden chair, his hands tightly clutching the arm rests. His face was partially shaded, making it difficult to make out his true features, but it seemed to be angular and strong. His mouth was slightly downturned, and his eyes a brown or dark gray. When the man finally spoke, he did so haltingly, as if he were under severe stress.

> *"If you are listening to this broadcast, I may already be dead. Therefore, you may be the only person remaining who can help save us from our own.*
>
> *"My name is Charlie Taglu. I am the assistant plant manager of the Birkshire Oil Company and have been for thirty years. As the APM, I am responsible for the safety and welfare of the twelve hundred workers at this plant.*
>
> *"On October 15, two newly-hired, but experienced operational controllers overrode security protocols and lockout mechanisms to sabotage the operations of the plant. The computer logs and*

reports on this data stick show conclusively that server security was disengaged, and access granted to outsiders who took control of our computers via SI-net. The IP computer addresses used can be traced back to offices within the Department of Environmental Protection. The logs also show the hacking of security controls within the plant's operations that enabled the outsiders to cause horrendous damage here tonight. They sent instructions to the flow-valve mechanisms throughout the plant, causing them to opened remotely. This led to a dangerous leak of partially-refined oil products. I believe the intent was to create a massive spill that would be blamed on the company and force the closing of this refinery.

"Unfortunately, some of these oil products were dumped near hot pipelines, which triggered a massive explosion. Half of the plant's capacity was destroyed, along with the lives of one hundred fifty-odd workers. Hundreds of others were injured.

"After the explosion, the computer files were wiped clean, and the two controllers fled. However, the outside hackers were unaware of real-time backups that were taking place offsite, and this is how the information on this data stick was obtained.

"My understanding is that the incident will be supposedly investigated by local police. But that is doubtful. Management of the company has been replaced by the board of directors and can no longer be found. We suspect the board was ordered to do so by the Department of Justice, who is also investigating. All computer backups were destroyed by the technology group under orders from the new chief technology officer. In summary, no witnesses or other evidence may now exist – except for this stick, that you now have.

"Please review the data and get it to whoever you can trust to get the word out on what really happened at this plant tonight. Those of us who are in positions to know are either in hiding, missing or dead.

"Good luck."

The video ended, and scores of documents and other files appeared, quickly scrolling past on the screen.

For the next six hours, Patrick combed through them. As someone knowledgeable of computer software, he was the right person to help decipher the arcane language of Berkshire's computer programs.

It was nearly midnight when Shea came home. She dropped her purse by the door and came in to give her husband a hug. "It's late," she said, somewhat perturbed. "Why are you up so late?"

Patrick fidgeted uncomfortably. He didn't like being secretive with his wife. "Oh, not much. Just looking over some things from work. How was your dinner?"

"Fine, I'd tell you about it, but it's late. By the way, where is your car? It wasn't in the garage."

"I was in a little fender bender coming home tonight. The car was pretty banged up, though. I don't know if we can fix it. I'll know tomorrow," he answered.

She looked at him quizzically. "If it were a fender bender, then why is it so banged up?"

"You know, honey, they just don't make cars like they used to."

"Well, I'm tired. I'm going up. You should come up too. It's been a long week," she said.

Patrick rubbed his eyes and looked at the old-fashioned, round clock on the wall. "Shea, yeah. I'm almost finished. I'll be up in a minute. I promise."

It took another hour, but what he found was compelling. The evidence suggesting White House involvement was overwhelming. Computer IP and Mac addresses, entry-access logs, security code breaches and attempted log-ins – it all came down to one thing. The Department of Environmental Protection had been involved, just as the man on the video had said. How far up the food chain it went was anyone's guess.

But he wondered, *Why didn't they at least try to mask their connection – like bouncing the instructions off SI-net sites all over the globe or using deep encryption? Did they have that much hubris to think it really didn't matter if someone figured it out? Had it really come to this?*

Getting online, Patrick managed to bypass the government's site-blocking programs and get into the SI-Net Underground, as it was now called. Si-Net Underground was the black market version of the SI-Net, filled with everything from illicit drug dealing, virtual prostitution rings, and illegal booze peddling to the sites that held the real truth about what was happening in the country and in the world. Although full of fabrications, mistruths, and even lies, there were those sites that were known to be reputable about their reporting. These were the most dangerous of all. The truth was what worried those in Washington the most.

One site called *Hydrocarbons* took an impartial view to the fossil fuel issue, beating up on the Administration for its lack of common sense in dealing with energy policy while at the same time badgering the oil and gas companies about their safety records and their occasional lack of environmental sensitivity. But it was one of their blogs that caught Patrick's attention. The discussion cited the Baton Rouge explosion and raised issues about the incident, including theories ranging from overseas terrorist organizations to a single, disgruntled worker. But it specifically referred to one that was most likely based on the information the blogger had obtained. He alleged involvement by the Department of Environmental Protection. Most damning, it pointed to the logons from computers inside the secretary's own office.

What remained unclear was whether the disclosure of all of this evidence -- short of having a video tape of the secretary herself inside the control room at Birkshire -- would have any impact. Things were corrupt, and these days, even the worst crimes were spun by the Administration so as to exonerate those involved. Their philosophy was to set things ablaze – the more things that burned, the more smoke would be created and the less anyone would be able to see the truth. Having been continually and intentionally confused and misdirected, people had become jaded and disenfranchised.

Patrick turned off the stick, watching the 3-D images recede back into the dime-sized receptacle. He was tired. It had all been punishing to his body and his mind. *Tomorrow would be another day,* he said to himself. *I'll tackle this again then.* But if he thought he would have more time later, he was wrong.

*****

CH 25 GOING CONCERN

Lenoir Research Labs, a once growing and thriving enterprise, was struggling. Cash was not coming in fast enough to hold off the creditors, and Shea was worried. She called a meeting of her finance group to discuss where they were and what they needed to do.

Flipping through the digital pages of narrative provided by her CFO and the charts and graphs forecasting the near-term future, Shea was despondent. "Annie, what else do you have for me? What does cash look like and where are we on our line?"

Shea was referring to the bank line of credit which they used to finance the business. Since there is always a lag between the time companies pay their workers, buy inventory for their shelves or invest in equipment to produce something and the time they sell their goods or services and eventually get paid by customers, businesses usually needed to borrow money from a bank. This was the line of credit they used until customers paid them; then, they would repay the bank when they received cash from their customers. For companies growing quickly or, in this case companies that ran into trouble selling their product or collecting on their outstanding accounts, repayment to the bank was a problem.

But that was the nature of business. It was risky. There were no guarantees. If customers chose another product to buy because prices got too high, quality suffered or not enough could be supplied, the company would lose business. But there were other reasons businesses could go under: someone could file a frivolous lawsuit, the company could over expand, management could fail to control costs, a competitor could invent a replacement product or service, or a consumer could misuse the product and create a nation-wide story, debasing the company's name and its product. These and other causes could derail and company and force it into liquidation.

"Well, not good, Shea. We've got 12.6 million borrowed from the bank on our line that has a ceiling of 13 million. That means ..."

"Yes, I know. We only have four hundred thousand available to borrow, which won't last the week. Will it?

"Cash isn't coming in very fast – customers just aren't paying," answered Annie. "I don't know if they smell the blood in the water, but it's almost as if they know we're going under, so they're intentionally not paying. I think we have to get tough with them."

"Do you think someone has leaked to them what our situation is?" Shea asked, probingly.

"I don't know. I really don't. The economy stinks right now – well, it has for the last eight years anyway. But I've never seen it this bad before," said Annie. "It's as if we're in the midst of a depression. No one wants to give up their money. It seems like our customers are hurting too."

"How long do we have?" asked Shea, a question more often asked by a terminal medical patient than a business.

Annie pulled up some 3-D charts on the holographic projector. "You can see here the trend line during the past six months. The trend is, obviously, down. Our borrowings have risen significantly, and so has our interest expense on what we're borrowing. If we can sell some of our receivables – the amounts due from customers – to a third party, we can get thirty cents on the dollar. That's horrible, but it may get us through the cash crunch that's coming."

"Where can we cut costs?" asked Shea. "Do we have to let anybody go?"

Annie showed several more charts and graphs – each one painting a bleaker picture. "Even if we sell off our receivables, that would give us about four weeks of operation based on current sales. All in all, I think we need to sell off any assets we have of value. We'll shrink our workforce to the point that we can't go any lower without closing the doors. That's about all we can do."

The day passed, but they didn't come up with any other answers. Annie suggested they go to a private equity firm and get money, knowing that they'd have to almost give away the company to get anything. Shea contacted a few people she knew, but they were quick to shatter that possibility, telling her that she would have to sell shares in the company for next to nothing to gain any interest.

"What about debt? Can we take on debt financing?" asked Shea.

"I don't think we can afford that either," said Annie. "With our dire situation, lenders will want an outrageous interest rate. We won't be able to pay that interest."

"What about our bank? Will they ..." Shea began.

"No. They've already told me that."

Shea shook her head. "I'm not giving up, Annie. We will find a way out of this. I know it. Patrick and I built this company through hard work, and I'm not about to let it all go down the drain because of some a**hole bureaucrats! We'll show them! We'll prove that you can't destroy Lenoir Labs without a good fight, and they haven't seen us at our best until we get into a good brawl!"

Annie grinned. She liked to hear that kind of talk from her boss. She too wanted to fight. But, when she looked at the numbers, she wasn't sure how. She could only hope that Shea and Patrick had a backup plan in their pocket – something sensational that would create a miracle. *They needed a miracle,* Annie thought. Kind of like an arrow shot at an apple balanced on top of her head, she wanted to know whether she should stand there with her eyes open or whether it was time to run for cover.

***

Annie worked late into the night with her staff, trying to figure out how to survive. They scoured the numbers in an attempt to balance the ins and the outs. At a minimum, the ins had to equal the outs for the company to make it to the next month. And by morning, they were no closer to finding an answer than they had been when the previous day had started.

It was mid-afternoon, when Annie got a call that she'd feared would come.

"Annie, it's me, Tim."

Tim Palmer was the company's bank representative. He had worked with Shea and Patrick for years as an intermediary between the bank's hard-core analysts who questioned everything about the company's numbers and their executives who wanted to maintain a great relationship with their customer. Tim was almost part of their corporate family, smoothing the rough times with the bank and giving them counseling on the side with how to best present the financial results during hard times.

"Tim, yes. It's good to hear from you. We're just putting together our analysis of operations you asked for. We are going to be a little tight on our borrowing this month. It looks like we may not make our debt covenants for the quarter. I'm just giving you a head's up. Things are hard here, but we expect a turnaround soon."

"Annie, we've discussed things here at the bank, and …"

"Tim, before you say anything. I just want to tell you that our forecast for the next quarter looks really strong. We think we'll increase our sales significantly next quarter with orders from Australia and Canada."

"Do you have any firm, written commitments?" Tim asked.

"Uh, no. Not yet. But our sales department tells me that they are coming."

"When?"

"Shortly. I'm told it will be soon."

"Annie, I'm afraid that ..." Tim began again.

"Tim, we've known you a long time. You're our advocate, right? You can talk with the people there who make the decisions. It's something that I think we can work out."

"Annie, the loan committee has decided to pull your line," said Tim. "They are asking that I send you a thirty-day demand letter for payment."

"What? You can't be serious! We have almost thirteen million outstanding, and you expect us to come up with that overnight?" asked Annie, the shock of the request registering with her.

"I know. I'm really, really sorry. I tried my best to talk them out of it. They said you'd have to find financing someplace else. They may give you more time than thirty days – probably can get you sixty. But you will have to look for someone else to cover your needs. Again, I'm really sorry," said Tim, his voice steady, but sad.

"I understand," said Annie. "I was afraid this call would come one day."

"Well, if there is anything else I can help you with, let me know."

Annie hung up with Tim. She sat, unmoving, at her desk. All the energy had drained out of her, and she wanted to just lie down on the floor and die.

How am I going to tell Shea? she thought. *This is the end of the line. It's only that miracle right now that will save us. That miracle. Yes, that miracle was what they needed. Would it come? And if it did, would it come in time?*

*****

CH 26 CROWN OF THORNE

"I want that damned technology!" shouted Thorne. "Does it take an act of Congress to get the stuff that I'm willing to pay good money for?"

He was, of course, referring to the forty million dollars he had promised to Angel Ratner for the software and technical blueprints of the SECE engine. He had, in fact, already paid her ten million up-front. The rest would be paid when the information was delivered. His Administrative Assistant, Kendra, had no answers, but then again, she knew her boss wasn't expecting that from her. Instead, she merely closed her notebook, got up from the chair and said, "I'll see where things are."

Thorne's Corporate General Counsel, Ellen Chou, was also in the room. She was not timid about confronting issues or people, and she could stand her ground against just about anyone. But she also knew to keep her distance from Thorne when he got like this. Instead of engaging him, she understood her best tact was to shut-up and listen, taking the blows one by one while he railed on her. She glanced down at the exquisite silk, Persian rug that covered nearly the entire floor within his massive office.

"Well, what do you have to say?" he asked Chou, turning his wrath toward her.

"Sir, I believe that deputy secretary said she is close to getting the answers for you. Her assistant told me that it would be only a few more days."

But Thorne was impatient. He wanted it, and he wanted it right away.

"Bull sh*t! Ratner was supposed to deliver the, design, specs -- everything by today. She promised me she'd deliver them. So where are they?" He glared at his general counsel. "Well? Where are they? You were in charge of getting that information for me, Chou. I don't see anything on my desk, do you?"

Ellen Chou was used to doing a lot of dirty work for her boss – even if it meant breaking the law. She was tough as nails, and although her Korean heritage had taught her to be loyal, she also knew what self-preservation meant. In this case, it meant hedging all bets and working for both sides. Thorne didn't know – he had no idea. However, Ratner did. She'd lured Chou with money – enough to make it easier to double-cross her EG boss, if necessary. It was a small price for Ratner to pay, sharing a few mil of her forty million in order to safeguard the deal. What Chou hadn't counted on was the debacle with Muntz when Sergei was accidently killed.

"No, sir. We don't as of yet have it."

"So, when am I going to get it?"

"I ... uh ... I'm not sure, sir. Like I said, I spoke with the DTA a few days ago, and I was told we would have all that we needed between today and the end of the week."

"That's not good enough, Chou! You're failing me. And you know how I feel when people fail me." It sounded like a threat, and it was meant to be.

"As of now, we still don't have anything, sir. I am pressing Ratner and her group hard to come up with what we need. But we'll also have to verify what they give us before we release the rest of the money."

"God damn it!" swore the big man seated behind the mahogany desk. "Do I have to fire every damn one of you people in my office and hire some competent bastards off the street to get something done?"

"No, sir. I will talk to the deputy secretary personally and see where she is with getting us the engine plans. We should have something soon, sir."

Thorne swiveled around in his pin-cushioned, burgundy-leather chair and reached for the Swarovski lead crystal decanter, pouring himself two fingers of expensive, 64 McCallum scotch. He gulped down the several thousand dollars-worth of liquor and poured himself another.

Chou left the same way Kendra had exited the office only moments earlier. As soon as she reached her office, she called Muntz. "Gunter, this is Chou. I just left Thorne's office, and he is really pissed off! He wants the engine specs now! Somehow, we need to convince Ratner to give him what she has. She has to fake the rest."

"She told us many times she'd give him the specs when she got the last parts of the software code that she's missing," said Muntz. "Without those crucial ones that were apparently omitted from the patent filing, the engine is worthless."

"Yeah, I know!" Chou shouted back. "But we have to come up with something. We can't continue the charade forever. Thorne will eventually find out. We have to tell Ratner something that will make her give up the specs now. She'll just have to fake the software piece of it."

"She's not going to unless she has the real codes. You and I both know she wants her cake and eat it too. She doesn't want to risk problems with Thorne later on," said Muntz. "If she gives him bad code, he'll figure it out soon."

"Yeah, but she'll already have her ... our forty mil. We can convince Thorne that the faked software is good. He won't know until much later when he applies it to the engine. By that time, we'll be long gone."

"What if he wants to hear it from the experts who will review the software they're given. What if they tell him it's a fake?" asked Muntz.

"Then, that's Ratner's problem," answered Chou.

"It's our problem if she turns us in to him."

"Just focus on the forty mil," said Chou.

"Yep, I know. But, I'm also thinking about the personalities of the two we are working for – Satan and the devil. Which do you choose?"

"Ok. So, what options do we have? Sergei's dead. Disone is the only other one who knows everything."

"Yes," said Muntz. "He is." At first there was silence on the other end of the line. Then Muntz said, "I'll get rid of Sergei's body. But, I'll need your help."

"Why do you need ..."

"I need you to connect with your friend that does electronic image and voice simulations," he said. "You can do that right?"

"You've got to give me more than that," said Chou.

"I will. But right now, just get a hold of him. Tell him we have a little project that we need help with."

*****

CH 27 SORTING IT OUT

The message of a call came up abruptly, and Maria pushed the automated button to answer it for her. "Congressman Sumner is currently indisposed. He will try to reply to your ..." she listened as the message unfolded. After it ended, she pushed another button to put the call on visual. "JC, I think you need to listen to this. It's from your friend, Patrick."

"Go ahead and put it up, Maria," said Sumner.

The two watched as the image of Patrick Disone sprang up from Sumner's PCD. "I know you're not in any condition to respond to my message, but I wanted to let you know what I found on the data stick. After I plugged it into my system, ..."

It was then that the message became distorted and garbled. The image of Patrick dissolved before them and then reappeared. He began again, starting over, but the message got stuck at the same place.

"Wait a minute," said Maria. "It wasn't like this a moment ago. Let me try to fix this."

Maria played around with the buttons on the PCD for a moment and scrolled through the setup codes to see if she could solve the problem. "There, I think that should work."

Sumner lay back in his bed, taking a sip from a glucose pack he'd been given for his evening dinner.

Maria turned off the device and turned it back on, rebooting it. "We'll try this again," she said, placing it back down on the bed next to them. The image reappeared as Patrick's face was front and center before them.

"... After I plugged the stick into my system," Patrick's image continued, "I got this message from someone who works or worked at the Birkshire plant." The 3-D picture then changed to show the face of Charlie Taglu of the oil company, repeating what he had already communicated to Patrick. After he'd completed his urgent message, the video ended.

Sumner and Maria stared in silence at the empty space where the images had materialized, revealed their chilling story and then faded again into darkness.

"What do you think?" Sumner asked her. His attempt to keep Maria out of the fray lasted all of one day before she broke him down. He finally told her everything about that night and how his life, and now hers, was in danger. She accepted it, and was more worried about her husband's than her own welfare. After all, she had said, it was he who had already taken a bullet.

"It's as serious as you told me. Probably even more so. If this thing goes all the way to the top, you are in danger. What are you going to do?" asked Maria.

Sumner rolled his head on the pillow towards her. "Unfortunately, I'm not in any position to do much of anything right now," he murmured. "But I worry about you, Maria. I think we should get a bodyguard for you twenty-four seven."

"Don't be ridiculous. I can take care of myself," she answered.

It was true that she had mastered karate at a young age, attaining the rank of second-degree black belt before she was twenty. But that was years ago, and she had not kept up with her training.

"I know you can," said JC, trying not to patronize her. "I just worry about you. That's all."

"I know," she answered sweetly. "But you're right. I think you need a bodyguard. We should look into that."

Sumner didn't feel like arguing with her. It was she whom he thought needed the bodyguard, but that battle would have to come later. "You just need to get some rest, Maria. The world will just have to do without us for a while. That's all. And it will. I promise. It will survive." He smiled and began stroking her dark, curly hair that fell to her shoulders.

"JC, you're the one who needs the rest. There isn't anything you can do right now. You said it yourself."

He huffed and rolled his head back to the other side of the pillow, away from her.

She started to get up from the bed to let him rest when he said, "But, you know they have to be held accountable."

"I know, dear. But right now, I have to be held accountable for you, and you have to behave until you get better. That means, you have to get some sleep."

A few minutes later, Maria kissed him on the forehead and left the room for the night after he had fallen asleep. But the nap didn't last long, and within an hour Sumner awoke when a night-shift nurse slammed a medicine cart into the white counter of the floor's central nursing station. The shattering of ampoules and clattering plastic pill bottles falling to the floor, got everyone's attention on Floor B, including Sumner's who shot out of bed at the sound. Startled and unable to go back to sleep, Sumner reached for his PCD.

"Call Sheriff Gauteaux," he commanded, articulating the name as clearly as he could. The line rang, and then there was an answer.

"Hello?" came the voice without an image attached.

"Sheriff Gauteaux?"

"Yes."

"This is JC Sumner, U.S. Congressman from Wyoming. How are you, sir?"

"Just fine, congressman. What can I do for you?" the sheriff asked cautiously, measuring whether to trust that he was indeed talking to a U.S. congressman or, perhaps, an imposter.

"Listen, I understand that there was an incident in Baton Rouge, at one of your oil refineries. There was an explosion there within the last few days. Is that right?"

There was initial silence on the other end followed by "Uh, well, I really don't know what you're referring to, congressman. We have minor things happen all the time around these parts. I'm not aware of anything major that's happened at an oil refinery here."

Sumner could tell he was lying. "I see, sheriff," he answered, typing furiously into his computer. He quickly pulled up data on Peter Gauteaux. He had access to several databases as a U.S. congressman that few outside of Capitol Hill had, and they often came in handy. Before him flashed several documents that summarized what was on file for the sheriff.

"Sheriff, let me try this a different way," said Sumner. "I can tell that you have a distinguished service record. You fought for your country in the war twenty years ago. You were honorably discharged, and you elected to go right into law enforcement – again, an honorable vocation. I salute you on both accounts sir."

"Well, thank you," said Gauteaux, now even more defensively than before.

"So, it seems to me that you're a man of character and that you generally do the right thing. Is that true?"

"Why, I like to think so, sir."

"Good. Then, I'll ask again, sheriff, what happened down there at the refinery? This is extremely important to that community in Louisiana as well as the nation. Do you understand?"

The sheriff did not answer this time.

"I'm sorry, sheriff. I didn't hear you. What was that?"

"I didn't say anything," came the reply.

"Yeah, I know. I was giving you another chance. So, sheriff, what will it be? Do you want to help me and your country or not?" Sumner asked pointedly.

"I'm sorry," said the sheriff. "I just don't know what you're referring to. Sorry I can't be of more assistance."

"Well, sheriff, I can tell that you're a man of faith, is that right?"

"Of course. Why do you ask?"

"Faith is important to me as well. I've been a lifelong supporter of religious freedom in this country. It's been under siege during the last several years. It's really a shame."

"Yeah, I agree," said the sheriff, hesitantly.

"But tell me," asked Sumner, "how do you reconcile your infidelity five years ago with your faith in God?"

"Excuse me?"

"You heard me, sheriff. How many people know about your extramarital affair with Amanda Perkins?"

"I don't know what you're talking about," Gauteaux answered, his defense mechanisms fully engaged.

"Sheriff, it's important that we find out about what happened at the oil refinery the other night. Can you help me understand what you know about it?" asked Sumner. It was a harsh tactic, but saw in the file and he'd heard on the street that the sheriff was a tough nut to crack, and using a heavy pair of nut crackers was the most likely way to do it.

Sumner could hear a deep breath on the other end of the line. There was still no visual – only an audio feed that connected the two men. Police stations were particularly careful not to allow visual calls unless the caller was personally known.

"There may have been an incident, now that you mention it," said the sheriff.

"I see," said Sumner. "What can you tell me about it?"

"Due to the importance of this matter," Gauteaux said, "I think it would be better if I called you back when I have more information. You will hear from me shortly." Then, the line went dead.

Sumner listened as a dial tone followed, indicating the communication had been disconnected. He shook his head, not believing he'd been cutoff. There was little more that he was going to be able to do. He hated to use veiled threats, but he thought it was his best chance at getting information. He knew the government had probably already used all of its power to intimidate the sheriff and anyone associated with the incident. It was a tactic they'd used time and time again, and he had no doubt they would stoop to that or worse.

Nearly an hour passed, and there was still no return call from Gauteaux. Sumner had written off hearing back from the sheriff that night anyway, but he would follow-up with him the following day.

The nurse came in and gave him his evening's dose of medication. A sedative was added to the list, as he had struggled with problems sleeping the night before. It was late, and the pain medicine, together with the sedative, made him drowsy. His eyelids began to close. But that is when his PCD sounded. He rolled over toward it and picked it up, pushing the *Video* button instead of voicing the command. "Sumner," he said, not realizing that his image was being sent to the person on the other end.

"Congressman, this is Sheriff Gauteaux. I'm now on a secure line. Let's talk."

Unfortunately, Sumner's eyes had closed, and he had already fallen fast asleep. He dropped his PCD next to him on the bed – the image of the sheriff scratching his head wondering what had happened to the person on the other end of the line he was trying to reach.

"Congressman? Congressman Sumner? Are you there?"

*****

CH 28 DIATRIBE

Cash to run the company was tightening, like the noose around a neck on a scaffold. Without the protection of the patent and, thus, the permission of the federal government to sell their product to auto makers worldwide, they were dead in the water. All of the years of late nights eating Chinese food, scrimping to meet the next payroll, and worrying about when they'd land the next customer and account were all a tragic waste of time and their life. Instead, they could have spent the time going to see the summer concert series in the local park, having many nice dinners out on a Saturday night, or even buying a boat and sailing on the calm, serene waters outside of Boston Harbor on the weekends. But no. They had to work. No sales meant no money, and no money meant layoffs, cutbacks and ultimately, closure.

At first, Patrick and Shea emptied their personal savings accounts to keep the business going and pay the salaries of long-time and trusted people who had become their best friends and part of their family. But eventually, even these resources ran out, and so did everyone's hope. The family began to fray, and keeping it together looked all but impossible.

Patrick sat in his office looking at the monitor and shaking his head. In front of him was a bottle of Johnny Walker Red scotch and a third short glass with ice cubes already melted from the previous pours. The light bulb from his green-shaded, brass table lamp illuminated the yellow notepad on which he was scribbling thoughts and doing some quick pencil-to-paper calculations. Usually, these were things that Shea would do, but he was restless and couldn't sleep. His spirit had collapsed, and his positive outlook had been sinking quickly.

Shea came in and pulled up a chair. "It's late hon. Let's go to bed."

"Can't," he answered. "There has to be a way out of this. Can't we get more money from the bank? What about our line of credit; can't we just borrow more?"

Shea shook her head. She hadn't yet told him about the phone call from Tim. He was just beginning to show signs of panic, and she didn't want to push him over the edge.

"They won't extend any more, Patrick," she said, down-playing the matter. "You knew they wouldn't. We're already on the hook personally to repay the thirteen million we've already borrowed. They'll take our house, our cars, our furniture – everything. There won't be anything left. I'm … I'm afraid that …" Shea hesitated. She too was starting to unravel, but caught herself. She smiled, putting on a brave face. "But, you know we'll figure a way out of this. We always do. Right?"

The answer wasn't the usual "of course honey" he'd come to expect from her, or rather, hoped would come from her. So, his face grew dark, and he robotically took another sip of his scotch.

"Really, Patrick. We'll get out of this," she said again, hoping to comfort herself as much as for him.

"And, if we have to file bankruptcy and start over?"

"We can do that. We built a company once; we can do it again." There was softness and compassion in her voice, and she could only hope that he would find the light and spirit he needed to claw his way out of his depression.

"I jus' don' know anymore, Shea. It seems hopeless. The government is breathing down our necks at every turn. The IRS, the FCC, the FTC, the Justice Department, the … well … whatever they call themselves these days." He picked up a small, blue rubber ball he used to exercise his hands, and threw it across the room in frustration. It struck a small porcelain ballerina on an end table, knocking it over and breaking off one of her legs.

Unfazed, Patrick continued. "I don' give a sh*t what they do anymore!" he exploded. His face was puffy and red. "I just don' give a crap. They can take everythin' from me … everythin'," he said, starting to slur his words. "But they'll have to kill me to take *you* away from me, Shea. As for anything else, it just doesn't matter anymore. It's not worth the pain. It's jus' not!"

She'd never seen him like this before. Besides being drunk, he was melancholy – even depressed. "Listen Patrick, there's a way we can work through …" she began, but he wasn't listening anymore.

"They have me by the balls!" exclaimed Patrick. "They know that, and they revel in it! But tell me. Wha' does it mean anymore when the country you've been born and raised in -- the one you love -- has a gov'ment that's willin' to destroy you because you don' agree with it? This isn't America anymore. It's not!"

"No, dear. It's not. It hasn't been the world Adams and Madison thought they were creating; that's for sure. But, honey, it hasn't been that for many years now," said Shea, putting her arm around her husband.

Patrick poured himself another three fingers of booze and drank half before putting the glass down. He was getting wasted, but he didn't care. "I grew up in a country that lived by the words … *We hold these truths to be self-evident, that all men are created equal, that they are endowed by their Creator with certain unail …* " he stopped and tried again, *"… unalienable Rights, that among these are Life, Liberty and the pursuit of Happiness.* So, where did it go so wrong? These aren't truths now. Life has become a commodity that only the well-connected have the money to buy. Health, or at least healthcare, and personal security for the rest of us is a thing of the past. The government promised us both, but doesn't deliver either one. Same thing with liberty; that was abandoned a long time ago too. Freedom to exercise free speech was killed off – first with political correctness and then, finally, with the Department of Prose and Language that they announced yesterday. Where does it end?"

"It's called censorship," said Shea.

"It's worse than that. They can throw us in prison if we utter or write certain things they don' agree with. And, of course, the *pièce de résistance* is the Pursuit of Happiness, which has morphed into a Right to Happiness. Of course, in the end, no one can guarantee that! It's not a *right* of every American to be happy. It's only an *opportunity* that each of us has to become happy, and we can have that only through our own labor. That's what was guaranteed to us – *the opportunity*! It was in the Constitution, for God's sake! But now, the Constitution … well … it doesn't mean sh*t anymore. They all but use it for toilet paper!"

He paused to gather himself. "It's sad, Shea," he continued. "It's not the country my parents toiled in for years to make a better future for me and my brother. It's closer to what they saw in the old Soviet Union of the 1960s and 70s. That's the America we're seeing now!"

He picked up his glass again and slammed the rest of his drink to the back of his throat, letting it burn as the eighty-proof liquid slid down his gullet.

"Patrick. Come on. It's going to be okay. It really is. No matter what happens … we still have each other."

Shea came over behind him and began rubbing his neck. She put her hands on his shoulders, messaging them lightly and then moving upward toward the back of his neck. She began giving him light kisses to put his mind onto other things. But he persisted.

"Why does it matter?" he asked rhetorically, paying no attention to the advances by his wife. "There's not a God d*mn thing we can do about it. They're going to do whatever the f**k they want, whenever they want, to whomever they want."

"It does matter," she said softly, stepping back from him, disappointed that she couldn't distract his mind. "But you matter to me more ..."

He was in no mood to be seduced, and he pulled away, leaning forward slightly. "I'm just one man. I only have one vote against two hundred million others. They have the power of the media, the education system, the courts, the police, FBI, CIA, Army, Navy, and Air Force, for God's sake! What do I have? Nothin'! I'm only one vote. One vote! That's it! And my vote counts just as much as some clueless dude who has no idea what the guy he's voting for stands for. No idea what the guy's voted for while in office. No idea what they guy really believes in. No idea. He wouldn't be able to tell you the difference between George Washington and George Lucas. He wouldn't know the difference between a Marxist and a makeover. Clueless – that's what he is. But you know what? His vote counts just as much as mine. All he's looking for is that P-Lever – the one with the People's Party logo on it. It's a lot cooler to pull that one than any other."

"Honey, we have to be optimistic about the future. Otherwise, what do we have left? Things must get better, not only for us, but for the rest of the country. Just think of it this way – things can't get any worse. Therefore, they have to get better, right?" implored Shea, backing away.

But Patrick couldn't control himself. He was beyond conciliation. "I just don't know anymore, Shea. It's hard to be optimistic. I mean, when you have people who aren't educated and aren't aware of what is really going on, and don't care to be, what can you do? Most don't even have a grade school education when measured by what they got back in the 1920s. They don't even know what communism means, for God's sake!" he said. "Marx who? Lenin who? Mao who? The average voter doesn't know the first thing about history or what led other countries into decline and ultimately toward collapse. At least the people of the Middle Ages had an excuse – they were all illiterate because they had no chance of getting an education. Today, people graduate from high school illiterate. Even those who can read and write were only fed propaganda during their years in school – three chapters on the glories of FDR and how he saved us from the Great Depression and two sentences on Thomas Jefferson, the white, racist slaveholder from Virginia. It's little different from the Soviet schools of the twentieth century that took young children from their homes to indoctrinate them into believing that socialism and centralized planning were the only viable forms of society. So, without being trained or educated on critical thinking, what else would they believe in – the virtues of Marxism or the evils of capitalism? It's obvious which bowl of poison they've been served up."

"I agree. It's all ten-second sound bites in commercials that push the ignorant to pull a lever to vote for a candidate. It's really sad, but ..." said Shea.

"Or worse, to pull the P-lever for an entire party, without thinking! That's the critical thinking that's completely gone today. We've created a bunch of ignorant sycophants who know nothing except the gruel of lies they've been fed since they were four years old. All you have to do is buy their votes through government welfare, food stamps, clothing credits, housing credits, medical credits, entertainment credits and God knows what other kinds of credits they've come up with – because, heaven-for-bid, they can't be left without – a distraction!

"Maybe, but ..."

Patrick belched inadvertently and covered his mouth. "Sorry," he said, apologizing. "The media will cover the positives of *their* candidate and play-up the negatives of the *other* one. At first it was subtle. Then, it was overt. Eventually, they didn't care."

Shea was finished with his soliloquy and ready for bed. "Are you finished?" she asked.

He turned and looked at her, realizing he'd been ranting far longer than he'd realized. "I ... I guess I am," he mumbled, having trouble with his words.

"It sounds to me like you're just going to give up?' asked Shea, tired but willing to turn the tables on him if it would change his demeanor. "So, that's it? That's all you have to give it?" Then, she said more directly, challenging him. "Is that what Reagan said in 1979? Is that what Churchill said in 1938? I don't think so. If I recall, Churchill said 'Success is not final and failure is not fatal, it's the courage to continue that really counts.' Patrick, you are the most courageous man I've ever known. We've struggled to make it through these many years – fighting to keep the dream of our engine alive. We've battled bureaucracies, environmentalists, competitors, and, at times, ourselves. But we always managed to stay the course. We were always able to see it through to the other side. And, yes, we're going to make it through this too ... we will, I promise."

Patrick smiled and squeezed her hand. "I love you," he said. "You are the most important thing in my life … the most important person who's ever been in my life."

"Will you come upstairs now?" she asked, her eyes longing for him.

"Sure," he answered, "I'll be up in a few minutes. You go up. I'll just finish a few things first. Then, I'll be up."

"Promise?"

He smiled. "Yes, I'll be up soon."

Shea went upstairs and climbed back into bed. She looked over at the clock and realized it was after eleven o'clock. She had to get up in another six hours. Checking the alarm, she rolled over and went back to sleep. What she didn't know was it would be the last time she would ever see her husband, Patrick.

Her life was about to change forever.

#####

Next Volume: *Atlas in Revolt – Book II*

American Secession

ABOUT THE AUTHOR

The author has written numerous novels, many of which are trilogies or multi-volume sets that span different types of book genre from fantasies and murder mysteries to horror stories and allegories. He has been cited for his creativity and fresh approach to books written in each of these book categories. The ATLAS Trilogies is the only novel series Gregory Phillips has penned using that *nom de plume*. Books authored in each genre are inked using a unique pseudonym most fitting to that style writing.

Phillips lives with his family in the Chicago area.

Go to www.blueMpublishing for more works by this and other authors.

*****

Book II
ATLAS in REVOLT

Book II, *Atlas in Revolt*, continues the story with the increasing power of the federal government and that of Angel Ratner, who becomes more ruthless in her rule over the lives of the citizenry. Shea's life begins to crumble from outside attacks to destroy her company, and Congressman Sumner finds a new calling – one that will raise awareness and ultimately change the direction and destiny of the entire nation.

*****

Blue M Publishing

FIND US AT: WWW.BLUEMPUBLISHING.COM

*****

www.ingramcontent.com/pod-product-compliance
Lightning Source LLC
Chambersburg PA
CBHW071335250626
47159CB00004B/1609